FUEL

Jeremy Chin

This paperback edition 2011
2

First published by Jeremy Chin 2010

Perpustakaan Negara Malaysia
Cataloguing-in-Publication Data

Jeremy Chin, 2010
FUEL
Includes bibliography
ISBN 978-145-38861-5-1;
1. Marathon
I. Title

Acclaim for FUEL

Very well written, in a precise, intelligent but "low atmosphere" kind of method (reminds me of the style of very good writers before WW 2). A moving tale that will change your life.
- *Keith Tan, via E-mail*

"Fuel" is a story you can wake up to every morning like the aroma of good coffee or the smell of roses after the dew has fallen. Not the typical romance novel, this book is a refreshing and welcomed addition to my collection of great reads. Packed with a wide array of solid but "i-didn't-know-that" facts, "Fuel" is for the hopelessly romantic but cerebral reader. The world has waited too long for Jeremy Chin to dish this one out."
- *Joshua Lee, Programme Director of StART Society*

It's a great read for anybody who's ever followed a dream, worked for 'the man,' or has been in love.
- *Thom Hiatt, President of Twin Bees Communications, San Diego*

I was inspired, in awe, fell suddenly in love, laughed & cried...
- *Alex Chong, New Jersey*

This debut novel is like a breath of fresh air. His writing style is lyrical yet poignant. It left me wanting more from Chin, and I sure hope this book won't be his last.
- *KLue Magazine, 10 Mar, 2011*

I just finished the book and wanted to let you know that this is by far the most moving novel I've read in my life. You've conveyed the story in such poetic fashion and I truly believe that Fuel unseats Romeo & Juliet as the best love story ever told. I look forward to many more books from you, Jeremy Chin.
- *Michelle Chan, Fuel Fan*

If I have just one word to describe FUEL, it is "potent".
- *James Chua, Sub-Editor Wolters Kluwer*

Your book has touched me deeply, emotionally and spiritually. I saw shades of myself in both Timmy and Cambria - as a marathon runner, and sadly, as a failed lover myself. I found it uncanny that, at times, their thoughts and struggles reflected painful facts and memories of my past which I've been struggling to understand and overcome for the past year or so. But thanks to your book, it has given me hope and a renewed sense of belief to continue persevering, to savour what life has to offer (good or bad) and to start off the New Year with a clean slate for myself. Jeremy, thank you for allowing me to believe once more...
- *Ray Mun, Fuel Fan*

Fuel proves to be an easy read and informative and manages to be inspiring without being preachy. It is riveting and there is this sense of anticipation as the protagonist works towards achieving his lifelong dream and learning many other lessons along the way.
- -*The Edge Newspaper, 18 Apr, 2011*

I don't remember reading a book that affected me so acutely. And that's saying a lot, considering I had just read Imran Ahmad's critically acclaimed Unimagined before yours. It was brilliant but didn't sink its claws and fangs into my psyche like this one did.
- *Alexandra Wong, Journalist (The Star, Quill and Going Places)*

Contents

Prologue

A pair of lionesses made their way to the edge of the tree line, and through the leaves, spotted a group of gazelle, grazing. Staying low to the ground, the uninvited guests crept up menacingly, the taste of their next meal forming in their mouths.

A dry, coarse wind blew from the North. Though slight, it carried with it sand and the scent of danger. Alerted by the winds, the herd of gazelle scampered for their lives in every direction. The lionesses tore forward with devastating force, churning a plume of dry dirt as they accelerated towards the dispersing herd. Their cold merciless eyes scanned for frailties in the group and locked on to a young pregnant gazelle. A silent understanding existed between the two cats—one actively closed in on their target while the other circled the hunting ground to cut off any corridors of escape. It did not take long before the weighty gazelle found herself sequestered from the group.

The two lionesses took turns to have a go at the prize. Once one had expended all its energy in active pursuit, the other on the periphery charged in to renew the chase. The pregnant gazelle was able to outmanoeuvre and outpace whichever lioness was after her. She stopped proudly in her tracks whenever she had put a safe distance between herself and her pursuer.

After an hour of cat and mouse, fatigue started to set in. As the expectant mother stood staring from a distance, she felt the strength in her legs leave. She buckled at the knees and sank to the ground. She tried to stand but again melted to the earth.

The exultant pair, recognising that their ruse had worked, calmly padded up to their bounty. The fallen gazelle looked around with desperate eyes, and spotted the herd in the distance, watching her. She caught a glimpse of her offspring from an earlier birth, and was overcome by a great sadness. In an attempt to return to her fawn, she made a last-gasped effort to move, but was not able to lift herself off the ground. The diminished mother, now resigned to her impending fate, rested her chin on her two outstretched hooves, and prepared to die.

The herd watched as one lioness locked onto the throat of the pregnant mother, while the other ravenously tore at the flinching child in her belly. It was a cruel reality to behold, but one they had witnessed many times before. Such was the law of nature, which ensured the strong prevail and the weak perish.

The herd were grimly aware of this fact: that the young mother had the speed and agility to outmanoeuvre the two lionesses all day, and that she would still be alive... had she not run out of fuel.

Common Grounds

On the road of life, the little things we encounter along the way, sometimes change us more than the big things. We may not know it at the time. We may not know it ever.

When Timothy Malcolm Smith was twelve, he watched a movie on TV. After the show, he went out to play—as he normally did every evening. Little did he know he was a different person, that he had been changed, forever.

~.~.~.~.~.~.~

Timmy could move mountains. And he could stop clouds from moving. That's what he believed anyway. He just hadn't figured out how to... yet.

You see, Timmy was a dreamer. But unlike any other. You could tell by his eyes. Looking into them you found fire and focus. And instantly you knew. That before you was no wishful thinker. No starry-eyed dreamer who built castles in his mind. This was a dreamer who knew his destiny. One who did not slow or stop or veer. Not until he arrived.

The movie Timmy watched at twelve was a fantasy adventure film about a dwarf named Willow. Despite his small stature, Willow was able to defeat a tyrannical queen trying to harm a baby that had come under his care. Little Timmy liked a line from the movie. *There is no dream too big and no dreamer too small.* Once a lithe-limbed wisp of a boy, he adopted that line as his life's mantra.

Timmy did not believe in magic or the supernatural. He believed there was a God. But he did not believe in him. Not anymore anyway. He, at some point in his life, decided to appoint himself the navigator of his own fate, confident that if he put his mind to it, everything was possible. It was with this same degree of self-belief that Timmy Malcolm Smith entered the boardroom that day, bringing with him nothing but his lovely assistant, and his two cents.

~.~.~.~.~.~.~

Common Grounds Coffee had been around for ages. They'd been around longer than penicillin. Longer than tea bags. Before sliced bread.

For some of the nineteenth century, and most of the twentieth, Common Grounds existed as the top coffee brand in the United Kingdom. Unfortunately for them, the last ten years saw their market share erode like flour in the wind, drawn away by trendy overpriced baristas, novelty brands from exotic parts of the globe, and American blends that in some parts of the world weren't even regarded as coffee. The world had changed, and Common Grounds hadn't done so with it.

Common Grounds had another nemesis, an age-old one. A foe that came not in the guise of a bean, but that of a leaf. That repulsive, characterless, sappy beverage—tea.

The owners of Common Grounds were convinced that tea was their biggest enemy. And so they drew their battle lines there. It turned out to be a costly mistake. By taking their eye off their competitors in coffee, they were blindsided by a foreign coffee company that had turned its sights on the British coffee market. The siege was relentless. After a decade of being outspent, outmarketed and outdistributed, Common Grounds found themselves on their knees, squeezed to one remaining breath. In the years leading up to their death throes, they were forced to close all but one of their business units — their headquarters in Hertfordshire, their birthplace from over a century ago. It was from here that they planned to make their last stand.

~.~.~.~.~.~

Common Grounds was steered by two partners, Robert Allen and John Wade, cousins, great grandsons of the company's original founders. Of the two, Robert was the older by three weeks.

Growing up as best friends, Robert and John spent almost every day of their sixty-one years together. They attended the same schools, entered the army together and married on the same day, in the same church. They even got circumcised together. The longest they were apart was the three weeks Robert waited for John to be born.

The two from Hertfordshire held the utmost respect for each other. All company decisions, no matter how inconsequential, were jointly made. Often it was the case where it was two nods or naught, to a point where Common Grounds became known as the company steered by two pairs of ears and one voice.

Oddly though, the boys were like night and day. They debated over anything and everything, but their exchanges were less argument and more playful banter — argument for the sake of it — to make sure the other did not have his way unchecked. Many felt that it was their opposite extremes which formed the glue between them, in the way two pieces of Velcro interact with each other. Of the very few things they had in common, was their love for the company. And they pledged their all to keep it afloat.

In their company's most recent board meeting, its internal auditors gave Common Grounds 6 months, a year at most. And then it would have to close its doors, for good. The news came to Robert and John as one just informed of a terminal disease; it was a sinking realisation that death had been dispatched, and nothing could be done to halt its progress. Grim as the future looked, the partners still felt they had a rabbit or two left in their hat, unused rounds in the chamber, that it was too early for the hour of eulogies to be upon them. In a rare moment of seeing eye-to-eye, Robert and John were unanimous on one thing, that there was only one way to go down—slinging.

As a last ditch effort to save the company, Robert and John called for a pitch, and summoned the *big four* London advertising agencies. Recognising they had little coin left in their purse, they invited a fifth to the table—*Cream*— a medium-sized local think tank that was rapidly rising to acclaim. *Cream's* fees, the partners figured, would be much lower than any of the large agencies. Also, as a home-grown company, *Cream* was more likely to have local insights that the others might miss or mistakenly forego.

Robert and John took the pitch process very seriously and blocked off a week of their time to hear each party out. Both were really impressed by what was prescribed by the *big four*, and saw potential in each of the four campaigns. But the partners were also gravely aware that their ship had entered uncharted depths, and that their vessel was now more a sunken treasure than a ship. They needed to pull a Lazarus to fish Common Grounds out of the deep. The proposals from the *big four* were good. But none provided the miracle needed to resurrect their company.

It was the fifth day of the pitch, and Robert and John felt all hope hinged on the underdog. They were privy to *Cream's* recent record of slaying goliath agencies ten times their size, and that *Cream* was currently one of the most sought after houses in London. Highly recommended by a friend of John's, the partners were not only hopeful, but confident, that the proposal from *Cream* would meet their expectations. But they were wrong.

The Pitch

Goliath. King Kong. Godzilla. Chucky. It did not matter. Timmy would take them on. And that was the mindset with which he would enter each advertising pitch.

Despite his great self confidence, Timmy was not cocky. Neither was he cocksure. He merely approached life with a *What's the worst that could happen?* attitude. Timmy did not like to fail, but he knew that as long as he had given an effort his all, failure was an outcome he could accept.

Timmy made Creative Director at *Cream* fourteen months back, and from that time, had slain every dragon that had crossed his path. He had just come off his fifth consecutive business win, and was looking for his sixth. To him, the presentation he had just made to Robert and John in their boardroom was business as usual. The only nervousness he felt was after the presentation, while awaiting their feedback.

~.~.~.~.~.~.~

Before the presentation that morning, Timmy had a breakfast deemed gluttonous by others, but light by his standards: four fried eggs, a couple slices of toast, a bowl of cereal with milk, a carton box of cranberry juice and a banana.

And a handful of nuts.

And half a panini, for the train ride.

Still, his stomach growled. He was not a big man. The opposite actually. He bore a distance runner's configuration — light frame, sinewy legs, high calf muscles, average height.

Despite his modest build, Timmy was always able to fill the room with his presence. His voice was neither big nor small, but full. A keen observer of the human condition, Timmy understood people well, and communicated at their level, seeing things through their eyes. Mostly, he talked to you as if he were trading vicinal news at the hay market. There was believability in his voice, and he had been told many times that he had genuine eyes. He found there to be no greater compliment. He always believed that eyes were peep holes into the soul. That if there was nothing but bile at the core, it showed on the surface, no matter the shape, colour or size of one's eyes.

At the presentation with Timmy was Cambria, a junior art director. In their brain storming sessions, it was often Cambria's ideas that formed the bedrock of their campaigns. Timmy's genius lay in his ability to polish her thoughts, turning them from great to legendary.

Cambria was like a sponge that had sat for years in the desert sun. She had an insatiable thirst for knowledge and was usually the one with all the facts and figures backboning the work she and Timmy came up with. Meticulous in her preparation, it was she who made sure their proposals were airtight.

Timmy and Cambria's close working relationship with each other came about six months prior. In their first pitch together, Stella, one of the people to whom they were presenting, interrupted Timmy midway through his presentation. She questioned the use of the colour purple in one of their boards. Before Timmy could conjure an explanation, Cambria pointed out to the client that seventy percent of their customers were women. Stella appeared irritated that Cambria had regurgitated a statistic that everyone in the room already knew. And she snapped at Cambria before Cambria could continue.

"Why not go with pink then?"

Unfazed by Stella's abrasiveness, Cambria came back without any hesitation, "The data we obtained from you three weeks back showed that ninety percent of your female clientele is above thirty-five and in the upper middle class. This information... it is still current?"

When she had received nods from everyone in the room, she continued, her face a study of calm concentration.

"Well folks, you've got on your hands a breed of women whose current aim in life is to obtain self-reliance and self-sufficiency, a group of suffragettes and bra burners willing to go the distance to establish for themselves autonomy from our male-dominated society. A study released by the National Organisation of Women early this year revealed that this segment of women... your segment of women, were inclined to progress beyond the confines of gender stereotypes. The study revealed that this group incidentally had an aversion to the colour pink, and generally preferred the colour purple. And to our delight, we discovered that your secondary target audience, metrosexual males in their early thirties, also favoured the same colour."

The room was impressed. From Stella—a curt nod of grudging approval. Timmy was dumbfounded by Cambria's response, and the fluency with which it was delivered. It was her ability to field questions like these that earned her a spot beside him at their next four pitches, and now the one for Common Grounds.

~.~.~.~.~.~.~

Robert Lane and John Wade shifted uncomfortably in their chairs. They frowned at each other and withdrew into their individual worlds of thought. Timmy himself was a little unnerved.

In all of his previous pitch attempts, he was able to tell if the room had bit on his idea before he concluded his spiel. But not this time.

The concept proposed by Timmy and Cambria to the partners did not meet their expectations. Nor did it exceed it. Or fall short of it. It was merely something they totally did not see coming, and they did not know what to think.

The most deafening silence filled the room as the partners contemplated the proposal. Timmy was intrigued by how dense the absence of sound felt. His breathing echoed inside his head like a whisper in an empty chamber. The air wisping out of the air vents suddenly became audible. He latched on to the ticks of Robert's watch. Picked up the groan of leather under each partner. And so there they were, John and Robert stoic and motionless in their leather chairs, Timmy and Cambria looking expectantly at them, like a tableau at a Wax Museum.

Then the aged voice of John Wade rasped its way across the room.

"There's a quote I really like. It is by Oscar Levant. He was an old American actor. Well before your time."

John paused and looked into space, searching his mind to make sure he still remembered the phrase word for word. Then he quoted Levant, *"There is a thin line between genius and insanity. I've erased that line."*

Timmy and Cambria did not know what to make of what John had just said and waited with bated breath for the explanation to come.

"Like Levant, this is what the two of you have done today. Erased that line."

The pair still weren't sure if they could celebrate, and were glued to their spots.

"You have developed a concept that combines genius and insanity. Brilliant. Simply brilliant!"

Laugh lines formed on Timmy and Cambria's faces.

"Robert? Your thoughts?" John turned to his half.

The pair from *Cream* were back on tenterhooks.

Due to their very different dispositions, getting both John and Robert to agree on the same thing was like trying to traverse a pair of swinging blades that criss-crossed each other. John himself, despite knowing the ins-and-outs of his best friend's mind, was clueless to how Robert would respond.

Robert Allen, still undecided, blew air into the pockets of his cheeks. Timmy and Cambria felt a nervous tension stretch across their shoulders. Robert, who was leaned back in his chair the entire time, leaned forward. He planted his elbows on the table and brought his hands together. His fingers interlocked, like rugby players in a scrum. Resting his chin on the seam of where his two hands met, he stared into nothing. It was clear that his mind was still conjecturing.

Robert maintained his blank stare when he finally spoke, as if he were reading off a teleprompter in his mind.

"I think this has the makings of a Chernobyl."

Cream

Timmy and Cambria shuddered. Their faces fell, John's too.

Robert continued, "Like Chernobyl, it's got the potential to seep into the earth and into everything around us... for a very, very long time. To make its way into popular culture, into the public's way of life, into their daily conversation. And..." Robert turned to John with a wry smile, "if executed correctly, it may just work."

John responded with a curt nod.

Timmy and Cambria knew they had done it again.

~.~.~.~.~.~

Cream was housed in a three-storey building in Clerkenwell, one of the better preserved parts of London that still held its charm from the past.

The team of creatives led by Timmy worked in the basement. More like a half basement really—the bottom half was concealed in the earth, the top half: a sweeping glass window running along the sidewalk pavement. Peering out from within, all one got was a worm's eye view of the street—the wheels of parked cars, the trunk of a lamp post, a glimpse of legs striding by, or the idle stance of *Cream* employees taking their cigarettes out front. Occasionally, the guys in the office would ogle at a chance upskirt. The female smokers at *Cream*, those who had worked there long enough, knew to stand out of view, on the stone steps at the front of the building—this a result of company-wide emails with subject lines like, *Lisa's wearing pink today*. Rather surprisingly, great restraint was shown by the guys in the creative department. The accompanying photos never circled, and to date, had somehow managed to stay within private archives.

When Timmy first made Creative Director, he pulled a prank on his team. He shaved off all the hair on his legs and slipped into a black Lycra mini skirt. Braving six-inch stilettos, he struck a seductive pose by the side of the building, along the window's edge. Without any underwear on.

Timmy was not inherently a prankster. But he was willing to go to any length (of skirt) to make people laugh. He believed in keeping things light around the office, and no one walked the talk and teased the line as fervently as he.

Housing a sundry of creative types, the basement was the liveliest space in the building. People buzzed from one desk to the other, small groups huddled for discussions, the whiteboard was always being doodled, and someone was always leaning over someone else's computer.

It was noise-filled in the creative department. But not a brand of noisy that was brash and distracting; more of an audible undercoat beneath the surface of your consciousness. Ever present was the signature thrum of an office environment—people on the phone, mouse clicking, typing on the keyboard, water cooler chats. This was supplemented at different times of the day by the muffled thump of a dart making contact with the cork board, the low rattle of dice within the padded enclave of a backgammon cup, or the crack of pool balls connecting with each other.

Evenings lent the basement a new voice. Conversation flowed more freely with more life, and the staff laughed more from their bellies and less from their voice boxes. Restraints on politeness relaxed, and people interrupted each other more frequently to make sure they got their line of humour in. More so than the other departments, the creative team at *Cream*, boisterous as they were, were like family. It was a culture that Timmy worked diligently to cultivate, and everyone was appreciative of it.

~.~.~.~.~.~.~

It was very different on the ground floor where client servicing was situated. The mood was a lot more sedate, the staff, more buttoned down. You rarely saw paper planes whizzing through the air, people sat at their own desks, they wore their clothes the right side in, and phone conversations were but a shade above a whisper. Client Servicers sat their tea mugs on coasters, unlike downstairs, where a napkin with a week's worth of coffee rings sufficed for one.

Things got more staid the higher you progressed up the *Cream* building. The top floor of the agency was nicknamed the *Creamatorium*, and harboured the grey matter of the agency. Here, the staff consisted of a team of researchers, statisticians, and analysts, all with doctorate degrees in unpronounceable areas of study. All day, the Consumer Scientists (as they were officially referred to) hunched over numbers, over charts, over graphs. They looked for recurring patterns and trends, and scoured for commercial opportunities their clients could seize upon.

You see, *Cream* was a different kind of ad agency. Unlike traditional shops, they approached advertising as ninety percent science and ten percent art. Their science was simple. They were very careful picking their lure, and knew not to use cheese to hunt sharks. If a target needed to be hit, they studied every relevant piece of intelligence before dialling in a strike. All recommendations made by them to their clients were extremely well thought out, and braced by an intricate web of logic.

Timmy stepped into his current role when Jonas, the agency's Creative Director of eleven years, retired. Despite Timmy only being thirty-two, many felt it was a position long overdue to him. From the time he took the reins, *Cream* had won every piece of business they vied for, and were gaining a reputation as one of London's creative powerhouses.

Jonas was by no means a lightweight. He had an acute business sense, a scarily keen understanding of consumer behaviour, and the gift to marry the two. Timmy learned a lot under him, and the two got along really well — Timmy, a willing and grateful apprentice, Jonas, proud to have no more worthy a protégé.

Timmy joined *Cream* when he was twenty-five, as a mid-level designer. Jonas singled him out early, after discovering that he was gifted as a thinker and a prolific problem solver. With great pride, Jonas watched as his student rose to take a place at his side, eventually superseding him in many aspects of the job. Timmy was well-liked, had a good moral centre, bore his moods well and did wonders to build camaraderie within the team, something that Jonas felt was his own failing. What made Timmy truly unique as a creative were his countless hues of thought. He had no reservations venturing into the grey; to look beyond the obvious, to utilise the third side of the coin, to view the glass as neither half empty nor half full, but as half-half.

As Jonas steadily relinquished his Creative Directorship over to Timmy, he was impressed by the leadership Timmy displayed. Despite being in a position of power, Timmy retained his humility and still got on well with everyone. Eventually, Jonas found himself in a position where he was learning more from Timmy, than Timmy was learning from him. It was at that point that he decided it was time. For him to step aside. To make way for the new guard.

~.~.~.~.~.~

Timmy had partnered Cambria on all of his six pitch wins, and she had become indispensible to him, his talisman for success. He synergised well with her and they built on each other's strengths. So naturally, each time a big piece of business stood to be won, it was Cambria who was summoned to the fore.

Timmy's choice to always stick with her stirred a little envy amongst the staff, especially those more senior than her. Timmy was aware of this, but his decision was one he measured carefully. Cambria's ability to derive sound ideas was unparalleled, and her talent to present those ideas with panache, unmatched. For that, Timmy thought better than to break apart their working symbiosis. There was speculation that the two had a thing for each other. But Cambria was nowhere close to being Timmy's type. Plus, he had his heart set on another.

Cambria was very pretty. Perfect skin. Beautiful eyes. Slender and demure. Tall for a girl. Bearing that shade of melancholia carried by most inward creatives, she was reserved, seemingly friendly and possessed a gorgeous smile that she revealed sparingly. She had silken black hair that ended at her shoulder blades, laser straight, worn down most of the time except when engaged in some kind of outdoor activity. Cambria was not a mingler, most of the time talking only when talked to. She lunched mostly by herself, at the second nearest park to the office, a book in hand, in her own world. Walking the extra eight minutes to the distant park sent a signal to her colleagues, of her disinterest to share company, and that she relished her time alone.

Cambria, just like Timmy, rose up the rungs very quickly. Starting out as an assistant to a senior designer, she spent most of her day performing the mundane—searching for stock images, doing paste-ups, preparing boards for presentations. But it didn't take long for her to win notice from the higher ups.

When Cambria first joined *Cream*, she fraternised mostly with two girls, both graphic designers; Bailey and McKenzie. For Bailey's birthday, Cambria assembled a sublime montage of old photos—classic toaster ovens, Cuban cigar emblems, vintage matchboxes, antique-coloured flowers. She combined those with quirky illustrations she hand-sketched. At the centre, she painted Bailey, posed semi-nude on a clam shell, in the fashion of Botticelli's *Birth of Venus*. Cambria transformed her art into a screensaver for her friend, who had the most delightful surprise when she got back from lunch and found her computer half asleep. McKenzie wanted one like that too. Cambria obliged. And after that, it was Mikey. And then Steven. And Julie. In a month, half the office had the most remarkable screensavers. It wasn't long before everyone realised that her talent was too precious for her to be doing what she had been doing at the time.

When Cambria and Timmy contested for Common Ground's business, Cambria had been in her role as Junior Art Director for a year and a half. Like Timmy before, she was merely waiting for a spot to open up, to assume the position she deserved. With their most recent win, her time was near.

The Campaign

The advertising campaign that *Cream* prescribed to Common Grounds grew into one of the most successful of all time, and became a case study for advertising scholars worldwide.

The idea started off as Cambria's, who in a roundtable discussion, was trying to moot the idea of *a coffee for everyone*.

Cambria was very methodical in the way she approached ideation, and had a knack to draw insight out of numbers. As a standard prequel to brainstorming, she pored through stacks of research findings, case studies, focus group results, learnings from past trends... whatever she could get her hands on to form a complete picture. At this phase of her process, her goal was merely to scrawl as much onto the walls of her mind, to quilt a honeycomb of knowledge she could later use to fuel her thinking. When her brain felt like it was going to burst, she was ready to begin.

Cambria's study of coffee started with a study of tea. She discovered that in Great Britain, a staggering one hundred and sixty-five million cups of tea were consumed each day, more than double that of coffee. Digging deeper, she found that things had not always been this way. Long before tea gained its popularity in Britain, there was only coffee. Coffee houses existed as trade centres, as a venue for men to gather and exchange business and political news. More so, it was a place to read the newspapers and to meet friends. Tea at the time, because it was rare and expensive, was a novelty item enjoyed merely by the aristocracy. But as the centuries wore on, British rule over the world's largest tea colonies drove its price down, and the opening of trade routes made tea accessible to the man on the street. Over time, tea became more popular than coffee. More popular than ale. More popular than gin. Eventually, it was declared the national beverage. Its place in history was sealed.

But Cambria felt that something was missing from the equation. She was convinced that for a beverage to become an institution, there had to be more. Forces at work more powerful than just price and accessibility. After careful study, she deduced tea's rapid rise and dominance to one more thing: its power to bring people together.

You communed over tea to announce a pregnancy. To share details of your weekend. Air your frustrations. Confess love. Boast of a sexual romp. More commonly, you got together over tea to talk about 'nothing'. Tea was the drink that brought people closer in dire times, the drink with the power to heal sad thoughts, patch frayed relationships, soothe weary minds. A cup between two people sometimes marked the dawn of something new. Sometimes, it served as the first steps to rebuilding a friendship. And other times, it was a way to say a final goodbye. Regardless of how tea was consumed, it was usually consumed in the company of another.

~.~.~.~.~.~

Cambria studied the coffee produced by Common Grounds. It was a Javanese Arabica with a delicate and mellow flavour. There was a certain roundness to it and felt velvety to the tongue. Taste tests revealed that their coffee wasn't something a connoisseur would outright fancy. But it was the joe of choice for every other joe.

Common Grounds was not an unknown brand. Younger people remembered it as the coffee their parents or grandparents drank. Because they were a long-standing home grown company, Common Grounds was still served at establishments that were set in their ways–old highway diners, greasy spoons, factory canteens, breakfast kitchens. Their coffee was also still quite popular out in the countryside. To Common Grounds' advantage, theirs was a heritage every Briton shared, their common ground so to speak, but a forgotten pride.

Cambria's position on the campaign was to establish her client's product as that bridge between people, a beverage enjoyed by all, irrespective of age, colour or creed. When she aired her thoughts to the team, she drew unenthusiastic stares from everyone. Everyone except Timmy. He thought it was brilliant. And he derived a landmark tagline for her idea, '*Common Grounds Coffee. Everyone's cup of tea.*'

Common Grounds spared no expense on the campaign. They viewed it, at worst, as a last hurrah. A mere two months after *Cream* were awarded the business, £10 million worth of print, billboards and TV flooded the marketplace.

The ads were simple. They featured people from all walks of life, all enjoying a cup of Common Grounds. The cast selection was exquisite.

In one, there was an old woman, looking sweet as pie, her reading glasses barely hanging on to her nose. She was posed next to a burly leather-clad biker, his long curly beard kissing the top of his belly. She gripped her coffee mug firmly. He held his daintily, his pinkie jutting.

Another ad featured players from rival football teams, arm in arm, all enjoying a cup of Common Grounds.

In another there was a priest, a monk, an Imam and a Jewish Rabbi.

Carried in all the ads, was Timmy's tagline: *Common Grounds Coffee. Everyone's cup of tea.*

The colourful personalities were modelled against a stark white background. Visually, the ads were elegant and eye catching. The main lure, however, was that it made a reference to tea. In England, just the mere mention of the word caused ears to perk, even if it were whispered counties away. Swiftly and with great precision, the ads cut through the clutter like the ping of a tuning fork across the silence. Their message reached every part of the country, pervaded every home, dipped into every pocket. Timmy and Cambria's idea warmed the peoples' hearts, reminded them of an old forgotten friend.

Because the ads were simple, they were easy to be copied, and parodies popped up all over. Late night talk shows made political plays on the concept, placing the likes of Osama and Obama in the same space. The public followed suit and took it many notches higher, spawning ads with every unimaginable pairing.

~.~.~.~.~.~.~

Following the first wave of media, Timmy and Cambria pro-duced and released a cute and catchy jingle. It featured a mon-tage of different people—young and old, colourful and drab, straight and bent—all singing a single word of a cheerful tune, a number that eventually became known nationwide as the Common song, the song for the common people. It went:

Rockaholic, jazzaholic, rapaholic, grungeaholic,
Workaholic, sleepaholic, danceaholic, alcoholic,
Shopaholic, diabolic, psychedelic, apostolic,
Soccerholic ,sexaholic, philatelic, chocaholic

Different as we all may be
We all gotta have some Common Ground
A common commonality

Near the end, as the jingle tapered off, they all slurped from their cups. "Common Grounds Coffee... ta da ta dah dum... Everyone's... ta da da... cup of tea."

As with their print ads, the public parodied the jingle, and churned out compositions of their own. It did not take long before hundreds of videos surfaced on the internet, with different treatments and lyrics.

Audiophile, out-of-style, versatile, paedophile...
Psychographic, demographic, geographic, pornographic...
TGIF, WWF, IMF, WTF...
Blue eyed, evil eyed, cross eyed, teary eyed...

The permutations were endless.

It was as Robert Allen had predicted. No one in the blast radius was spared. A revolution had been sparked. A cultural Chernobyl. This was going to stain for a long time. A very long time.

In a mere two months of their running the campaign, a third of coffee drinkers who drank competitor brands switched over to Common Grounds. The majority of Brits, who on average drank six cups of tea a day, started to only drink five, opting for a mug of Common Grounds to switch things up. To a coffee company in a nation of tea drinkers, it was a wet dream come true.

~.~.~.~.~.~.~

Timmy had a gift few possessed. He always found a way to the essence of things, to extract from day-to-day living, the little pleasures that warmed your heart and touched your soul. Such was his brilliance. In some circles, his name was mentioned in the same breath as the few who had made it into the upper echelons of advertising: the J. Walters, the Ogilvys, the Bernbachs. It was never Timmy's dream to pursue such a legacy. His was merely to do that which came naturally to him.

Fame usually comes to those who are thinking about something else.
                                            - Oliver Wendell Holmes, Jr.

Timothy Malcolm Smith

I spent most of my life collecting skills I never used. I learned how to play the piano, picked up all my certifications, but never touched a single key after that. I learned how to ride a bicycle when I was five, but since then, always opted to run if I needed to get some place quickly. At fourteen, my father taught me how to saddle a horse, how to spur it into a gallop, how to slow it to a canter. But horse riding hurt my testicles. So I never got on a horse again. (I once thought to myself, that were I ever the Tsar of my own country, women would ride astride, men—side saddle.)

My mum was Danish. So I spent many summers with my grandparents Kirsten and Jorgen, on Laeso, an island off the northeast coast of Denmark. There I learned to draw honey from a honeycomb, hang and dress a deer, birth a calf, spear-fish, identify edible berries; all skills I mastered but never used again the following summer. It wasn't that I lost interest. I merely was a curious little bugger, and was always on to learn-ing new things.

I enjoyed spending time in the kitchen with my grandma. I felt like a chemist who got to eat his lab work. Through her, I learned to bake virtually every type of bread on the planet— rye, kibbled, baguette, ciabatta, Spelt, panetonne, sourdough, brioche, sprouted grain, pumpernickel and fougasse to name a few.

On Saturdays, I followed my grandparents to the flea market to scour for finds. I thoroughly enjoyed flea market days, and developed a deep appreciation for old things – turn-of-the-century farm tools, traditional costumes, old photos, costume jewellery, antique ornaments. I enjoyed discovering how gadgets of the past were used, how they came about, and when, and with what, they got replaced. Over time, I think I developed an eye for value, and a feel for quality. I learned how to test genuine jade with a drop of water, how to date antique furniture by the different articulations of its finish, how to pick a worthy thermos by holding it to my ear.

Of all my varied interests, there was only one I kept at. Running.

My interest came early. As a boy, I enjoyed running as fast as my legs would carry me. I loved the feeling of the wind tugging at my cheeks. And I loved that no one could catch me.

In my teenage years, speed became less important to me, and was replaced by distance. I enjoyed the high of being pushed to the extremes of fatigue, to run till I was forced to stop. I felt that running great distances tested my inner limits more than running fast in short spurts. And I derived no greater sense of achievement than notching new milestones in distance. Running for long stretches also gave me a chance to strike a lullaby-like rhythm, something I found soothing to the soul. Above all, running afforded me time alone to think, to untie the knots that were clogging my mind. I often discovered, that by the end of a run, many of my problems had percolated into solutions.

~.~.~.~.~.~

When I was sixteen, reality in its crassest touched me—my parents were taken in a car crash.

I was at a friend's birthday party on the outer edges of the city, and my mum and dad were on their way to pick me up. After the party, when everyone had left, and my folks had not yet arrived, I got mad at them. It wasn't the first time they were late picking me up. Figuring that they had forgotten about me, my friend's parents decided to send me back. My world caved in when we passed the wreckage on the way home.

Following their death, I became a very angry person, angry mostly at myself, and after that, at life's unfairness. I used to marvel at the might of tragedy, of the way it swept you away, made you a passenger on its winds; and how afterwards, everything which has been thrown out of orbit, just fits back perfectly into place, solely because it no longer mattered that the pieces fit. Everything lost its shape. The things that once held meaning, no longer did; were robbed of their configuration, their definition, their distinction.

My parents were pious Catholics, and I followed in their footsteps. I've not shared this with anyone, you'll be the first. I used to confide in Jesus throughout the day, as if he were my alter ego. These conversations took place in my mind, in street talk, as one would with a chum. I even had a nick for Jesus. 'Jezza', I would call him, sometimes shortened to 'Jez'.

"Do ya believe dis here? What would ya do if ya wuz me, Jez? What would ya do?"

I regarded Jesus not as a distant being in the sky, but as a friend I had allowed to reside in me, a friend I thought I could count on to watch over the people I loved. After my parents were taken from me, I expunged Jezza from my life, and adopted a new religion. Running.

I knew no better way to release my pent up anger than to deplete every joule of energy on my runs. I pushed myself to the limit and ran further each time, for longer periods. My longest run lasted six hours and thirteen minutes, before I blacked out in a London alley. For me, this was a period where there was no medium, only extremes. It finally got to a point where I just couldn't dedicate that kind of time to running insane distances. So I upped my pace, and capped my runs at 26.2 miles, the length of a marathon.

Seared by the embers of my past, I exiled myself from everyone I knew. I declined invitations from anyone who tried to include me in their lives. Invitations to Christmas dinners, birthday parties, baptisms, Easter lunches. I resented that people were trying to absorb me into their world, chiefly because mine had been shattered, and I did not want their pity. One day, the invitations stopped coming.

~.~.~.~.~.~

I died once before. It was six years to the day of my parents' fatal accident. From the time I woke up that morning, I was stalked by a dark loneliness that would not leave me, a nettling sadness that buried itself like a splinter in my flesh. I dealt with my grief in the only way I knew how. Laced up and headed out the door. That morning, I had the urge to break my body, and I exerted myself harder than I'd ever done in the past.

I deviated from my usual running route, opting instead to go by the hospital my parents had been rushed to after their accident. As I passed the entrance, I punished myself to run even harder. My blood felt like lava coursing through my veins, and my body felt like it was tearing from its bones. Eventually, my world faded from grey to black.

When I opened my eyes, the doctors told me I had a cardiac arrest at their doorstep, that my heart had stopped beating, and that I'd been clinically dead for three minutes.

My ribs were broken when CPR was administered, and they had to tape my chest tight. I didn't remember much of what happened. My only recall was my chest pulling tight like a trampoline. And then the lights went out.

Hospital bound, and advised to lay off running for at least two months, I felt like a straight-jacketed heroin addict denied his poison. They held me for a week, primarily for observation and to run some tests. The hospital staff constantly reminded me of how lucky I was to still be alive, of how I was one of the fortunate ones not to have suffered any brain damage or long term side effects. That really annoyed me. At the time, I was uncertain if I was happy to be alive, or if the hospital had done me a disservice by resuscitating me.

I always had a heart rate monitor strapped around my wrist when I ran. The device, which logged each minute of my run, showed that my heart failed at 198 beats per minute. My doctor told me that 198 was a good gauge of my MHR, or Maximum Heart Rate, scientific speak for how fast and hard my heart could beat before it got into trouble. For the future, I was advised to stay within eighty-five percent of my heart's fail point. They also warned that each year of aging knocked that ceiling down by one.

Confined to the boredom of the cardiac ward, I started to contemplate my 'beingness'. I looked at the world around me and the world within me. It wasn't pretty.

For the time I was kept at the hospital, I did not receive a single visitor, a single card, a single phone call. It was as if I no longer existed in the universe. But what disturbed me the most was when I started to grow envious of Noah, the eight-year old kid across the curtain. Noah had a pair of balloons tied to his bedposts and a bedside table full of get-well-soon cards, each colourfully splayed open. He received a fresh basket of fruit every two days, and had family who snuck in home-cooked food for him, food with flavour. Noah had a terminal disease with weeks to live. I knew this. But it did not stop my jealousy. I realised that to be envious of a child with a death sentence only meant one thing: I had hit rock bottom. Strangely, I was comforted knowing that. That I could sink no further.

~.~.~.~.~.~.~

Switchfoot is a term for when a surfer flips his footing on the board to get new perspective, to take a new stance in the opposite direction. My heart arrest knocked me off my feet, from my mantel, and I found myself reacquainted with my mortality. I was shaken by the fact that I had technically died, and each day, I grew more and more perturbed that my experience of the afterlife was not what I'd expected. There wasn't a light I could walk towards. Just darkness and silence.

I always believed that when I walked past the gates of death, my spirit would un-dock itself from my body, and I'd be able to look down on the spot where death had taken me. In the after-life, I thought I'd hear angels in hymn. That my parents, bathed in a frosty silver glow, would be waiting to welcome me. But I experienced none of that.

I fell into an existential panic, realising there may not be a *hereafter*, just a *here and now*. Reckoning that the life I was currently living was possibly all there was, I felt I had best make the most of it. This became a turning point in my life... and I switched my feet.

~.~.~.~.~.~.~

As I was emerging out of my purgatory, I fell in love with a student nurse at the hospital, and she became the centre of my universe for two years. Although things between us did not work out in the long term, it was through her that I learned to love again, to laugh again, to live again. She helped reopen my soul to the things I once cherished, and she convinced me that happiness hinged more on my disposition than my circumstances, that the world is lush with beauty to those with the eyes to see it. My near death experience, she felt, was a big blessing, to remind me of how fragile life is, and how it should be coddled as if it were the most precious thing in the world.

After I got back on my feet, I took a new approach to running. I became enamoured of running as a science and grew fascinated by the mechanics of the human body. I knew that the road to perfection was an endless pursuit, but I stayed the course, and worked tirelessly to refine my form. Looking beyond emotional relief as its sole purpose, running took on new meaning for me.

It took me many months to arrive at new plateaus, to train my muscles to adopt new ranges of motion as part of its natural, to derive from my body all that it was capable of. The process was long and arduous, but the end was rewarding. When I was on song and fell into perfect rhythm, I experienced a oneness with myself, a rapport with the earth. And this was a feeling for which I found no replacement.

~.~.~.~.~.~

After I was discharged from hospital, I devised a game which I played with myself each time I ran. I tried to guess my pulse rate, and matched my answer to what my pulse reader showed. I became real good at the game and was never more than one or two beats off.

Following my brush with death, despite emerging a better person, my inner demons never left me completely. They skulked in the wings, waiting for every opportunity to re-emerge. It was a long time before I allowed family to seep back into my life. I always feared that their direct link to my past would evoke emotions I wasn't strong enough to handle. So I stayed away from the big events, and limited myself to quick house visits, where I'd drop in on a moment's notice for a quick exchange.

~.~.~.~.~.~.~

During the two weeks I was confined to the hospital, I developed a maudlin attachment to Noah, the dying boy next to me. The boy enjoyed hearing of my little adventures and misadventures on Laeso. I found that by retelling those stories, I was able to relive my time on the island, and that gave me joy. After being discharged, I continued to visit Noah, every day, for seventeen days.

Kim, Chloe & Monica

When I made Creative Director, I inherited my predecessor's personal assistant, Chloe, a decorous pink-cheeked lass. Of my flaws at work, being organised was my biggest. As such, I appreciated the assistance Chloe provided. From day one, she was on the ball, and no one worked the Rolodex with her speed and efficiency. Proudly, she embraced her role as a sentry regulating my personal dealings with others, functioning as a switchboard connecting me to my every need.

Chloe had a friendly face, not drop dead gorgeous, not a head turner that guys wanted to bed for a night. Hers was more of a classic, timeless beauty; Audrey Hepburnesque. She was one of the sweetest people you could ever meet, and people always felt an obligation to protect her from our abrasive world. Because she was often overly polite, she always sounded like she was apologising. This was something I took awhile to get used to.

Late one evening, while working on a presentation, I looked up and saw Chloe at my door. She had the reports I had requested. With one hand on my jaw, I ratcheted my head to one side to release a crick in my neck. After placing the reports on my desk, she proceeded behind me and started to knead my shoulders. I welcomed the midnight massage and told her it really helped. I was taken by surprise when I felt her hair brush past my shoulders. She then kissed me on the neck. I immediately withdrew myself from the situation, and explained to her that my interests lay with another. She apologised profusely and left the room, tears running down her cheeks.

Things very quickly got awkward between us. Embarrassed by the whole situation, she threw in her resignation a short time after. I was unsuccessful in my attempts to get her to stay, and granted her request for immediate release. I felt awful with the way things had turned out. So I slipped a letter into her hands on her last day, when she came to say goodbye.

Dear Chloe,

I feel really flattered to be the choice of your affections. It was merely a matter of timing. My heart, as I've already explained to you, is with another. I hope you understand.

But let our friendship not end on this note. With time, I feel we will be able to work out this awkwardness between us. Coffee this Friday?

Timmy

It took many months of *Friday coffees*, but I was eventually able to nurse her heart back to health. We went on to being really good friends.

~.~.~.~.~.~.~

At the time, I was set on a different skirt — Monica de la Pena, an intimidatingly beautiful senior account manager at *Cream;*

dark hair, tall, tawny complexion, with amazing presence. Eyes locked on her whenever she entered a room, and conversations paused, as if to offer a bow.

Some are endowed with it, and some aren't, and she was. She possessed 'a glow', a cloud of magical dust surrounding her person; intrigue, awe, success, reverence, magnificence; all specks of her allure. She also had the gift to voice without the need to speak, who with a smile, or disapproving nod, could sway pillars of belief. Hers was a beauty that blurred the line between want and need.

There was a magnetism to Monica, not just in her physical appearance, but in the way she carried herself and a conversation. Her father was an ambassador for Peru, so as a child, she was suitcased all around the world, to whichever location he was assigned to. Having attended her share of state dinners, she came well-trimmed with savoir faire, and held her own at any function. I believe she possessed what Renaissance author Baldassare Castiglione described as *sprezzatura*, that most subtle veil of nonchalance and reticence, intended to make that which is difficult, appear effortless; a mask that also disguised her inward thoughts, feelings and desires.

At socials, Monica enthralled for hours, with tales of distant lands, and with the colour of how she lived her day-to-day. I had limited dealings with Monica at work, and my one-on-one conversations with her seldom exceeded a couple of minutes. Mostly, I watched from a distance, as she stood within the circle that always seemed to form naturally around her.

I could not, however, pinpoint the true reason for my captivation; if it was the resumé of her experiences that enticed me, or if she was merely a highly-prized feather every male in the office desired to obtain. My attraction to her somehow lacked the warmth one normally experiences upon finding true love. And for that reason, I always wondered if another woman, someone with a little less fairy dust, a little more earthly, was better suited to me, if someone more like Chloe, was what my heart truly yearned for.

~.~.~.~.~.~.~

I felt as if I were driving on a roundabout without an exit. Frustrated that the same stale ideas were eddying in my head, I rose out of my chair and decided to get some coffee from the café around the corner. It was on this cold damp night, on the front doorsteps of *Cream*, that I met Kim for the second time, the man who would eventually be my new personal assistant. We had shared a brief encounter the day before, when he was shown around on a statutory first day tour. At the time, he was a temp filling in for an account executive who had gone on maternity leave.

Kim doused his cigarette just when I exited the building, so I invited him to Marie's for coffee. He appeared reluctant at first ,but eventually relented with, "Oh, why the bloody hell not!"

Over coffee I learned that Kim was not usually a smoker, but changing circumstances in his relationship with his girlfriend changed that, brought back his cravings from years ago. Her name was Liz and things between them had ended awfully. Upset by the breakup, his first instinct was to buy a pack of twenty from the store. He told me that feeding his lungs with smoke helped fill the void in his chest that she had left.

After we had broken the ice, I expressed to Kim that his was an odd name for a bloke. He explained that with his father being Malaysian, and his mother, Norwegian, his first name was a test on the tongue. It was only after he revealed his full name to me that I concurred that 'Kim' was the most pronounceable part of his name. Six foot, with blue eyes, a squarish jaw and dirty blond hair, Kim showed very little of his oriental genes. Except for a smattering of an accent I could not quite place, Kim was as Nordic as they came.

Kim and I found we had a lot in common, especially with the way we approached life and extracted meaning from it. We traded stories through the night, and even shared our dreams, past failures, our secrets, our fears. Overall, I was impressed by his fluency, and the profoundness of his thought. I found it peculiar though, that Kim, well into his thirties, was still temping for a living. I later discovered that he had taken seven years off to see the world, picking up odd jobs wherever he went. Though there was some transience left in him, he opted to settle down in London after meeting Liz, whom he was going to marry, or so he thought anyway. Kim shared stories from his travels, and I listened with interest, having seen quite a fair bit of the world myself.

I had never told anyone about New York. But I told Kim. Of my dream to one day win my maiden race, the New York Marathon. This, I always felt, was the perfect precursor to my other dream, which was to work for *Oddinary*, New York's most prestigious advertising think tank.

Because I was aware of its improbability, I never shared my dreams with anyone. I preferred not to have an audience, were mine to be a failed endeavour. But I discovered a level of ease with Kim I had never enjoyed with anyone else. And I was thrilled that I finally met someone who 'got' me.

~.~.~.~.~.~

An individual I could trust with my trust.
A person with candour who would tell it to me the way he saw it.
One with a sense of adventure, verve, who took life by the horns.
Someone with genuine eyes.

These were all the things I was looking for in my personal assistant, and I saw those qualities in Kim. I was going to offer him the position on the spot, but figured I should ponder on it further and decide in the morning. But with an ad to produce by sunrise, I had very little time to sleep on it.

It was past two when I got back to my house. My eyes were tired but my mind felt like a loofah that had just been dipped in a bucket of water. My late night conversation with Kim opened up new arteries, cured my paucity, and left me with fresh fodder for creativity.

The ad was to be for LIFE, a pro-life charity organisation I volunteered at. LIFE offers advice to pregnant mothers who are planning to abort, and presents them with alternatives. To help with the raising of the child, they offer financial support, housing, and above all, a support system.

The message that my client was hoping to get across was that life is precious, and should be preserved at all cost. As I sat in my living room with a notepad, a piece of my conversation with Kim re-entered my mind. I had shared a fear of mine with him; that were I to participate in the New York Marathon, victorious or not, my life would be stripped of purpose afterwards. On hearing my words, Kim countered with a stern reply.

"Timmy! You've been running since some of your earliest memories, and your feet have touched the earth ten thousand times more than the average person. Everything you've done, from then to now, has steered you to this moment. You've gotten within half a minute of some of the best running times clocked in New York marathon history. Dreams exist to be achieved, not to be skirted around. Don't even bloody think of backing away from your dreams. You've got a real chance here. Don't squander it. Many people would count themselves lucky to be in your shoes, to have this opportunity before them. Half the people on this planet can't bloody afford shoes. Some are born without feet. Some without legs. Some don't even get born."

That night, Kim's words resonated in my head, and a suffocating sadness came over me. Some are indeed denied the most basic gift of breath, their lives, sometimes intentionally extinguished before they had come to being, before they had a chance to prove themselves worthy of a place on earth. I was moved to tears by this sad reality, and I started to write.

IF

When I went to work the next morning, I headed straight for Kim's desk and asked if he would consider a position as my personal assistant. Kim gladly accepted. I submitted my request to human resources, and afterwards, excitedly conveyed the news to Kim—that the paperwork was being processed, and that he would be able to start the next day.

When I walked into work the morning after, everyone in the office turned their attention to me. Work ceased. Water cooler chats froze. People who were on the phone covered their mouthpieces and paused. Some had tears in their eyes. It was austere.

Sensing that something terrible had happened, my heart sank, and I felt my gut tighten. Slowly, everyone started to stand. They vigorously clapped, their eyes fixed on me.

My piece for LIFE had been published that morning.

~.~.~.~.~.~.~

That day, Timmy redirected all the praise to Kim, for sparking off the great idea. For Kim, it was his first taste of what it was like to be under the leadership of Timmy. And a great first day it was for him.

On the night Timmy conceived the ad, he realised that

whilst a picture speaks a thousand words, none would ever be good enough to convey what he wanted to say. So he wrote a poem about chances, of what life could be were it allowed the opportunity to flourish.

If I could see
I'd commit everything to memory
So when darkness comes and daylight dies
I'd paint the sky without my eyes

If I could speak
I'll not lose my words behind my cheek
Will never leave any songs unsung
And thoughts shall never stale under my tongue

If I could hear
I'd want my heart to be my ear
I'd sit alone on the quietest quay
And try to hear what my eyes couldn't see

If I could smell
My nose will tell you if I'm unswell
It will crinkle when I smell something bad
And it will run all day when I'm feeling sad

If I could laugh
My grin would cut my face in half
For awhile my eyes would disappear
And if I'm really happy they'd start to tear

If I could taste
I'd savour every bite and not chew in haste
Eating right, I wonder how tall I'd grow
But Mum I guess I'd never know

When it appeared crisp and bold on the full page of the Metro, the ad generated the buzz and word of mouth that LIFE had hoped for. Millions of emails carrying the poem circled the globe, and LIFE received a deluge of requests from all over, asking for permission to re-publish. The piece for LIFE was the first mark Timmy left as the head of his department, and a signal to the world that a new rainmaker had just stepped into town.

~.~.~.~.~.~

Timmy and Kim became really close in the ensuing months, inseparable, and discovered they had a common love for foreign films. They spent many weekends catching movies at the Stratford Picture House, in East London. The typical movie lasted two hours, but the duo normally adjourned to the Theatre Royal Bar afterwards, a sleepy establishment with cosy patio seating. To their delight, the bar's kitchen served some of the best Jamaican food in London. It was here that they engaged in post-movie debate that lasted twice the length of the movie; stretched longer if they stayed on for the poetry reading or open mike comedy afterwards.

Following the success of LIFE, Timmy hopped back on the war path and launched a campaign for a different client. And he turned more heads.

Bell Inc. was a bicycle helmet company from California that was looking to make a mark on the British market. Timmy worked closely with Cambria on the campaign, and together, they produced an effort that saw sales rocket through the roof. At the time, Timmy had known Cambria for three years, and he utterly enjoyed working with her. Having made Creative Director, there was at first a little awkwardness between them; with him now her boss, instead of one of the crew. But Timmy rarely pulled rank within his team, and his new badge was more a mental divide if anything.

Timmy believed there to be no greater force than chemistry between two people. Just as lichen is a marriage of algae and fungus, such was the relationship between him and Cambria: a mutually beneficial partnership whose coming together exceeded the sum of its parts. What made his collaboration with Cambria so potent was that they both had very different thoughts, but thought the same way. Being on the same intellectual trajectory as Timmy, Cambria easily locked-on to the far-flung ideas he sometimes found difficult to convey, and she helped fish them out of the shallows of his mind. Timmy contributed differently. He was a master at drawing the acute from the ordinary, and making it remarkable, iconoclastic. He wasn't smarter than Cambria. Or harder working. Or more eloquent. He just viewed the world with different lenses.

Equipped with a great analytical mind and a keen eye for design, Cambria was in Timmy's mind a viable successor to him, one who could easily assume his position should his move to New York ever materialise. What Timmy found truly amazing about her was her ability to beautifully craft copy, a quality not commonly found in designers. The thing that impressed him more was that her eloquence lived beyond the tip of her pen; she spoke as she wrote, full of nuance, poetry — her thoughts — always captured in the purest and most beautiful of ways.

For Bell Inc., one of the first things Timmy and Cambria did was to persuade their client to take on a new tagline, which they did. And so *'Bell Helmets. We've got you covered.'* became the breath of their new advertising campaign.

Their target was inner city cyclists. They came in many sizes, shapes and shades. Some were milk men, some were men in suits. A handful were couriers and newspaper delivery boys. Others; kids learning to ride and recreationalists. A diverse bunch they were. And the best place to connect with them was on the street, where they could be found.

In their first effort, the team at *Cream* scoured the city for bus stops that met this criterion: they had to be beneath trees and power lines frequented by birds. *Cream* then replaced the roofs of these bus shelters with giant fibreglass Bell Helmets. And they stood back and watched.

The display amused all who passed it: bus commuters sheltered under poo-covered giant helmets; behind them in the background, the tagline, *'Bell Helmets. We've got you covered.'*

Cream backed up their first initiative with an idea that sprang from one of Cambria's insights, this when she drew parallels between the dampening function of car bumpers with that of a bicycle helmet. Both were made of lightweight material designed to crash on impact, absorbing the blow that would have otherwise been transmitted to the passenger.

After knocking on many doors, Cambria managed to convince a major cab company to carry bumper stickers with the words, *We take a beating so that you don't.* Trailed, of course, by their tagline.

Timmy and Cambria also flooded the outdoor space with billboards, each differently flavoured.

A few offered counsel: *Be swell, not swollen.*
Some carried caution: *Wear a Bell before one tolls for you.*
And some were laced with sex appeal: *Nice top.**

*Lana Laine, the famous centrefold, was used for this one. The two helmets used to shield her breasts were auctioned off for a pretty penny, the proceeds going to charity.

At the tail end of the Bell Campaign, with spare change, *Cream* bought really cheap billboard space in a secluded part of the city that rarely got any foot traffic... except when the AIDS walk took place. Their billboard shouted, *Protection is not only for sex,* with all the letter 'O's replaced with the circles of different coloured condoms. That billboard touched a massive amount of eyeballs that day, and got coverage on national TV. All for a pittance.

All of *Cream's* creative executions fell brilliantly under the umbrella of Timmy's big idea. Each of his initiatives for other clients also found success, but none like the work he conjured for Common Grounds coffee. Within the advertising community, it was the Bell campaign that put him on the radar. But it was Common Grounds that made him a target. Timmy received many job offers, including one from New York. *Oddinary* had come knocking.

A Night To Remember

To celebrate the success of the Common Grounds campaign, *Cream* reserved a restaurant in Islington for the night, the Rodizio Rico, an all-you-can-eat *churrascaria*, or Brazillian meat barbecue. The restaurant owed its origins to the fireside roasts of gauchos in the southern regions of Brazil. At Rodizio, *passadors* (meat waiters) came around every few minutes, with giant skewers of beef, lamb, chicken, pork or ham, which they carved straight onto your plate. The restaurant sat a hundred and ninety comfortably, but no one was sitting that night.

Cambria enjoyed parties, but only amongst people outside work, amidst close company where there was no claptrap, where she felt she could let her guard down. Cambria whiled away her days falling deep into her thoughts, and she enjoyed engaging in intellectual discussions with people. It allowed her the opportunity to air her ideas, battle test them, arrive at new conclusions. Above all, it gave her a chance to showcase a side she was very proud of.

In public, Cambria was very proper in her mannerisms — grammatically abiding, never swore, was seldom drawn into gossip–and people had a hard time breaking the ice with her. She was stringent with her reveal, and gave away very little about herself. Mostly, she preferred to linger on surface topics before divulging anything personal... almost as a rite of initiation one had to endure to get a peek into her private world. Funnily though, those who made it past the small talk found it arduous to engage at her level, and often wished they had remained on the plane of frivolous chit chat. Not wanting to feel unsmart, most of her colleagues avoided one-on-one conversation with her, especially suitors who were merely looking for a quick lay.

At parties, through years of being cast aside, Cambria grew good at detecting boredom in one's eyes. She knew precisely when your mind started to wander, the precise moment before you'd excuse yourself to the washroom so you could rejoin the party someplace else. But she seldom let it get to that. She'd ask to powder her nose before you could. On her re-emergence, she would secure herself a place in an idle corner of the room, and smile, and be smiled at.

Because the party was thrown primarily to celebrate her and Timmy's achievements, Cambria figured it would be polite to position herself close to him, just so people could collectively rather than individually toast their success. Although she recognised she played a big part in each of their campaigns, she felt undeserving of the garlands of praise bestowed on her. Deep inside she felt that her role was insignificant, that it was Timmy's ability to swirl in the meaningful bits that put their work in a league of excellence.

To make matters worse, Timmy never took credit for his work. Instead he'd say, "It was all Cambria.", "It was all Kim.", "I have a great team." Never would he say "Thank you" and leave it at that. Cambria held the opinion that this was his way of diffusing the awkwardness of being lauded. On the contrary, Timmy truly believed he stood on the shoulders of giants, and he deflected praise to where he felt it was due.

For the six months after Timmy was promoted, Cambria worked closely with him on a variety of accounts, and she found him a joy to be with. He always showed a keen interest in the lives of the people around him and had a funny habit of asking, *How are WE doing today?*, as if to suggest you and him were interlinked; that he was in your boat, for better, for worse. On a personal level, what Cambria appreciated most about Timmy was his ability to sense when something was wrong. And he had this gift to spot silver linings even in the grimmest of situations.

Timmy was always able to stay calm and collected under every condition, regardless of its magnitude. Whether he was addressing a boardroom full of company directors, or facing an unruly gaggle of reporters, Cambria had never before seen him fazed by a situation, up until that evening, when Monica de la Pena made her entrance at the restaurant. She noticed that the minute Monica walked in, Timmy's eyes shifted to her, and he was distracted from that moment on. It did not surprise her though that Timmy was fixated on Monica. She had, after all, everything a man could desire; status, fortune, a sinusoidal figure, dazzling eyes, lips that could draw nectar from stone, and indisputably (and enviably) the mother of all tits.

~.~.~.~.~.~

Timmy's heart raced as Monica made her way over to him. Effulgent in a one shoulder white Grecian dress, its scalloped hem cut just above her well-toned calves, Monica looked like a goddess who had taken a wrong turn to Earth.

"Good evening," she crushed him with her piercing olive green eyes.

"Just wanted to say brilliant job on the Grounds campaign," she continued, acknowledging only him and not those around. Timmy knew not how he could be breathing so heavily, but still be breathless. He scrounged for a reply and managed his usual.

"Oh, no, no, no. It, it was all Cambria. Yah! She was the real hero in the war."

Cambria rolled her eyes and smiled.

"So Timmy, achieving all you've achieved, what's next on the horizon?" He found Monica's queenly confidence intimidating.

Kim, who overheard the brewing conversation as he was passing by, caught Timmy's vacant expression, and saw Timmy could do with a breather to unknot his words.

"Kids," Kim swooped in. The circle of people parted to allow him in. Knowing that Timmy was head over heels for Monica, he proceeded to highlight that Timmy was for the taking. "We've got to find Timmy a good woman. Get them married off. And then bloody bug them to have children, to make sure his brilliance is passed on."

The group chuckled. Timmy felt relieved that his wingman had arrived on the scene.

"How about you Monica? You plan to have kids someday?" Timmy asked.

"Well someday maybe. But I'm wary about you men. You've got a tendency to unload your seeds and then leave them screechlings entirely in our care."

A flurry of coughs rippled through the males in the group, followed by a deep, collective "Nah!"

Someone threw in, "We're not all like Timmy."

The weight of Monica's gaze shifted to Cambria.

"Now Cambria's a woman. She knows what I'm talking about."

A petition for support.

Cambria jerked. With all eyes turned to her, awaiting her response, she went stiff across the shoulders, and bore a contemplative smile as she ironed out a reply in her head. Personally, she was always peeved by Monica's stuck-up demeanour, and had never been so keen to deny her an accomplice. But did she have grounds to disagree? She found she did.

"Well, I may have a slightly different point of view in regard to this matter." Everyone waited anxiously for Cambria to continue.

"How so?" Monica asked curiously.

"Well... I like little babies." As she spoke, she folded her arms as if she were cradling a real baby, and she gently swayed from side to side.

Monica pouted her annoyance, then offered Cambria a polite but slightly disappointed smile.

Timmy was spellbound by the heart-warming display of affection Cambria showed for her make-believe baby, and he felt as if the world paused, to afford him the chance to etch that moment in his mind. He was always privy to Cambria's kind and gentle nature, but he merely wrote it off as timidity, as part of her non-abrasive demeanour. But after her display, he was now convinced that those soft qualities were the essence of her, and he felt he had just been allowed a peek into her centre.

For the rest of the evening, Timmy could not get that image of Cambria out of his head, of her softly rocking her arms, her eyes cast downwards with the warmth and tenderness of a mother truly in love with her child. As he worked the crowd at the party, he found himself constantly stealing glances at her. And when she looked back, he turned away, afraid that she would discover he was observing her. And the unexpected occurred. He experienced an emotion he had never before encountered with regards to her–jealousy. Each time a guy struck up a conversation with her, he felt protective of her, and he wanted to ward them off. The worst was when Gavin, *Cream's* most drooled-over designer, his hand guiding her back, ushered her to one corner so they could talk privately.

Gavin had a bit of a reputation, of lodging himself into every woman he set his eyes on. Even though he usually only bedded one at a time, he had a contingent of willing subjects on call, a relatively public list he did little to hide. Quite detestably, his lack of discretion did not seem to bother any of them. In fact, many brazenly bragged that they were a part of the deck, and didn't at all mind being shuffled. The guys at *Cream* were constantly baffled by how the fairer sex were so madly drawn to Gavin, hovering over him like seagulls at a pier. Amazed by his tally and curious of his allure, they always watched to see if Gavin stood further from the urinal than other guys. He did. Only because he knew they were watching.

Timmy was certain of Gavin's intentions as he leaned in close to talk to Cambria. And he loathed the way Gavin was appraising her with his opportunistic eyes. Each time Cambria smiled or laughed at one of Gavin's comments, he felt the urge to rush over, to disrupt the conversation, to make it awkward for him to pull any prurient moves. Timmy breathed a huge sigh of relief when Cambria pulled away from Gavin. But in the next instant, he became tense again, realising she was walking over to him. He forced himself to take a couple of deep breaths to quell his panic.

"Timmy. I shall be taking leave from our little soirée and just wanted to say goodnight before I head off."

"So soon?"

"I'd really love to stay, but I've been fighting a losing battle to convince my eyes to stay open. I think the events of the week have finally caught up with me. And it's a pity that they had to have this do on a Thursday. So no sleeping in tomorrow."

"No, just take the day off. Seriously, Cambria. You've been a star all week. All month actually."

"No. There's just so much to be done. I think by this time next week, everything will be out the door, and we'll have room for a breather."

With some reluctance, he agreed with her.

"I saw you talking to Gavin earlier."

Cambria twisted her face into a pretzel, "Pffffft, that nutter?"

"Why?" Timmy asked, anxious to know.

"I've never met someone more forward with his advances, with more presumptuousness."

Timmy flashed a knowing smile.

"You wouldn't believe what he said to me."

"What?"

"This isn't going anywhere, right?"

Timmy nodded.

"Gavin asked me if I had any plans after the party, and I told him yes, I've got a date with my bed. He replied, what a coincidence, after this, I've got a date with your bed too. I chuckled and told him, ha, ha, that's funny. He then attempted this licentious confession on me. He professed that he has had his eye on me for some time now, and that if I were up to it, he'd really like to pollinate me."

"Noooo," Timmy's eyelids peeled open fully, "did he really use that word... pollinate."

She nodded.

"He didn't."

"He did so," Cambria sternly confirmed. Timmy tried to smother his amusement but failed. And she, surprised that he would be so amused by the whole thing, laughed along. "The nerve," she topped up. They laughed even harder, clutching the giggles in their bellies. There was silence as they both caught their breath.

"Timmy..." Cambria swallowed and paused for a moment.

"Yes?"

She timidly lowered her eyelids. "For some time now I've wanted to thank you for being such a great mentor to me. And for giving me opportunities that most could only dream of. I know that all the favouritism you've shown me causes some disconcert in the group. And I know it's hard to justify some of your decisions to stick me in the big projects. Thank you for investing so much belief in me."

This was the most heartfelt praise Timmy had ever received, and he cast frantically for a reply.

"Well thank you."

And he left it at that.

"See you tomorrow then."

Shyly avoiding her eyes, he replied, "Yeah, see you."

Cambria swung away, and weaved her way to the restaurant's entrance. As she was walking out the door, she looked over her shoulder. She noticed that Timmy's eyes were fastened on her. So she raised her hand, and curled her fingers lightly, to again bid him goodbye. Caught unexpected, Timmy felt embarrassed and instinctively reciprocated with a stiff wave. He watched her walk out the restaurant, taking his heart with her. As the door swung close, cutting off that last glimpse of her, he felt as if the party had lost its lustre, and he found no reason to be there anymore.

Timmy suddenly felt claustrophobic in the room packed with people. Perplexed by this surge of emotions for his protégé, he wanted to be alone, to have some time by himself. Time to analyse and understand this new tangle of emotions that had manifested itself in him.

Timmy made a quick round to excuse himself, citing the same reason that Cambria used for her departure. And he left.

~.~.~.~.~.~

When he got home, he threw his keys on the dining table, proceeded to the couch in his living room, and became a frozen silhouette in the dark. Staring into the unlit doorways of his house, he experienced a deep loneliness he had not felt in a long time. Looking at the lap of luxury that surrounded him, he sighed, *The guy with everything... but nothing.*

When Timmy's parents died, they left him with a huge fortune he had no idea they had. Based on who they were and what they did for a living, Timmy always figured they were rich. But it was only until their will was read that he discovered they were eight million rich.

Growing up, Timmy lived with his parents in a medium size

townhouse in a decent part of the city. They lived comfortably, not lavishly. As a child, he got to travel frequently, a lot more than his peers. And this was their only indication of affluence. Following their death, Timmy chose to fend for himself rather than rely on the help of others. He always felt that he did not deserve his parents' money, and only used what was needed to get himself an education abroad, in America.

A year after his studies, upon returning to London, Timmy had his close brush with death. This was the time he ran his heart to a stop in Whitechapel, in front of the hospital that pronounced his parents dead. It was there that he fell in love with the student nurse assigned to change his bedding every day. Two years into their couplehood, his relationship with the nurse ended abruptly and badly. Reeling from the break-up, and at that time feeling the need to meet his eccentricities as a budding Art Director, Timmy spent a sizeable chunk of his inheritance to design and build a house in the sky. Composed in a Balinese style, his four-bedroom home sat on the rooftop of an eighteen-storey luxury apartment building, right on the water's edge in Canary Wharf, London's upscale financial district. In the building stages, he even belted up and applied whatever woodcraft skills he had acquired from his summer months on Laeso.

This dream home of Timmy's was fashioned out of dark tropical hardwoods and plant fibres, and nested within a lush rooftop garden of creepers, ferns and fish-filled rock pools. A thatch roof supported by dark teak wood beams kept the place cool and dry.

To regulate the extreme conditions found on the rooftop, Timmy made sure the house had a wrap around veranda and ample slatted shutters. This permitted airflow and controlled the light coming into the house. Despite being close to the sun, Timmy's architectural marvel stayed cool in the summer and glowed with a gentle warmth. The house dealt with the cold differently. It was designed to capture the thermals rising from the apartments below in the winter time.

Without upsetting its natural aesthetic, Timmy contemporised his living space with indulgences you wouldn't find in your typical Balinese hut. A state-of-the-art sound system, which he concealed in the ceiling and beneath the floor boards, offered a subliminal auditory experience. To help ease him out of sleep each morning, Timmy programmed his home to come alive with natural sounds. Each day it was a different theme. Some days he woke up to the purr of the sea and the fleeting call of seagulls. Some mornings he was in the forest–the sound of rustling leaves, distant bird calls and crooning insects filling the air. Other days, he awoke by a gurgling brook with restless fish (trout that announced their presence by arcing out of the water, and plopping back in).

Timmy's bed sheets were made of 1500-threadcount Egyptian cotton, and he always felt as if he lay on butter. Because he had ample space in his bedroom, he treated himself to an elephantine mahogany bed, two feet broader than a King. He had always envisioned having a wife on the opposite end, and two kids sandwiched between them. Timmy's bed choice was a decision he later regretted. Sleeping on it he always felt insignificant, as if he were a life raft lost at sea.

"Cambria? Who would have thought?" He shook his head.

Timmy was well familiar with the dreariness of post party blues. But what he was experiencing was far more heavy. By himself in an empty house, beset by the melancholy of an old unplayed piano, he felt irrelevant to the world. That night, to not magnify his insignificance, he opted not to subject himself to the vastness of his bed. After kicking off his shoes, he prepared for sleep on the recliner in the living room. Eyes closed, he allowed his mind to journey into the quiet corners of his soul, to try and learn what incited the flurry of emotions that had gained control over him. The only thing he was sure of was that it all started at the party, as Cambria rocked her arms. *I like little babies.* Those words, spoken so innocently in her creamy voice, repeated themselves in his mind. He wasn't certain of Cambria's age, but reckoned he had eight candles on her, maybe more. He considered it, and concluded that it was a gap wide enough to churn gossip, to raise an eyebrow or two in some circles. And he started to question if what he was feeling for her was love, or merely some fetish for mothering ingénues he was unaware of. Over the years of working with Cambria, he had felt nothing for her. Nothing.

His eyes still closed, he allowed snippets of their past to play through his mind, like movie trailers spliced onto a single reel. Now and then, he paused and rewound, to try and spot any forming of a latent desire that may have fallen beyond his knowing. He dipped into the crevices, sieved through the scrapings, but found nothing to justify his passion.

Timmy had a pre-determined set of attributes that he looked for in his *only*, and he carried it with him like a glass slipper. The qualities that he revered did not match Cambria's. He veered towards women with a stately confidence. Mostly, they tended to be outspoken, someone he could listen and talk to for hours. Cambria was just too reserved to be his type.

Who is this voice, this voice communing with my soul, he threw into the dark.

Growing more restless by the minute, Timmy started to wonder if maybe he needed to reconsider 'his type'. With his career going places very quickly, he questioned if he was too caught up with trying to find a partner to match his celebrity. He sometimes wondered if this was the case with Monica de la Pena, that maybe, he was not attracted to her as a person, but to the social status she carried.

Despite the glass slipper not fitting, the only thing that occupied his mind that night was Cambria, the image of her, her smile, her demeanour. Timmy scoured for a reason to call her, to hear her voice. He floated up some, but none that were valid for that time of the night.

To try and quiet his mind, Timmy deployed his thoughts to other things: to ongoing projects at work, to new running techniques he was planning to experiment with, to memories of past romances. The diversion worked, but was fleeting. Each time his mind relaxed and lowered its guard, it meandered back to her.

Friday After The Party

"Am I asleep?"

Timmy hated how that question answered itself.

He reached into his pants pocket and pulled out his cell phone. 5:30, the time showed. Realising that he was past getting any decent sleep that night, he got changed and went for a run, an hour earlier than his daily usual.

Timmy felt sluggish and ached all over. But stepping out into the cool dawn renewed him. He enjoyed his runs each morning and felt incomplete if this part of his day was unfulfilled. His daily routine was such. Wake at 6:30. Freshen up. Run. Back by 7:30. The three Ss. Watch the news over breakfast. Head to work when the morning rush had eased.

There were a lot of things that Timmy loved about the early hours. He found the light soothing; the air—crisp and sweet. He also liked the deadness. It was a good type of dead, not of a life that was, but of a life to be. It was life on the onset of commencing, full of hope and promise, like seedlings in the moist earth waiting to be coaxed out by the sun. He enjoyed watching the day unfurl into a hive of activity, easing from quiet to vibrancy. He loved the smell of dew glistening on leaves, the aroma of waking bakeries, the sound of cars stuttering to life, the flit of hands poking out the front door to retrieve the morning paper. He also obtained an odd sense of fulfilment seeing store owners flipping around their signage from 'closed' to 'open'. Each morning, as the sun kissed the cool earth and left her radiance everywhere, he felt as if the world had been cleansed of the previous day, and renewed itself.

Timmy knew his route well, was well-acquainted with every crack, bump, and recess on the asphalt. The pavements of London were his domain, his escape, and he knew he could count on his morning run to still his mind, stem the recurring thoughts of Cambria. To his chagrin, his workout turned into an extension of his midnight ruminations—she was all he thought about the entire time. Starting out earlier than usual, Timmy headed home before the sun had fully risen, the city still in a yawn.

After each run, Timmy relished the sensation of being lacquered with sweat, loved the feel of his soaked jersey sticking to him like cling film. Sometimes, he would stick out his tongue to catch the sweat pouring down his face, just to savour its saltiness. That day, it was different. He fell into a panic, was seized by an urgency to get out of his clothes, to jump into the shower and drench the sweat off his body. He had but one thing on his mind that morning: to get in to work as quickly as possible.

~.~.~.~.~.~

The cold wind curled the collar of his overcoat into his cheek. He hugged the warmth tight to his body by crossing his arms, and he quickened his step. When he arrived at *Cream*, the corrugated steel door shielding its front entrance was still anchored to the ground. Not wanting to leave his hands exposed to the cold he reached into his trouser pocket and browsed for the right key. He had locked-up after work enough times to single it out by feel alone.

The first in, he was not greeted by the lovely receptionist usually at the front desk. Each morning he'd stop and talk to her for a bit, to get a measure of people's mood.

Timmy descended the stairs into the basement and stopped at Cambria's desk. Being around her things intensified his longing for her. Of all the creatives, Timmy noticed her desk was the neatest. Storyboards were in sequence, slanted against the inner edge of her low cubicle divider. Stacks of research, organised using colour coded tabs, were arranged in perfect vertical alignment. She only had three items pinned to her board. A birthday card she had received from Bailey, her best friend at *Cream*. Next to it, there was a magazine tear-out of what was probably her next dream destination. It featured the luminescent cliff houses of Oia in Santorini, set against a deep blue Mediterranean sky. The third item was a close-up photo of Cambria, cheek-to-cheek with a girl of five, maybe six, possibly a niece. Timmy could not see their eyes. Their smiles had taken up all the real estate on their faces. He could tell from the off-centeredness, and from the tight crop, that the photo had been self-shot with the camera held out at arm's length.

"You're in bright and early," Kim's voice rang across the room.

"Hey Kimbo," Timmy looked up and walked in Kim's direction, a little guilty that he had been caught snooping.

"I tried to reach you last night. Where were you? Not like you to leave a party early. I called to make sure everything was alright." As Timmy got closer, Kim noticed the rings under Timmy's eyes. "Jeez, you look like death. Late night romp?"

"If only," Timmy managed to roll his heavy retinas.

"I'm headed to the deli. Care to join me?"

It was signature for Timmy to have two, sometimes three breakfasts in one morning; artery cloggers when he was in the mood: bangers, hash browns, eggs, bacon, fried tomatoes, beans, mushrooms, sometimes all heaped onto a single plate.

On a regular day, swallowing over twenty miles of road from his morning and lunch time runs, Timmy felt thermal throughout the day, his body an internal furnace combusting everything it was fed. As such, he paid little concern to his diet. But that morning, his heart residenced in his belly, he felt not a twinge of hunger.

"Nah, I'm fine. Have a nagging pile of things to get through today. Should best get a start on it."

Kim raised an eyebrow, crinkled his forehead, then caved in, "Alright mate."

Kim dropped his things off at his desk and went back up the stairs. Timmy was by himself again. He had the urge to go back to Cambria's desk, just to be near her things, but fought off the disturbing voyeuristic urge.

As he sat at his computer to go through his emails, he found that nothing he was reading was registering. So he started to reorganise his desk, a first for him. Timmy was the poster child for untidiness. To start with, his desk looked like autumn ground cover beneath a shady tree, layered with years of reports, project briefs, chewing gum wrappers, meeting notes, receipts. He never found any reason to reorganise, figuring that things fell in their natural order, chronologically, like the rings of a tree. When he needed to find something, all he had to do was peel into the past. The things he needed the most, usually lived on the surface.

Timmy's desk served as a template for the rest of his room. Clothes lay strewn all over—on the couch, beside it, under it, behind it, before it—a mingled mass of dress shirts, running jerseys, neckties, socks, pants of every length. Most of his apparel was half worn, some brand new and still in their crisp plastic sheets.

Timmy ran a hundred or so miles a week. As a result, he wore out his shoes very quickly, a pair every two weeks. He retired his trainers in the corner behind his desk, in a heap Cambria once referred to as the Elysian Fields for shoes, the place where dead soles go when they die. To everyone's surprise, despite being a breeding ground for bad odour, Timmy's room smelled good, thanks wholly to a portable air ioniser that vacuumed the air the same time it wisped a scented herbal mist. This gift from heaven came from his former personal assistant, Chloe.

As the office started to fill at 9:30, Timmy found he could no longer focus on tidying his table. Each time someone descended the metal stairs into the basement, he felt his chest tighten, and relax soon after, after he discovered it was not Cambria. Stuck with a half-organised desk, he regretted ever starting, seeing how there was no longer any order to the disorder. At 9:42, his heart lurched forward. The footsteps coming down the stainless steel stairs were distinctly hers. He was amazed that he recognised her sound. He must have subconsciously picked it up through the years. Males generally thudded down. Females *clinked*. Cambria *clanked*.

Cambria was never comfortable in heels, no matter how low they were. She only wore them to work and big events. Over the course of her professional life, she grew more accomplished with walking and standing in them, but had never been able to master the stairs.

Clanking occurs when your footwear flaps as you walk, and this is more likely to happen upon descent than when walking level. It all had to do with leverage. To avoid *clanking*, sufficient downward pressure needs to be applied to the front of the shoe, so that the rear of the insole is tipped upwards, against the heel. This was something Cambria had a problem doing. She could not curl down her toes enough. It would have helped if she wore heels with a closed back, or shoes with straps, but she chaffed easily. So she avoided those styles like the plague.

Cambria was happy that she did not stay long at the party. Though it was the most thrilling February of her life, the late nights at *Cream* were starting to wear her down. Rejuvenated after her 10-hour sleep, the spring in her step was more pronounced than the day before. As she made her way to her desk, she noticed Timmy peering through his door at her. She bypassed her table and headed straight for his room. Timmy scrambled to look busy.

With as much life as she could muster, she asked in jest, "Good morning Timmy. How are WE this morning?" mimicking the trademark phrase he used throughout the day, every day. It was only after she greeted him that she noticed how awful he looked. And she wondered if the joviality with which she delivered her question was out of place. It was typical of Timmy to look artistically dishevelled, but today he looked unkempt, and haggard.

"Morning Brie. Couldn't be better," Timmy answered with a smile. To his own surprise, he wasn't lying. As Cambria walked in, he felt as if an angel had descended upon him. He wanted so badly to hold her in his arms, but at the same time felt unworthy of her touch. His heart, which raced as she was making her way to his room, started to steady as she stood there talking to him. At first, he was certain of this, that were he to come face-to-face with her, he would be overwhelmed and suffocated by his emotions. But what he experienced instead was a sense of peace, a displaced tranquillity restored by her presence.

"Any plans for the weekend?" Timmy asked.

"Just going about my usual."

"And what is that? Your usual?"

"Oh! Laundry, ironing, prepare my lunches for the week. Read a book."

"You cook much?"

Cambria chuckled. "Does anything that takes less than three steps count as cooking?"

"In my world it does."

"I cook a fair bit if that's the case." They traded smiles.

"So what's the book for the weekend?" Timmy enquired, trying to prolong the conversation with her.

"I'm at the tail end of a book I've wanted to read for years now. *Prozac Nation*. Have you read it?"

"No, I've not. What is it about? Is it any good?"

"It's about the author's paralysing journey through mental illness and depression. Many of her accounts are scarily lurid. I like books with real life accounts, not so much biographical work, but stories with slice-of-life descriptions. If you like, I'll lend it to you when I'm done. But I hope it won't cast a shadow on your day."

Timmy kept a library of books in his office; in disarray on the shelves they lived on, much like the room they lived in. The selection was telling: books on religion, conspiracy theories, political books, bathroom humour, marriage survival guides, transcendental meditation, de-motivational books, even books for cigar aficionados. Eating up the most shelf space were books on running; every dimension of it..

"Sure, I'd love to read it... when you're done with it that is."

"Just give me another day or two."

Timmy struggled desperately to think of something else to say to her, to keep her in the room longer, but words failed him. The silence became awkward.

Placing her hands together, Cambria resorted to, "I should probably start my day."

Timmy disagreed, but nodded in agreement.

He watched as she made her way back to her desk, her heels accentuating the movement of her hips as she walked. As she leaned forward to switch on her computer monitor, her knee length skirt rode up her legs, conceding a glimpse of her inner thighs through the split. He took in the svelte lines and sensuous tone brought about by the light strain on her calves. Timmy felt dirty defiling her in this lewd fashion. He turned away, wrestled with his urges, and in the next instance, found his attention fixed on her again. Afraid someone would notice him staring, he forced his eyes from the door and stared goggle-eyed at his computer screen, befuddled by the ghost that had taken him over.

Throughout the morning, Timmy made several attempts to do what he failed at the night before, and that was to figure out what made this whole thing with Cambria come about. Frustrated when his self investigation turned up more questions than answers, he grew resigned to the possibility that this anomaly fell well beyond his comprehension. The sensible thing to do, he decided, was to just closet up his inclinations—a foolish endeavour he discovered soon after, almost immediately. To try and shut her out of his mind was as effective as an attempt to dam a river with gauze. He could not stem it, let alone contain it... this urge... this unrestrainable passion... it seethed through the pores, poured from the seams. He couldn't take it anymore. He decided he was going to ask her out for coffee.

Timmy stopped halfway out the door, arrested by the need to compose what he was going to say. He was taken aback by his sudden loss of spontaneity. What once came as a routine "Let's discuss this over coffee," was now a jittery effort akin to one buying his first condom at a store. Tight in the gut, as if someone had braided his intestines, he made his way up to her and proposed coffee, citing an upcoming project as the purpose for their meeting. She upped and went with him, taking a pen and a notepad with her.

At the café, he was unusually quiet throughout their discussion, and found himself grasping none of the ideas Cambria was parading. He developed a new cognisance of her and found himself fully focused on the details of her manner, on her accentuations. The curls of her mouth as she spoke, the way she used her index to twirl her hair when deep in thought, how she leaned forward when conveying the interesting parts of a story, how she bit her lower lip and looked upward when reconsidering a thought she had just announced.

Cambria had mesmerising hazel eyes, which in equal degree, pierced as much as they lured you in. Timmy made several attempts to look directly into them, but found himself breaking contact before he could fully dip into them. He was smitten by how talkative she was, now that he wasn't hogging the conversation, and how his approval meant so much to her; the way her face lit up whenever he agreed with her on a point. Timmy felt that he could watch her for hours, analyse her like mathematics, and not say a word.

Towards the end of their hour-long discussion, Cambria noticed that Timmy had not touched the strawberry scone he had ordered.

"Are you going to eat that, or poke it with your fork all day?" she cheekily asked.

Timmy looked up at her, and back down at his scone. Amused by her forwardness, he drew a one-sided smile.

"Nah! I haven't had much of a stomach of late. Would you like to finish it for me?"

"Not after you've Jack-the-Rippered it like that," she goofishly grinned. "Half an hour ago, maybe."

"Why the loss of appetite?"

"New girl in my life has filled my stomach with butterflies," he revealed jokingly, but only in manner. Although it was his natural instinct to hide his feelings from her, a larger part of him wanted so badly to share them with her. He enjoyed the exhilaration of dropping the idea into her head, of flirting with the possibility of her learning of his desire.

"Really?" Cambria reacted excitedly, but withdrew her enthusiasm immediately, until she could determine from his face if he was joking or serious. His face did not give away much. But Cambria knew from experience, that whenever someone was in love, there was always an inclination to want to talk about it. So she enquired further.

"Who is it?"

"I was just joking, Cambria."

Timmy felt a tingle when he spoke her name. He always thought she had an alluring name, but only at that moment was he fully cognizant of how beautifully it rolled off his tongue.

"You can tell me. I swear, your secret's safe with me." She placed her hand on her chest, in the fashion of one pledging allegiance.

"I was joking. Seriously."

"Try again, hombre." Her grin turned into a giggle. "Is it Monica?"

Timmy's eyes widened.

"Everyone's been speculating that you have a fancy for her. It's her, isn't it?"

She sensed she was on the cusp of getting a confession from him, and leaned in fully to catch his answer.

"No, it's not her."

"Aha!" Cambria exploded deliriously, her synapses pricking to life. "You've just admitted to a someone. And that the butterflies do exist. So, if it's not Monica, who is it?"

Timmy smiled as he shook his head, amused and bewildered by how quickly she dissected his words and arrived at conclusions of her own. Now feeling the heat, he veered the subject away from himself.

"You mentioned that everyone was speculating it's Monica. Who's this 'everyone' anyway? And why on earth would they think I had an interest in her?"

"Well, we just always see how you crawl into your shell whenever you're around her. How your eyes never leave her when she's in the room. How you hang on her every word."

"You said 'we'. I take that as admission on your part that you are a member of this 'everyone' you were referring to?"

Cambria laughed, amazed by how Timmy so smoothly turned the witch hunt around. "No, I just happened to eavesdrop on a few conversations."

"And you agree with what THEY were saying?"

"No. I did not agree with what they were saying." She paused. "I merely, did not disagree." She leaned back in her chair with a guilty cheek on her face.

Satisfied by his riposte, Timmy breathed a sigh of relief. A little too soon.

"So if it's not Monica, who is it? Is it Chloe? Let me guess. Her sudden departure left a big empty in your heart, and you are only now starting to realise it?"

Timmy palmed his forehead and smiled at her persistence. He was always bedazzled by her power of conjecture, but this was the first time he saw it applied outside the realm of work, in gossipy gossip.

"No. It's not Monica. And it's not Chloe."

She waved him on. "Keep going."

"Who knows... maybe it's you," Timmy dared to say, figuring the self allegation was preposterous enough to be disregarded.

Cambria felt a warm blush spread across her face as Timmy's eyes connected with hers. From the flatness of his voice, she could not fully tell if he was pulling one on her. But she got an inkling he was half serious more than he was half joking.

A moment of uneasiness hung between them, but Timmy let it steep. When it got unbearable, he diffused the awkwardness by asking, "You sure you wouldn't care for some of my scone?"

They both laughed. The witch hunt had been called off.

The Ensuing Weeks

Timmy: Where can I score some Prozac? Your book has gotten me really down. Think I'll buy some blades OTW home. /----

Cambria: LOL. What's up Timmy?

Timmy: Just looked over your mocks for the new account. Wasn't so sure about the font choice.

Cambria: What's wrong with it?

Timmy: Nothing wrong with it. Just find it a bit overused across the work we've been producing.

Cambria: Oh?

Timmy: We've used Century Gothic for Bell. Century Gothic for Common Grounds. And now this.

Cambria: Oops. Century Gothic's my fall back font. When in doubt... Cent Goth. :\

Timmy: Ya, I pretty much guessed.

Cambria: Do you have a replacement font in mind?

Timmy: Hmmm! No one knows fonts better than you.

Cambria: True. But no one applies them better than you.

Timmy: Maybe we could try a sexier font like Cambria, bold but elegant. Wonderful curves, pleasing to the eye. ;)

Cambria: Ha, ha. Don't like the uppercase Q. Her tail is too big.

Timmy: Yeah, I've noticed her tail too. Looks fine to me.

Cambria looks over her shoulder and shoots me a look of amused disbelief. Through my door, I respond with a Cheshire grin.

Following the dawn of my feelings for her, every conversation with her became unnatural, every invitation for coffee more contrived, and I preferred to chat online with her, flirting with her in ways that decreased in subtlety. It was really difficult to concentrate at work whenever she was around, so I tried working from the café down the street, only to soon learn, that I did not have to see her, to see her. I started to spot her likeness in other women — random strangers — and it took but the slightest semblance to renew my needing.

Despite my years of working with her, Cambria had remained an enigma to me. Because we shared so much in common by way of work, that was all we talked about. She also had this habit of deflecting questions aimed at her back to the enquirer. The chatterbox I was, I often bit on the bait, and divulged more than I indulged.

But now it was different. Each time her name was brought up in group conversation, I seized the opportunity to inconspicuously enquire about her. And every chance I got, I tiptoed into subjects inevitably linked to her to try and learn more. Funnily, the more I uncovered, the more intrigued I grew, as each door I opened led to three more. Soon, my discovery of her became much like an attempt to cure thirst with sea water.

To see if I could pick up any indication of how she felt about me, I got close to everyone she was even mildly pally with. Recognising that they were a channel to her, I treated them nicer than I normally did, in hopes that they would drop in a good word. And throughout the day, I sat glued to my computer, anxiously waiting for her to make an entry on her blog, or post an update to one of a handful of social networking sites she belonged to.

One day, I stopped and questioned if I was going too far with my infatuation. I felt I had become the hunter, and she the prey, and it shocked me that I had unconsciously become a different person. Someone I did not want to be.

Before I became consumed with her, I was proud of the way I lived my life; to the fullest, with little pause, with little regret. The only thing I bemoaned in recent memory was the decadent home I had built for myself, an indulgence which caught me at a moment of weakness. I almost sold off my property, figuring the money could have been better used to aid the needy. But I pulled back at the last minute. I wanted to keep it as a reminder of a mistake never again to be repeated, a reminder I woke up to and went home to every day. Eventually though, I found a way to atone for my folly. I arranged for every penny I earned at *Cream* to be deposited directly into the bank accounts of five causes I supported. Bolstered by my inheritance, and not having to work to survive, I sometimes found it difficult to find meaning in my job. But knowing the charities counted on my paycheque each month gave my work purpose.

~.~.~.~.~.~

It was a flicker that persisted into a flame, that doused the fire in my eyes.

Sleep continued to elude me, and I looked more and more gaunt each day. The torment that I lived with was from having no outlet for my feelings. I felt as if the chambers of my heart were not large enough to contain my love for her, that at any point, my sternum would give. The twisted irony that plagued me each day was this, that thinking of her served to both fill and contribute to the ravine of emptiness within me. Yet I never felt more alive. I now had something real to live for, something to look forward to every day, and life held new meaning for me.

Each night, trapped in the loneliness of my house, I slid into a state of brooding disquietude. It was usually in the breathless silence of the late hours that I pined for her and longed to hear her voice. So I started to save voice messages that she left on my phone, each a sparkly little gem. I listened to them over and over again. Of the constellation, my favourite was, "Hey you. The funniest thing just happened [giggle]. It's all gone pear-shaped. Those muppets printed the piece in greyscale. Just like you suspected they would. Will just wait for you to get in on Monday. And we'll sort them out together."

She possessed the roundest, most natural laugh. And it poured a rainbow into my heart each time I heard it. I found this message special not because of her giggle, but in the way she concluded the message; with the words 'we' and 'together' in the same line. Often, as I lay in bed, I snuggled my phone against my cheek, and played my favourite recording till I slid into sleep, my ear on her voice.

An Invitation

I studied my First Class ticket, flipping it to its back, and then to its front, and to its back again. I squandered the minutes away, quite certain of my decision, and watched my lifelong dream strain through my fingers.

~.~.~.~.~.~

"In heaven's bloody name, what are you still doing here?"

Kim was in total disbelief as he rushed into the room.

"You should have left a bloody hour ago," he half shouted.

Timmy was stunned out of his reverie, but resumed his pre-occupation with the ticket. In a dull voice, he acknowledged Kim's presence, "Hey Kim."

"Traffic's going to be a bitch. You know better. What with the mad rush home for Easter. It'd be a knot. You'd better leave now. I can't bloody believe you."

With dogged determination, Kim searched the room for Timmy's travel bag; along its periphery, beneath Timmy's desk, under the piles of clothes. Finding none, he shut the door behind him.

"What's going on?"

"I'm not going."

"What do you mean you're not going?"

"I'm just... nn nn not going"

"WHY NOT?"

"I'm happy here."

"You?" Kim enunciated sarcastically. "YOU?" More pronounced this time. "You are happy here?"

Timmy had never heard Kim's voice reach that level. As he watched Kim pace around the room, puffing through his nose, his mouth, his ears—bull-like—Timmy sensed that worse was to come.

"Happy?" he huffed, his anger compounding. "Well, that sure as hell explains the last two weeks. Why you've been completely drawn out of character. Why you've been looking like horse shit. Why half your nights are spent here, why we find you here in the morning slumped over your desk. Why you carry the rancid breath of a drunk each morning. What's bloody going on Timmy?"

Timmy knew that it was a matter of time before someone confronted him on the poor state he was in, and he wasn't at all surprised it was Kim.

"Well, I met a girl."

"You met a girl?"

"Well, I didn't really meet her. Well, I did. A long while back."

Timmy appeared confused, so Kim summed it up for him. "So it's someone you met awhile back, but just developed feelings for."

"Yeah!" Timmy responded with great excitement, as if Kim had just resolved one of life's great mysteries.

"I don't believe you. I really don't bloody believe you. You've come this close," Kim pinched air, "... this close, and you're copping out."

"I'm not c..."

"Don't give me that load of crock."

They stared at each other.

"You told me to always tell it to you as it is. So don't give me that look, like I've just shot your dog or something."

Timmy straightened his face.

"On the day we met, you told me this—that your dream of dreams, your so called 'doorway to the next paradigm', involved you accomplishing two things."

"To secure a job at *Oddinary*." He thumbed. "And to debut as the winner of the New York Marathon." He pointed.

Kim paused, to let his point sink in. "You've been working half your life towards this moment, Timmy. You've come within seconds of the world's best runners. And you've got *Oddinary*, your dream agency, knocking on your door. How many agencies fly their candidates in First, and put them up at the Carlton, on one of the busiest weekends of the year? When? The job's damn near yours, Timmy. The first of your two piece puzzle. Mate, you can't let your dreams gestate forever. Your hour has arrived Tims. Seize it."

"But she is..."

"Stop. Just stop," Kim superimposed his voice over Timmy's. "I know you're going to give me all that *'she is the one'* bollocks. That you have found *true love*, your *raison d'être*. You need to just trust me on this one mate. To help you see clearly."

Timmy knew he wasn't going to get any words in.

"You read widely. You probably know this line." Kim changed his voice, and spoke slowly, "The day that man allows true love to appear, those things which are well-made will fall into confusion..."

"...and will overrun everything we believe to be right and true. Dante's Divine comedy," Timmy steered the quote to completion. He was surprised by how easily the words left his tongue. He had his English teacher to thank, the one he had a crush on when he was fifteen.

"Are you familiar with the Mexican concept of the *acomodador*?" Kim asked.

"No I'm not."

"The *acomodador* is something that happens in our life that shakes our foundation and causes us to stop living. To stop pursuing our dreams." He explained further, "Many things can come in the way of our dreams. A death, a birth, a car accident, a woman. Regardless of its source, one thing is certain. The *acomodador* is deleterious, can derail your life, and you need to bloody flush it away. Or else you will waste your life and never arrive at your true potential."

Timmy was always blown away by Kim's ability to draw from renowned European scholars, and in the next instant, lean on folkloric teachings from obscure cultures. He always regarded Kim an odd choice for a personal assistant, and thought him more fitting as a writer or a literature professor. A politician even. But never a PA to a Creative Director. It crossed his mind to push Kim on to bigger and better things, but Kim always seemed happy at his job. Thankful for it even. Today being one of the exceptions.

Timmy let a brief moment of quiet pass.

"I've given it a lot of thought Kim. And I think you know me well enough... to know that I would have. And let me assure you that I'm not giving up on my dream, but just setting it aside for awhile, while I unknot my situation. I've kept you out of the loop on things. I shouldn't have."

"You remember your first love, Kim?"

Kim nodded.

"Correct me if I'm wrong, but back then, you loved this person unconditionally. And you were prepared to spend forever with her. And if someone asked you why you loved her, you responded with something daft like, 'Just because'. And nothing anyone could say would change how you felt for her."

Kim nodded again, fully aware of where Timmy was taking his point.

"Well Kim, she is the one. I have found her at last. And nothing you say will change that. Please realise and accept that."

Timmy detected a glint of disappointment in Kim's eyes.

"Kim, from the day we met, there's been no greater a friend than you've been to me. And now, more than ever, I need your support on this."

Kim sighed.

"Let me tell you about your 'one'. And I don't know how to break it to you lightly. But I'll bloody call it as I saw it. She was clubbing at The Roof Gardens last weekend with a guy, rather distinguished looking, as you'd expect of her taste. And they were kissing."

Timmy felt his heart clench into a tight ball, and he struggled to breathe out his next question.

"Kissing?"

"Was it a hello, goodbye kiss? Or a kiss, kiss?" Timmy knew the answer before he even asked it.

"Let's just say, she looked like she was trying to eat his lunch. I know she holds herself really well here at work. Courtly and cultured. But that night, she took on a different manifestation."

Timmy was crushed. Just like that, his Eden had turned into Hades.

Robbed of the only thing that occupied his nothingness, he felt his life force leave his body. Tears gushed to his eyes, but found no outlet, dammed just in time by his masculine pride.

"Nightclubs are dark. Are you sure... " His voice crumbled like a wafer. "Are you sure it was her?"

"They were seated in a well-lit section of the club. Under the cover of the crowd and flashing lights, I was able to get really close to catch a good glimpse. It was definitely her. No mistaking her signature green eyes."

"Brown eyes." Timmy was quick to correct Kim. "Cambria has brown eyes."

Kim's eyes widened. "Cambria?"

After a two-hour conversation with Timmy, one that he was asked to keep in the highest confidence, Kim exited the room, still unsure of what to think of the whole situation. Timmy had a thing for Monica de la Pena. Everyone was certain of it, he included. But Timmy had ten arms, a surprise up each sleeve. That he knew too. Never had he met anyone like Timmy, so fluctuant, whose every pattern seemed fashioned to elude prediction.

Kim wanted to be happy for Timmy, but he couldn't. He was greatly unsettled knowing that his boss, now also his best friend, was going to get his heart broken. Cambria had never before expressed the faintest shade of interest in Timmy, had displayed no romantic inclinations of any sort to anyone. And for that, Kim's week at the Lakes was not as peaceful as he had intended it to be.

Cambria waltzed up, rapped her knuckles on the door frame, and stuck her head in.

"Happy Easter!"

Timmy tore his eyes away from what he was not really doing, and looked up.

"Yeah, to you too."

"Any plans for the weekend? Doing anything? Going anywhere?"

She had to push her way into the room–his door had long lost its ability to fully yawn open, thanks to the hoard of clothes, gym bags and sports rackets hanging on the back, dangling like meat at the butchers.

"Nope. No plans for the weekend. Just me and Mark."

That was secret code that he was going to be by himself.

Makers Mark was a smooth Kentucky whisky bourbon he developed a liking for when studying in the States. Each year, around Christmas, a collection hat went around. Depending on how well the drive went, two, three or four bottles, a ribbon on each, waited for him when he walked in to work in the morning. One to live each day as if it were his last, Timmy always insisted that the 'spirit' of Christmas be enjoyed by all, without a moment's waste. The bottles got lighter as they toured around, and by midday, he and his crew would be lit brighter than the tree up in reception. Adhering to tradition, the party carried over to the Sekforde Arms, a cosy neighbourhood pub from the 19th century. To repay the gesture of the gift, Timmy always bought the flock lunch and a round.

"No really, you're going to be by yourself this Easter? Just you? You and your bronze refreshment?"

Timmy acknowledged with a smile.

Cambria knew of the death of his parents when he was sixteen, and realised the holidays was probably a painful time for him. She didn't know if being in the company of another's family would hurt more than being alone, but she asked anyway.

"My sister and I are headed to my folks in Lechlade. You should come."

Timmy was utterly surprised by the invitation and instinctively turned down her offer.

"They have sublime outdoor trails up in Lechlade. Perfect for running. You'll love it."

"Nah, I don't even have any clothes packed."

Secretly, he hoped she would convince him harder.

Light sprang into her eyes. "You can do your laundry there," she excitedly suggested, averting her gaze to the clothes that were strewn all over his office.

"Hey, you even have your running shoes. Come, I'll help you pack."

Cambria strode over to Timmy's couch and gingerly started gathering a few items.

Timmy grinned and shook his head. "Pardon my ignorance, but how far is Lechlade from here?"

"Only one way to find out."

She bent down to pick up one more article of clothing.

"We're all set," she gasped. "You can pack your own underwear," she continued, trying to suppress the smirk that was forming on her face.

Timmy could not stop grinning, his face a revelation of his inner delight. Right as rain, he flicked off his table lamp.

Mark was spending Easter by himself.

Trip To Lechlade

Cambria often thought back fondly of her first day at *Cream*. Cold and lifeless that morning was, not a cloud in the sky, not a bird in song. But still, the air was ripe with promise.

Not wanting to be late on her first day, she was at *Cream's* doorstep at eight, even though she was told to come in at half nine. To avoid looking like a punctual nerd, she waited on the bench across the street, a book in hand, an eye on the office.

That morning, at a quarter to nine, Timmy showed up and unlocked the place. By the time she tucked her book away and ran across the street, he had already made his way into the building. She rapped on the glass door. He was a fair way in. He looked over his shoulder, and on seeing her outside in the cold, jogged to the door in the most ridiculous fashion— his knees rising high above the ground, almost touching his chest. It was the most random, silly thing she had ever witnessed. He opened the door. She could not stop smiling.

"Hello, I'm Cambria," she introduced herself.

"Oh, you must be Cambria then," he responded chirpily. He scooped her hand up in his and rigorously shook it.

"You've got Freon in your veins," he remarked. "Come I'll fix you a warm drink. Kitchen's this way."

She dutifully followed him. He punched her in the arm, to let her know he was just playing.

In the kitchen, Timmy showed her where all the things were stored; the confectioneries, microwaveable lunches, teas, coffees and silverware. He even let her in on where the receptionist kept a secret stash of Pop-Tarts. Before they left the kitchen, he warned her about the bread toaster, how it confiscated your toast if you fed it heavy breads like rye or multigrains.

On the way down to the basement, he told her all about the *Creamatorium*, and what went on up there, and he cautioned her about wearing short skirts on the sidewalk next to the office. Finally, he introduced her to people at *Cream* she had yet to meet.

At 9:30, as the office filled up, Timmy took her around to get acquainted with the lot. Through each introduction, he learned more about her from the information she divulged, and like a cotton candy seller flossing a stick, his synopsis of her got more voluminous. His introduction of her started out as, "Hey guys, Cambria joins us today as a junior illustrator." This snowballed into something like, "Hello chaps, this is Cambria of Lechlade. She's a talented artist who just graduated from Falmouth, and she joins us today as a junior illustrator. She's a cellist who teaches yoga to children, takes two sugars and milk, loves to read, can't sing to save her life, and just like you Thom, suffers the District Line from Earl's Court to Monument on the way to work."

Timmy used to set his own working hours, usually walking in at ten sometimes eleven. No one minded him walking in so un-early. They knew he was always the last to leave, the light from his room, like a beacon in a sea of dark. Timmy dreaded being alone in an empty house, and always preferred to be around people. To shorten his time at home, he always stayed back at work, till the last to leave left.

It was only a month or so later, after observing Timmy's work patterns, that Cambria realised this. That to see her settle in comfortably, he made the effort to be there early on her first day. But it wasn't just her. He did that for all the new people joining the team. At the time, Timmy was only second-in-command, but she always felt that it was he who admiraled the ship.

Within minutes of meeting Timmy, Cambria knew he was special. It was only a little later that she knew how special. Her feelings toward him went through different phases, progressing from general friendliness, to admiration, to fondness, and eventually into an unbearable schoolgirl crush. This all occurred within a week of meeting him.

Her first three months at *Cream*, now when she looked back, were her most tormented. She recalled her jitters each time Timmy was near, and she loathed how her best side went on hiatus when face-to-face with him—her humour, her ability to think straight, her charm, her smile, her personableness; basically all things great and good about herself. Initiating any kind of conversation with him also became a tense sweaty-palmed ordeal; very much like the moment before the nurse punctured your skin with a needle.

It actually came as no surprise to her when she started to develop a thing for Timmy. He had, after all, all the qualities she ever wanted in a life partner. Well, most of the qualities anyway. There were a few things she would have preferred changed. His general untidiness was one. His obsession with work, another.

Timmy had a face that was as pretty as it was handsome, and people who met him for the first time studied his features closely, to try and assay which he was, pretty or handsome. Often, they arrived at thinking he was neither. Timmy's mum was half Danish, half Inuit, his Dad more English than he was Chinese and Icelandic. This mixed parentage lent him a mosaic of features that was hard to place. He had nicely rounded cheekbones that did not match his squarish jaw, and black Asian hair that contradicted his dark green Icelandic eyes.

To even out the incongruence, Timmy dyed his hair a dark auburn. More from lack of effort than choice, he wore his brown locks in an artistic mess, something which irked Cambria. She always thought he looked like a person who hadn't quite shrugged off an afternoon nap.

But over time, what Cambria initially regarded as blemishes in Timmy, became marks of his character, an ensemble of little quirks that made Timmy, Timmy. With her feelings for him deepening through the years, she eventually found herself marooned on a dreamy plane where he could do nothing wrong, do nothing that did not endear himself more to her.

~.~.~.~.~.~

When Timmy agreed to spend Easter in Lechlade with her, she felt as if it were Christmas in April. To her it was an opportunity to foster a friendship with him outside work. And she was thrilled at the prospect.

Cambria had never before brought a guy back to the house; this despite her parents always hoping that she would. Every holiday season, her mum dropped in the same reminder to her, *'If you have a friend you'd like to bring home, oh I don't know, maybe he or she is stuck without a place to go...'* Although it was unspoken, it was always the preference that this stranded friend had a penis attached.

Cambria's folks were always curious about her well-being; if she was happy, if she blended in well, if the city had grown on her. But Cambria did not share much of her personal life with them. It wasn't that she wanted to shut them out of her world. She merely felt there was little about her life that was newsworthy. But that wasn't the case anymore. Timmy was single, good looking, brilliant, successful, and she was excited about showing him off.

Her excitement came with a tinge of sadness. He had yet to be hers to show.

So that he too could be on the lookout, Cambria described to Timmy what her sister's car looked like. They waited inside, at the reception area, their eyes fixed on the front door.

A beat up car clattered into view, a white 1983 Ford Escort Cabriolet, its edges scalloped with rust. The car strained to a stop and vented a nerve-pinching squeal. Timmy winced, and breathed a sigh of relief when the car progressed no further. The '83 shuddered on the spot, like a washing machine on a final spin. Cambria instantly recognised the eyesore to be her sister's.

"That's Lenka," she announced to Timmy.

As they exited the building, Lenka reached over to the passenger side to unlock the door. Timmy saw through the window that she looked like a carbon copy of Cambria, only with frizzy Maharishi hair. Cambria opened the car door and poked her head in.

"Would you mind popping the boot? Timmy's coming back with us to Lechlade. We'll need the back seat."

"Back to Mum and Dad's?" Lenka asked, very surprised.

"Yes. He'll be spending the weekend with us. You remember Timmy, don't you? My Creative Director. I've mentioned him before."

"Yeah, yeah. I think so."

Turning her eyes upwards, Lenka looked into the folds of her mind, rummaging for any recollections of 'a Timmy' from the past. "*Ah, yes. Timmy,*" a voice formed in her mind.

It was unlike her sister to do things on a whim, and it was completely out of character that she bring someone home unannounced, a man on top of that.

It had been years since Cambria had let anyone into her life. Lenka presumed she would be the first to know if that ever happened. Unless of course her suspicions were real. That all these years, Cambria indeed had a someone. A man in her life who just had yet to be a part of it, his mere existence forming the emptiness that completed her. Lenka was reminded of an argument she and Cambria had when they were in their teens. Cambria had taken the position that unfulfilled love was the most powerful form of love. *Most powerful, yes. But what fulfilment is there in being unfulfilled.*

Cambria defended it this way. That with love, the exhilaration comes not from its attainment, but in its pursuit. That love, once fulfilled, becomes bankrupt of desire, and loses its lustre, its depth.

She was always capable of such twisted love tragedy.

Lenka unbuckled herself and circled to the back of the car to open the boot. As the three of them congregated at the rear, Cambria made the briefest of introductions. "Lenka, Timmy. Timmy, Lenka."

Lenka's hand jangled as Timmy shook it. He noticed heavy brass bangles bunched up at her wrists, about five of them, each finely laced with curly Celtic knots. With his pub eye, he inconspicuously gave Lenka a quick scan. She had a tattoo on her ankle he could not quite make out. Her hoop earrings matched her bangles. She was a tad meatier than Cambria. And she looked the older of the two, but maybe because she wore heavy eye shadow. He also found her very oddly attired. Dressed in a long crinkled skirt, and sporting a sequined vest over a gauzy long sleeve blouse, she looked like a member of a gypsy troupe.

After Timmy stored away his and Cambria's bag, he closed the stubborn boot. The sisters hopped into the front seat and he slid into the back. It occurred early on to Lenka that her sister might have been trying to match-make her with Timmy. But she knew that if those indeed were Cambria's intentions, she would have done a better job with the introduction. Nothing as unflowery as *"Lenka, Timmy. Timmy, Lenka."*

Lenka was notorious for converging on the scene of a brewing romance. When two people were in love, but afraid to confront the other about their feelings, she saw it as her cue to jump in, to act as an emissary between the two parties. She thrived on helping unconnected people discover their common ground, and was exultant when the seeds she helped sow, turned into something meaningful.

"*Lenka*... that's a very Slavic name," Timmy expressed.

"Our mum moved here from Macedonia. Donkey's years ago. Before it was Macedonia."

"Interesting."

Lenka cheekily looked into the rear view.

"All strapped in?"Timmy looked for his seatbelt. Cars that age did not come with seatbelts at the back. He got her joke.

Lenka put the car into gear and they pushed north, through the heavy outbound traffic.

"Timmy," Lenka peeped in a high curious voice. "My sister has told me very little about you."

The meddling started.

~.~.~.~.~.~

Lenka was quite the opposite of her sister; bold, gregarious and outrageous, talking as loudly as she dressed. She was highly animated when she spoke, and very bubbly; like a vitamin tablet effervescing in water. Twenty minutes into the journey, the radio station played '*Holiday*' by Madonna. Lenka knew all the words and put on a performance while driving, complete with the accompanying head shimmies and wobbly hand gestures. Timmy could only stare wide-eyed in amusement.

Timmy discovered a lot about the girls during the car ride, the biggest revelation—that they were twins, Cambria the elder by over an hour. Cambria was born at 4:42 a.m. on a Saturday, by way of water birth. Lenka, who enjoyed having the whole place to herself, decided to stay put. On failing to be coaxed out, she was introduced into the world by way of a scalpel.

"Who wakes up that early on the weekend anyway?" Lenka joked.

Of the twins, Cambria ate less, exercised more, and hence was the more slender. But Lenka attributed the difference to this, that by oozing through the birth tract, Cambria was squeezed thin for life.

Timmy also learned that the sisters were artistically inclined from young. Both enjoyed painting and sketching. But Lenka hung up her brushes at fourteen when she developed an interest in handicraft. They both attended Falmouth, an arts college in Cornwall, but to their parent's disapproval, Lenka took an early bow, to join a repertory theatre group in London's Soho district.

It did not take Lenka long to work her way into prominence within the arts' circle. One of the most prolific actor-dancers to grace the stage in years, she was a fortnight from the launch of *Lenka*, a musical comedy about a tomboyish country girl, who through an endearing series of missteps, landed herself where she was, as the lead in a musical comedy about herself.

Of the two, Lenka was by far the more outgoing. When Cambria was curled up at home reading a book, Lenka was out on the town, chatting the night away at a café, or at a party fraternising till the wee hours. As a child, Lenka found every excuse to be out of the house. Often, she'd engage in things you'd not expect from a girl—corralling fish by damming a brook, threading a dragonfly, raining fire on ants' nests or helping her father with the repairs. Cambria was more of a homebody, and did more in the way of chores. Each day, it was Cambria who helped her mother tend to the laundry, prepare the meals, keep the house in order. Cambria was the daughter her mother always wanted, Lenka, the boy her father never had.

FUEL

~.~.~.~.~.~

It was past midnight when the trio arrived in Lechlade. Except for the taverns, all the town was asleep. The place was not big, and it did not take long to drive through and out of the town centre. On the outskirts, Lenka took a sharp turn onto a loose gravel road. It was pitch black all around, except for the beam of the car's headlights. Timmy could see a speck of light in the distance, like a stationary firefly. As they progressed deeper into the darkness, the speck turned into the kitchen window of a thatched roof cottage.

Box planters of bright coloured foliage shrubs lined the base of the cottage. And the outer walls were covered almost entirely with several varieties of flowering climbers. The main entrance to the house was typical of some farmhouses, through the kitchen, via a half door designed to allow fresh air and sunshine in, but keep the livestock out.

Before their car came to a standstill, the upper tier of the kitchen door opened inwards. Standing within the square of the door frame was Cambria's mother. She pulled her cardigan close to her body, and came out. Cambria was the first to exit the car, and ran to give her mother a hug. Lenka stayed behind to gather her stuff–cigarettes stashed above the vanity mirror, her cell phone from the dashboard, an MP3 player and a toothbrush from the glove compartment. Timmy felt a little awkward, and was a bit tentative getting out of the car, seeing that he was uninvited and all. Through the car window, he saw Cambria point, and both she and her mum looked in his direction. He saw that as his cue to get out of the car.

Cambria's mum strode excitedly up to Timmy, and shook his hand with both of hers.

"Hi Timmy. Cora. Welcome to our home."

Cora was happy to finally meet Timmy. Although Cambria had not volunteered too much information about him in the past, his name always popped up in random conversation.

Timmy apologised for imposing, and effusively thanked Cora for having him on such short notice. But she assured him that the surprise was a pleasant one. As Timmy alternated gazes between Cambria and her mother, he was amazed by their physical likeness. It was apparent where Cambria had gotten her pretty features from. The differences were minor. Cora had a deeper, more mature voice, wore a slighter frame, with a more golden tinge, probably from tending to the fields. Of Cora, Timmy was certain of this. That she had exceeded the beauty of her youth, the years adding graceful lines to her face, which did more to deepen her stunning features than take away from it.

Cambria's Dad came out of the house to meet his girls. He was a mountain of a man, his frame almost as big as the door's. He wore plaid, had his sleeves rolled up to his elbows, suspenders hanging down at his sides. By appearance alone he matched the profile of a ruddy-cheeked lumberjack. Lenka raced up to greet him, lifting both her feet off the ground as they hugged. She looked diminutive in his arms. Timmy could see immediately where the lines of favour were drawn; Cambria to her mum, and Lenka to her dad.

Greg put his daughter down and swung to Timmy.

"Hi, I don't believe we've met. I'm Greg."

"Timmy."

They locked hands, Greg's swallowing Timmy's.

Cora shuddered on the spot to highlight the obvious. "Come, it's frigid out here." And she ushered them in.

~.~.~.~.~.~

It was nice and toasty in the cottage. A buttery aroma of baked goods clung to the walls, hung in the air. You could almost stick your tongue out and taste it. The kitchen by which they entered was lush with gun metal grey cooking ware that hung from above, mostly utilitarian than decorative. The black stone kitchen countertop was worn from years of use, and was now grey, complementing the dark oak cupboards it had grown old with. Hand-painted pots of herbaceous plants, pretty on the window sills, completed the country charm.

"Should any of you be peckish, I left out a couple slices of rhubarb crumble," Cora announced to the girls and Timmy. "Am sorry. Would have saved more if I knew you were bringing a guest."

Although he was, Timmy claimed to not be hungry, and told the girls to proceed without him.

"You've got to try Ma's rhubarb crumble. It'll be a sin if you don't. Come, I'll share mine with you." Cambria pulled out a fork from the drawer, and using its flat edge, cut herself a corner. She closed her eyes as she took in the taste.

"Mmmmm," she testified.

She cut another segment, slid her fork under it, and balanced it to Timmy's lips.

"Here, you have to try this."

Timmy was a little surprised, thrilled actually, that Cambria was granting him use of her fork. The very fork, that a moment ago, she had christened between her tightly sandwiched lips. To align his appreciation of the crumble to hers, he closed his eyes as she did, and let the full mélange of flavour lather the walls of his mouth.

"Heaven," he concurred.

As Cambria continued to feed herself and Timmy, Lenka, wolfed down her piece. She rolled her eyes at the lovebirds as they revelled in the intimacy of sharing silverware.

"Mrs Lane."

"Cora." She was quick to correct Timmy.

"Cora," Timmy accepted with a nod and a smile, "... my trip here to spend Easter at your home was unplanned, and I feel really awful for showing up empty handed. If you..."

"Don't even worry about it Timmy. It's a pleasure that we are graced with your company. Greg and I have always encouraged the girls to bring their friends home for the holidays."

Timmy sensed Cora's genuine delight but went on with his offer.

"Actually, I was thinking. If you have no plans for lunch tomorrow, it would give me great pleasure to prepare lunch for you and the family. All I need is for Cambria to point me to the morning market, and for you to afford me the use of your kitchen."

Everyone looked surprised. Cora was thoroughly impressed that a stranger—male—who had only clocked five minutes on their property, three minutes in her kitchen, would make a lunch attempt for people he barely knew. Her first thought was this. That growing up, he must have spent a summer working in the kitchen of a restaurant. Her second, that he had Italian or Greek in him.

"It's the least I could do," Timmy continued.

Before Cora offered an answer, she turned to look at Cambria, then Lenka, then her husband. They all were wide-eyed on hearing Timmy's offer.

"Sure. It would be our pleasure."

Cora thought for a second about what she had just agreed to, and then nodded to reaffirm her decision.

"It would be a great pleasure."

Everyone was surprised that she accepted Timmy's offer. Timmy included. They thought she would stand her ground and insist that he sit back and enjoy his weekend.

"There's most of what you'll find in the market here on our farm. If you need a hand with the livestock, Greg can assist you."

Wonderful Timmy exclaimed, *great*, Cora replied, *okay-eee*, Cambria mumbled under her breath.

Greg brought his hands together. "Alright. It's pretty late, and you all must be knackered from the long journey. Timmy, I can show you to your room."

"Super."

"Did you bring any bags with you?" Greg asked.

"No just these."

Greg looked amusedly at the bundle Timmy was carrying; a long sleeve shirt knotted into a makeshift satchel, containing what he could only guess to be clothes.

"Came prepared, I see," Greg flashed a wide grin. "Come. This way."

Timmy followed, Cambria to his side. As they proceeded to the living room, Cambria leaned in and whispered to Timmy, "Are you sure about lunch tomorrow? I could have just shown you to the local grocer. And you could have just picked up a bottle of wine or something, you know?"

"No shit?" Timmy feigned surprise. "Too late for that now. I'd eat a big breakfast if I were you!"

She bumped his shoulder with hers.

"I'll give you a hand. I'm pretty good in the kitchen."

In the living room, the interior was light and airy, the walls, painted in a light colour. White or cream Timmy could not quite tell. This, because the room borrowed its colour from the fireplace, and from a scatter of votive candles. Shadows drew in and out like seaweeds in a sea current. A large four-seater sofa, dressed with a crimson cashmere throw, sat in the centre of the room. The couch demarcated the sitting area from the dining. In the far corner, a weary-looking rocking chair, painted in distressed white, lent a nostalgic ambience to the whole space.

From the living room, Timmy was led down a broad corridor. He was shown the second door.

"Well, here's your room." Greg opened the door and ushered Timmy in.

"It's not much but you should have all that you need. A slight draft comes in from the window on the right. But it looks like a still night so you should be fine. But just in case, there are extra blankets on the top cupboard shelf."

"Alrighty."

"If you need anything, just let us know."

"Actually. Don't happen to have a spare toothbrush do you?"

"The Mrs keeps them stashed some place. I'll have her pull one out for you."

"Super."

"Alright, I'll leave you to settle in."

~.~.~.~.~.~

Timmy studied the interior. The walls were buttered with white plaster, the floor, laid with terracotta tiles. Square lattice windows, trimmed in natural wood, nestled between pigtailed curtains. Rustic accoutrements ornamented the walls: tarnished copper pans, retired oil lamps, old washboards. Like an art enthusiast browsing a gallery, Timmy stopped at each item to take in the details.

Himself a bit of a woodcraftsman, Timmy was captivated by the furniture in the room—a bedside table, a roughly rendered sitting bench, the bed and the clothes cupboard. He ran his fingers on the furniture, over the embellishments and joints, and across the finish. He knew right away they were all handmade, each piece with its own soul. Caressing the silky complexion of the wood, he knew a great many hours had gone into the effort. A smile formed on his face when he discovered some words indiscreetly etched on the headboard of the bed. *Lenka loves Jamie Adams forever and forever.* Although he had only known her for one car ride, he felt those words fell so aptly within her character.

A knock on the door surprised Timmy.

"Yes?"

The door squeaked open and Cambria peeked in.

"Are you dressed?"

"Sorry to disappoint. But yes. Fully."

They both smiled.

"I brought you a toothbrush. Pa mentioned you needed one."

She walked into his room and handed the toothbrush to him. She had slipped on a cream, satin nightie. Relaxed against her skin, her gown surrendered every nuance of her body. Timmy investigated her deeply, to see if he could draw any shade of what she was wearing underneath, if anything at all. To his disappointment, the material was spun too tight to be breached.

Once or twice, over the recent weeks, Timmy pictured himself having sexual intercourse with Cambria, but he stopped himself almost immediately, and felt guilty that he had sired such thoughts. This was a reflex that was ingrained in him, but only towards girls he felt a deep connection to, those he regarded as the special ones, his true loves.

He did not know for sure why. Why sexual fantasy was impermissible for his 'one-and-onlys'. Perhaps it was the bible preaching to him. Perhaps, recognising the transience of earthly pleasures, he felt that sex was shallow, and to think of her in any way feral, soiled the essence of her. Timmy always believed you had to look beyond the flesh to discover the meat of a person. So maybe he felt that to deprive was to nourish, that the only way to arrive at the core, the pure, was to discover the beauty beyond the beauty. For him, the attachments he formed to the special ones were sacred, and lived on a higher plane, above the realm of the physical, in a world comprised of heartfelt gazes, walks on the beach and the sharing of hearts. In a place where two could exist side by-side and be the equal of, neither dwelling above nor beneath, at a level where two could be apart, but at the same time, be one.

It was a lot less kosher for Cambria. She always felt Timmy was doused in sex appeal, this going as far back as her tender days of knowing him, long before her desire for him had reached full blossom. Convinced by the yearning in her loins, she was certain that he was put on earth for a single purpose; to mate with her, exclusively, intently, fervently. Awash in a sea of carnal wanting, she allowed her imagination to flare unabated, and pictured in lucid detail what intercourse with him would be like. Taking into account the athlete he was and his stallionesque physique, she foresaw their love making to be long and glistening, his thrusts smooth but decisive. She promised herself, if fate so decreed, that were they ever to bed, she would make herself fully accessible to him, malleable, bending to his every desire, whispering words he lusted to hear, groaning the way he wanted her to groan. She relished the notion that she, despite being in a position of servitude, would be in firm control as she drew his yolk from him. Him breaching her, surging, extracting every dimension of pleasure from her; and she, an eager receptacle, sheathing and unsheathing him, walking his pent up urges over the edge; the thought of it was unbearable.

In the end, Timmy still was human, a man with the defects of a man. Like a twinging compass needle, his eyes helplessly found their way back to Cambria's body, drawn into its svelte defining ridges. She caught him staring. He realised it. She realised it. He felt embarrassed, and she, smug.

"Alright, hombre. Goodnight, sleep tight, don't let the field snakes bite."

"Snakes?"

Cambria flexed her eyebrows and then chuckled naughtily.

"Goodnight Timmy."

"Goodnight."

She eased the door close. He trapped in a last glimpse of her. And she was gone.

Flipping off the lights and settling warmly into bed, Timmy lay awake with his eyes open. Swaddled under the same roof as his beloved, and separated but by a facade of brick and plaster, he was overcome by a feeling far stronger than the rustic country charm that permeated the air. The walls breathed with her; he was breathing her air, and she, his. And he felt blissful.

Sleep came to him slowly, gently, softly, like a whisper in the wind, and brought with it an overwhelming peace he had not felt in years.

~.~.~.~.~.~.~

While unpacking her bag, Lenka expressed casually to Cambria, "Timmy..." She slipped a hanger into a dress, dangled it, and hung it , "I think he is a really nice guy."

"You think so?" Cambria chirped.

"Genuine smile, honest eyes." She threaded and hung another dress.

"I think so too." Cambria plopped her bum onto her bed and smiled to herself.

"Hey, since you don't appear to have feelings for him... you mind if I have a go at him?"

"No. Don't you dare," Cambria snapped at her sister. Her reflex was not disapproving, but aggressive defensive, like the caustic hiss of a cornered cat. Cambria smiled deeply to herself, and shook her head, amazingly aware that she had just fallen prey to her sister's cunning.

With Cambria's territorial markings now uncovered, a mischievous grin formed on Lenka's face. Shaking out a long skirt, she smugly enquired, an eyebrow raised, "So how long has he been your heart's only desire?"

Cambria fought down the urge to tell her sister everything. But failed miserably. Their conspiratorial girly exchange went on till the sun came up.

Easter Eve

Timmy's eyes were still closed when he woke. The air felt cool against his face, and carried with it an invigorating potpourri of scents: thatching reed, sage, vanilla, thyme, lavender, apricot and manure. He opened his eyes and sat up. He spotted Greg through the window, scraping mud off a double shovel plow. One to normally be awake by the wee hours, Timmy was surprised to see the sun as high as it was. He tore off his blanket, slipped on his shoes and went outside.

He looked around him and knew they were on the onset of spring; the drab of winter giving way to great swathes of colour. The sun was brilliant.

Timmy ambled up to the low stone wall separating the house compound from the farmed land. There, the air was suffused with the smell of freshly turned soil; the stretch of scored earth before him, like corduroy. Prim patches of flowers grew amongst the produce, bestowing upon their plot the charm of an ornamental kitchen garden, or French potager, except one done in grand scale.

When Timmy was young, his grandfather, Jorgen, imparted to him many lessons of the land. Jorgen Jorgenson had a way of turning the uninteresting, interesting. By incorporating a sprinkling of science, history and wit into his teachings, he was able to hold young Timmy's attention for hours on end, and Timmy retained many lessons of his youth.

Timmy enjoyed discovering how things originated and got their names. Dandelion, he learned, came from the French words *dents de lions*, which meant 'lions' teeth', identifiable by the flower's jagged leaf.

Primrose was *prima rosa*, which in Italian meant the first rose, or the first flower of spring.

Celandine was a spring flower too, lending from the Greek word *chelidon*, the word for swallow. It bloomed in time for the coming of the first swallow in April, and wilted when the birds left.

Timmy stood and admired the beautiful landscape before him. Not all the flowers were in bloom. The ones that were–dandelions, primrose and celandine. Spring was indeed upon them.

~.~.~.~.~.~

"Good morning Timmy!!" The greeting left Greg's throat with the vigour of a leaping spring.

"Morning!!!" Timmy returned with interest.

"Sleep well?"

"Like a baby."

"Come, let me show you around."

Timmy nodded.

"This all...." Greg pointed with one sweeping motion, "is ours. From the fencing to the lone maple, from there to the old barn. Two acres in all."

"What do you grow?"

"Carrots, broad beans, purple sprouting broccoli, spinach and potatoes."

Greg proceeded to introduce Timmy to the neatly partitioned herb garden within the house compound; dill, mint, rosemary, tarragon, chives, chervil and parsley, all residents of the patch. Sage, thyme, camomile and bergamot lived at the back of the house, beside the wind pump, in a hotter, drier part of the garden.

"In the stable we've got two horses and a cow. Molly's our cow. She provides our dairy. In there, we've also got chickens, most of them layers."

"That lovely lady there," Greg pointed, "wandering by the log pile, is Josephine, our resident goose. But the Mrs would not be too pleased if she showed up on the lunch table. We've had her for ages, and she and Cora have gotten really close."

Timmy grinned. He felt at ease around Greg, and could tell that Greg had taken a liking to him.

"We've got ducks over by the far fence. And pigs in the pen. Feel free to use anything you need. Except the old goose."

The distinct purr of roosting pigeons caught Timmy's ear, barely. He turned to look.

"How about them pigeons over there?"

Greg turned around and saw Timmy peering up at the roof.

"I'd love to do them up for lunch," Timmy said.

"You want to do them in for lunch?" Greg asked quizzically.

"Mmm-hmmm."

Greg examined Timmy's face to see if he was joking, but saw that he was dead serious. The mischievous boy scout in Greg came alive.

"I don't see why not."

He smiled sheepishly at Timmy.

"I'll be right back."

Greg marched into the shed by the house, and came trotting back, a double-barrelled shotgun cradled in his arms. Timmy was a little troubled by Greg's enthusiasm. He also did not think Greg would take him seriously.

"You ever fire one before?"

"Nope."

Timmy grinned from ear-to-ear, still in disbelief that a flock of sleepy birds stood to be executed because he went off-the-wall with his lunch idea. He thought about it for a second before deciding, "You can have the honour, Greg. Blast away."

Timmy figured everyone would get as much a kick from eating pigeon, as he would from cooking it.

"If you like, I'll show you. She's a side-by-side 12-bore, *Webley & Scott*. Fairly easy to use. I've had her since I was thirteen."

Timmy, like most boys growing up, dreamed of the day he'd fire a weapon; a crossbow, a pistol, a rifle, a machine gun, a tank gun.

"I'd be flattered," Timmy replied.

Greg flicked the top lever to the right, pushed the barrels down to open the breech, and loaded two cartridges into the empty chamber.

"I've just put in number 6, high-base birdshot," Greg informed Timmy as he snapped the gun close.

"Urrrmmm. In English please?"

Greg chuckled.

"Inside each cartridge, there are little pellets. You know that right?"

Timmy nodded.

"Number 6 indicates the size of the pellets. The higher the number, the smaller the pellets."

"Is number 6 considered big?"

"Yes, we're using fairly large pellets. For the power. This is because feathers are pretty hard to pierce. But if we were shooting something more delicate, like say, clay pigeons, contact is more important than penetration. In those instances, we would go for a higher number, maybe number 9. When the pellets are smaller, you can pack more of them in. So there is greater spread, and a higher chance of contact."

"I see."

"And high base means high brass. High brass shells typically carry high-powered ammunition, and give us the punch we need when hunting live game."

Timmy was in awe.

"Here, take this." Greg handed the gun to Timmy. "This is the safety," he pointed out. "What you'll want to do is stand about forty degrees to the right of your target."

Timmy did so.

"Nuzzle the butt of the gun in the pocket of your shoulder. You can use the line between the twin barrels as your sight. Exhale as you fire. As you pull the trigger, lean slightly into the shot, to compensate for the kick. This girl has two rounds."

Timmy got tentative. "Hmmm! Maybe you should do it."

"No worries sport. If you miss we'll just head over to Charlie Wyble's barn down by the creek. He's got lots of these winged devils in his roof. We can have a second go there."

Greg laid out the plan of attack.

"I'll drive them out with a handful of pebbles. You take aim slightly above the brow of the roof. When they take flight, you take the first shot. You may lose your balance a bit. If you regain your feet fast enough, squeeze off a second shot."

Timmy nodded.

"Ready Sonny?"

Timmy lined the gun to the crest of the roof, then nodded to indicate he was ready. Greg took a big step forward and launched the pebbles. There was a loud flutter of wings as the birds broke from the roof. Timmy nervously squeezed the trigger. His shot went high. But the round still managed to find a couple of birds, evident by the plume of feathers that burst into the sky. The blast was much louder than Timmy expected, and stunned him a little. Despite planting his feet firmly on the ground, he was knocked backwards and barely kept his balance.

Timmy noticed the flock had turned east. So he swung right, this time aiming a little lower to compensate for his earlier mistake. Another shot rang through the air, followed soon after by a loud metallic clank. Timmy's eyes widened. The weathervane on the roof swivelled uncontrollably, like a basketball spinning on a finger. Timmy and Greg turned to look at each other, agape. Wrought in disbelief, they reverted their attention back to the roof. The weathervane wobbled on its axis as it started to settle. Timmy was able to make out that the rooster was now headless. And the arrow pointed not North, South, East or West, but towards Venus.

"Holy, Mary, Jesus. For crying out loud. What are you boys up too?" Cora marched out of the house and demanded an explanation, her tone unforgiving. Cambria and Lenka darted out of the house in a panic and joined their mother.

"What happened? Is everyone alright?" Cambria asked with great concern in her voice.

Timmy and Greg were on the ground, writhing in laughter. They tried to get words out of their mouth but choked on their mirth. Tears in his eyes, and clutching his belly, Greg pointed to the piece of twisted metal on the roof.

Spotting her father's rifle on the ground, and looking up at the maimed weathervane, Cambria pieced together what had taken place. But why the two were playing with guns still escaped her. In her mind, she just wrote it off as 'boys being boys', and she was glad that no harm had come to her Timmy.

Cambria felt fuzzy inside seeing her dad help Timmy up by the elbows, and dust some of the loose grass off his shoulder. She could see that a bond was starting to form between them, and that made her happy.

"Really sorry for the alarm everyone," Greg apologised to his wife. Cambria found it comical how the two boys looked like students reprimanded by their school principal; standing next to each other, hands behind their back, in front of a Cora who did not look a bit amused.

"Timmy here," Greg brushed his nose with his hand, "was simply helping me with some pest control."

Timmy chuckled. Cambria and Lenka laughed. Cora smiled. All because Greg snickered.

~.~.~.~.~.~.~

Cora made herself available to Timmy as he searched the compound for lunch ingredients. She was utterly impressed that he employed the right techniques when harvesting herbs; pinching basil off at the split of the stem, pruning chives three inches from the base, snapping sage off one sprig at a time. For basil, he picked only the leaves that were drier and starting to curl, to make sure he got the ones with the most intense flavour; for the rest, he took only the young leaves, to avoid their being woody and coarse.

Timmy learned a lot walking alongside Cora through her garden. He discovered that Cora did not cook with bergamot, that she cultivated it to perfume the air, and to lure bees to the garden. And he learned about the different herb families, and what was unique or similar about them. She shared with him that savory could be used in place of thyme, parsley to replace cilantro, anise seed as a substitute for fennel.

As Timmy was reaching down for oregano, she stopped him.

"Use marjoram instead."

"Why, what's the difference?"

"Well, they are both very similar in taste. I just have an emotional fondness for one."

"How so?"

"No, it's silly. Really. Pick the oregano. You're probably more adept at using it."

Timmy smiled at Cora and waited for an explanation.

"Marjoram has a long and colourful history. It was proclaimed that if a girl placed marjoram on her bed, that the Greek goddess Aphrodite would enter her dreams and reveal her life partner to her. Marjoram eventually became a symbol of eternal love. In ancient times, newlyweds crowned themselves with wreaths of marjoram, as a symbol of everlasting love and happiness."

"Interesting!"

Cora's story brought her closer to the topic she was most interested to raise.

"Are you married, Timmy?"

"Nope."Timmy offered a regretful smile. "Unmarried, un-engaged, unattached."

"Have yet to find that special someone?"

"Yeah. But I think I'm close."

"Who is she? Is she someone from work?"

Timmy chuckled. "Well, it's still very early. I'd rather not jinx it. Yes, it's someone from work."

The look Cora gave him told him she knew. Having collected all that he needed from the garden, they wore their smiles into the house.

~.~.~.~.~.~

"Cambria at your service," she announced from the kitchen doorway. "Need a hand?"

Timmy wanted badly to impress the family with his cooking, and thought better of inviting distraction into the kitchen.

"No I'm fine. Really."

"I could boil some water," Cambria offered. "Remove the feathers for you."

"Nah, I think I'll leave the feathers on. It adds a nice fluffiness to the dish I'm making."

"Ha, ha smarty pants."

Cambria started to curl an apron around her waist.

"Seriously, I'll get some water going for you."

"No, I'll be fine," Timmy insisted. "Scout's honour. It's a lovely day. Go soak up the sun or something. Shooo!"

She measured his seriousness.

"Alright Master Chef," she conceded amusedly, "I'll leave you to your mischief. If you need me I'll be out in the living area. Just flail your arms and scream if something catches fire." She grinned and left.

Timmy's food preparation methods kept everyone curious and left them baffled. At one point, he marched out of the house, tore himself two handfuls of sphagnum moss, and marched back in. The moss was being dried out by Greg for horse bedding. A few minutes later, he stormed back out, and asked Greg if he could start a pit fire. Greg obliged. Before going back into the house, Timmy gathered two large gobs of mud in a pail. Greg reported the news to the girls.

About an hour later, Timmy marched out with the pails, and sank several blobs into the deep bed of red coals that Greg had prepared for him. Cora and the girls snickered amongst themselves, and wondered if it was a lunch or war preparation.

Cambria popped into the kitchen just one other time, to see how Timmy was doing. He had his act together. Herbs and spices sat in neat clusters on a large plate. He had marinades and sauces mixed into separate bowls. All the burners on the stove were roaring. To her surprise, nothing was boiling over, and there were no dark plumes of smoke. He was quite a joy to watch actually, his movement around the kitchen deft and precise. In the ninety seconds he allowed her to stay, he poured a brownish-burgundy sauce into a pan to reduce, swivelled to the worktop to chop some carrots and celery, bruised some mint with a pestle, and following that, swept different islands of garnish into their respective pots and pans.

Cambria drew great pleasure watching the excitement Timmy had brought to her household. She joined the rest of the family in the living room, and in great anticipation, waited with them.

Bon Appétit

They spoke, but without words, using their eyes to telepathise their amusement. Timmy pretended not to notice, but inside, he was deeply entertained by everyone's quiet, with the way they sat at the table, hands on their laps, silent as a flock of sheep, each too polite to ask about the grey orb on their plate.

The lunch setting was immaculate. It was a gorgeous day out in the Cotswolds; cool breeze, warm sun, the air heavy with the scent of blossoms and herbs. On days like these, the Lanes liked to dine outside, beneath the shady tree next to the house. The rustic trestle table at which they sat was fashioned out of weathered oak, and had been on the farm since Cambria's earliest memory. It had only been moved once, and it took six grown men to do it. Greg vowed never again to move that table, and was thankful all these years for the tree's shade, and its long life.

Timmy saw to the finer details. A sprightly sprig of fresh mint was placed on each plate to keep the flies away, silverware was lined in the proper hierarchy and a dainty vase of flowers graced the centre of the table. Timmy chose one of spring's early flowers for the centrepiece, one suited for the occasion—the pasqueflower—which he found on the steep bank bordering the farm.

Pasqueflower got its name from the Hebrew word *Pesach*, or Passover, which to the Christians was synonymous with Easter. Though very rare nationwide, the largest population of pasqueflower occurred in Barnsley Warren, a national conservation nine miles away. Timmy was elated when he discovered the flower had spread east to these parts.

Timmy stared at them staring at their food, and did not say a word. Once the awkward meter moved into the red, Greg spoke, the three women, glad that he did.

"So what do we have here?"

Timmy grinned. "Furthest from me," he pointed, "caramelised potatoes with a scatter of chives and basil. Next to that, a summery salad of rocket, romaine, cherry tomatoes and pomegranate wrapped in a tangle of green, red and yellow peppers. In the pourer is a citrus and sesame vinaigrette you can dress it with."

They were all impressed.

"In your bowls is a soup I plagiarised from my favourite Caribbean restaurant. Lentil, potatoes, baby carrots and onions in a tomato and orange base." Timmy paused for a second before introducing the main dish. "And on each of your plates, mud-baked pigeon."

Not including the weather cock, Timmy had made five kills. Greg was very impressed by the number.

Timmy demonstrated what needed to be done. Holding a dining knife backwards, he firmly tapped on the grey orb. The crust neatly split open in the middle. With two hands, he pulled apart the halves. The feathers came off with the clay, unveiling a fully intact pigeon.

"Anyone need help with theirs?" Timmy offered.

There were no takers. The process was simple enough.

Cora was the first to take a bite.

"Never had anything like it. This is absolutely delicious. How did you do it?"

The rest eagerly dug in.

"Well..." Timmy started, "the pigeon was cooked with its feathers on, so it had to be marinated from the inside. The marinade consists of ginger, thyme, honey, star anise, onion, garlic, red wine, and..."

A pause.

"...and marjoram."

Cambria noticed the smile that passed between Timmy and her mum, and noticed they had the look of two people with a shared secret.

"Because of the red wine, my marinade had a light consistency and wouldn't adhere to the meat. I didn't want it sloshing inside the pigeon's cavity, so I needed something to contain it. This is what I did in the end. I sponged up the marinade with tufts of sphagnum moss, and plugged it into the pigeon."

Cora raised her eyebrows and continued to listen intently.

"As the pigeon cooks, the fibres in the meat separate, and the feathers start to draw away from the flesh. This coming apart of fibres also opens the meat up to be flavoured. This is important. You see, once the heat penetrates deeply enough into the bird, the marinade in the moss turns into a flavourful and aromatic vapour, and passes the body tissue of the pigeon, fusing the flavour with the meat and moistening it. This steaming effect is also important because it keeps the clay moist on the inside, and prevents it from cracking. We need the clay to be pliant, so that it retains enough gummage. This is so that when you break the clay, the feathers are rooted out, not snapped off."

"Did you just use the word 'gummage'?"

Timmy laughed as he poked his finger at Cambria.

"I knew you wouldn't be able to leave that alone."

Lenka leaned forward, and like an art curator trying to determine authenticity, examined her meal from every conceivable angle. "I see that the skin was left pristine, without any clay on it. How is that possible?" she asked.

"It is technically still winter, and the birds retain a large layer of fat under their skin to insulate against the cold. When heated, this oil rises to the surface and allows the clay, in theory, to hydroplane off the skin."

As Lenka examined her food further, she excitedly remarked, "Hey, I think I found the entry and exit wounds."

Laughs erupted around the table.

"So where did you learn this intriguing technique from?" Cora enquired, her voice thick with curiosity.

"It's all made up," Timmy joked. Switching to a more serious voice, "From all over I guess. Mostly from TV. I got the clay idea from an episode of *Survivor*, during which a local group of Aborigines cooked with mud. Watching *Man Vs Wild*, I learned that sphagnum moss is non-poisonous and retains fluid well. Heston Blumenthal taught me that star anise enhances meaty notes in a dish. I also attended a pottery workshop one summer, and it was there that I learned how the properties of clay changed in a kiln. Everything else, I learned from Denmark."

"Denmark?" Only one of the four Lanes thought out aloud.

"My grandma lived there. She was the most amazing cook. When she was alive, I learned a lot from her." Timmy smiled to himself. "I really miss her."

Everyone sensed that she meant a lot to him. There was a brief silence at the table, in her honour, for her contribution to their meal.

Greg looked at Timmy and asked, "Cambria mentioned that you are a runner. What kind of distances do you run?"

"Oh, I run the marathon."

"How long is that?"

"26.2 miles."

"Yes, I always remembered it to be a rather odd number. I've always wondered how it came about."

"Great story behind that," Timmy answered enthusiastically.

Everyone stopped carving, and gave their attention to Timmy.

"It happened way back, when the Greeks faced off the Persians near the village of Marathon. For the Greeks, victory was crucial to deny the Persians free passage to Athens. Though outnumbered, the Greeks prevailed. Pheidippides, an Athenian messenger, ran 25 miles from Marathon to Athens to announce the victory. Having run over 150 miles two days prior, he collapsed and died from exhaustion, right after he announced these words, *Nenikékamen*. Translated, it means, *we have won*."

They were all intrigued.

"How the marathon turned from 25 miles to 26.2 is another matter. For many years, there wasn't a specific length to the marathon, and the distance varied from race to race in the first few Olympic marathons. All that mattered was for contestants to run the same distance, and that distance had to be about 25 miles. It wasn't until the 1920s that 26.2 was set as the official length."

"Why 26.2?" Greg enquired.

"They adopted the distance from the 1908 marathon in London, between Windsor Castle and Great White City Stadium."

Greg was about to throw in another question but Timmy answered before he could ask. "And why use the 1908 Olympics as a benchmark?"

"Politics?" Greg took a shot.

Timmy smiled to affirm.

"I've got another question, Timmy. And I hope I don't offend any of the ladies by asking it."

The three readied their claws.

"In almost all sports, men have the upper hand on women, this, usually because of biology."

Timmy agreed with a nod, and waited for Greg to get his real point across.

"But to me, long distance running appears more a test of endurance, than a test of raw physical strength, which I feel should even up the field. But still, there seems to be such a huge time difference between the men and the women."

"Yes, the gap is quite big," Timmy confirmed.

"I mean, look at Paula Radcliffe. Our female runner from Great Britain. Long, lean and muscular. Probably capable of completing the marathon in half the strides of those small emaciated fellas... well, what I'm trying to say is, if I were a betting man, my money would have been on Paula. She's like a machine."

"You seem to know a fair bit about running. You a runner yourself, Greg?"

"Oh no, no. But I developed an interest in the sport years ago, and have since kept a keen eye on it. Plus, you've probably already realised this. There isn't much to do out here in the Cotswolds. And there's only so much you can jaw on regarding the declining rains and receding water table. So we treat every page of the newspaper as a precious commodity. It's our way to stay in touch with the rest of the world."

After acknowledging Greg's point with a smile, Timmy proceeded to shed some light on the situation.

"There is something you first need to know about the world's best Kenyan and Ethiopian runners. They come from a part of Africa called the Rift Valley, and the altitude there is between 8,000 and 10,000 feet. There, the sun is harsh; the air, because of the altitude, is cool. There are no rivers, not a lot of trees, just red dirt roads filled with cattle herders and people carrying anything and everything on their head."

Between mouthfuls, Lenka interjected. "Have you been there? You sound like you have been there."

"Yeah. I travelled there for a month, on foot. From one dusty village to another. Since I was a child, I'd been interested in long distance running. So it was a dream come true for me, to see where the best did their training. It was an eye-opening experience. Life in the Rift Valley is not easy. Everything is done by hand, and those who reside there are toughened from childhood on farms or in the fields. Theirs is a kind of resilience born out of hardship, forged within a crucible of famine and strife. Because transportation is limited, children, from the time they start schooling, run as far as twenty miles a day to get to and from school. At that altitude, running twenty miles is equivalent to running fifty miles at sea level. By the time they complete their secondary schooling, and decide to run competitively, most would have run a hundred times further than the best athletes from other parts of the world. Also, because of the high altitude, and because their diet is simple, their bodies are conditioned to use very little oxygen, and very little energy. To top it off, they have light and slight frames."

"But I'm sure there are women runners from those parts who run as far each day, work as hard," Lenka pointed out. "Why haven't they emerged to give the men a run for their money?"

Timmy now felt like he was on the stand. They were all anxious for his answer.

"Yessss. Good question."

"This is where biology plays a part. Women, because they need added padding for pregnancy and child birth, carry around more fat. More fat means more weight."

"Isn't that a good thing?" Greg asked. "I mean, doesn't the fat get converted into energy, and come in useful, especially in a long race? The same way camels travel impressive distances."

"Well, yeah. You have a point. Unfortunately, the fat only gets converted at the latter stages of the race. You see, a well-conditioned athlete carries glycogen to last about twenty miles in a race. Only after that does the body start to draw from its fat stores. Fat is an excellent source of energy. Each pound supplies about 3,500 calories of energy. Unfortunately for women, they carry a lot more than required to complete a marathon. And this becomes more a burden than an advantage."

"How about muscles?" Greg asked. "Men have more. Does that play a big role in a marathon?"

"Well, men have about fifty percent more upper body strength, and twenty percent more in their lower body. But that doesn't always translate into better running times. In long distance running, what matters is the type of muscles you have, not the size of muscles. For marathons, a body that has a greater proportion of slow-twitch muscle fibres always has the upper hand. This is determined by genetics."

"Wait. What are slow twitch fibres?" one of the girls asked.

"Slow-twitch muscles contract with little force, for long periods of time, and are suitable for endurance running. Fast-twitch muscles are better for sprints, as they contract powerfully, and quickly. But they fatigue very rapidly."

"Wow! I didn't even know there was such a thing," Lenka admitted.

Timmy took a breather to assess if he had gabbled on too long on the subject, and if he should go on. He could not help himself.

"To add to the list of things going against women," Timmy continued, "men are able to store more glycogen, and hence have more energy. Also, women carry about ten percent less haemoglobin in their blood, which restricts their ability to transport oxygen to their muscles. Lastly, women are more prone to injury. There are at least a couple of reasons for this. During childbirth, women produce a hormone called *relaxin* which relaxes the pelvis. This hormone causes the joints to become looser. Women who run after childbirth have a higher risk of knee injuries. Women also have wider pelvises, so their feet hit the ground at a sharper angle, which can result in overpronation. Overpronation can lead to injury if not corrected with the right shoes."

"So, do you think a woman will ever be able to beat a man at the marathon?"

With the three women glued to his every word, Timmy knew he had to be careful with his answer.

"I think anything is possible. But women do have the odds stacked against them. With the current field of women, I think it will be awhile before a woman will break the men's record. As it is, the women have been struggling to break their own world record, which was set by Paula on home soil, in the 2003 London Marathon. It's been ages, and no one has come close to that time. Not even Paula herself."

"Your knowledge of the sport is impressive. You run professionally? Won any competitions?"

"No, Greg. I don't run professionally. And I've not run in any competitions."

"No?" Cora was surprised. "Why not?"

"Welllll..." Timmy hesitated on his answer. "I have a dream I've been working towards."

"And what is that?" Cambria asked.

"I've always dreamed of one day winning the New York Marathon. And I wanted to do it as a rookie runner." Everyone raised their eye brows.

"Why'd you pick New York? It's such a slow course?" Cambria asked.

Lenka jumped in. "Wait, what do you mean by slow course?"

"In marathons," Timmy explained, "it is to the runners' advantage if he or she can maintain a steady rhythm and pace throughout the race. A slow course is one with lots of dips, inclines and curves. New York is considered a slow course because there are a lot of turns in the route. The race also takes you over five bridges through the five boroughs of New York, and each bridge has a steep incline leading up to it. Also, because the route is close to the sea, wind often comes into play and can be disruptive to a runner's rhythm."

"Is London a fast course? Where the women's record was set?"

"Yes Lenka. London is pretty fast. But even faster would be Berlin, where the men's world record was set."

"So why New York?"

"For some time I've dreamed of working at *Oddinary*, an ad agency in New York, deemed by some to be the best in the world. I know this may sound a little juvenile, but I always had this vision of starting my career there with a bang, by winning the New York Marathon."

Cora looked at her daughter, and knew her pain.

This was the first time Cambria had heard of Timmy's plan for the future, and her heart sank. The thought of being a continent away from him was unbearable. She questioned if she was willing to leave everything and everyone behind to be with him. It didn't take her long to decide. And so she searched her mind for all the potential ways to get herself there.

"So when do you think you'd be running in New York?"

"Ah, I don't know Greg. When I feel I'm ready I guess. Or if *Oddinary* offers me a job."

"Have you applied for a position there?"

"Well actually, they wanted to fly me there this weekend."

"What happened?"

"Well, call it cold feet. But I thought about it further, and realised that I'm happy where I am. At *Cream*. Where my heart is."

After Pigeon

Lunch, Timmy thought, was a great success. After the meal, the twins insisted that they do the dishes. So he had a moment by himself in the living room. He looked all around him, at the timeless family treasures adorning the shelving and wall space—elaborate hand-fired ceramics, personalised wall hangings, wood and metal sculptures, hand-blown glass vases, elegant candle holders, photos of family and friends. He could tell from the spread that the Lanes showed a keen interest in the arts and valued travel to near and distant lands. It was also obvious they cherished the memories of their time spent together.

Timmy walked over to the hearthside to look at the photo frames on the mantel. There was one of Cambria sitting in the bedroom, a cello snug between her thighs. A shaft of morning sunshine had cut through the bedroom window, casting bold slants of shadows across the floor. Head tilted to the left, her long silky hair covered one side of her face. She was lost in a soulful sway.

Timmy was spellbound.

The photo next to it featured Cambria with very short hair, tears running down her cheeks. The light in the photo was so drab you could barely tell it was a colour picture.

"That was me when I was eleven."

Cambria's voice reached to the other side of the room like church bells across the valley. Timmy met her with his eyes, delighted.

Like the colours of autumn, her voice took on many hues; sure and thoughtful most of the time, coarse in a whisper, but otherwise, velvety. Amidst close company; warm and embracing. And in the still silence; celestial, like the note of a chime that hangs in the air. He loved every manifestation of her voice and wished there was some way to bottle it.

Timmy learned from Cambria, that at eleven, she had to have her hair cut short due to lice. Scarred by that episode, she had since kept her hair long, in the same exact style; straight, black, ending at her bra strap. Timmy looked at other photos. Unlike Cambria, Lenka had experimented with bobs, weaves, nests and frizzes, and her hair had seen more colours than a piñata shop. She even went shiny once, to protest government legislation against stem cell research for cancer.

Timmy proceeded further along the living room wall and stopped to look at some of the paintings.

"All the ones on the left are mine, the rest are Lenka's."

Timmy noticed that their styles were very different. Lenka's work was uplifting and playful, and she experimented with an ambitious and iridescent colour palette; whereas most of Cambria's pieces were dark and heavy, with less contrasting colour pairings.

Timmy found himself drawn to a painting Lenka had done. It featured a pink elephant with a filigree of blue and green vines within. Cambria explained what Lenka was trying to convey in her art. Their mother always complained of varicose veins on her feet, a result of standing in the kitchen for too long. Lenka reckoned that elephants, themselves standing for long periods, would be plagued by the same problem. But weighing what they weighed, Lenka imagined their varicose veins to be severe enough to spread to their entire body.

Lenka's art was simple. She would discover an interesting fact about a thing, and convey it through a colourful and over-imaginative lens. But of the twins, Timmy could tell that Cambria was the more accomplished artist, her work more sophisticated, both technically and in its subject matter. The piece of hers which stole his attention was painted in sombre tones; stark greys, rich browns, black, and brilliant white.

Cambria detected Timmy's interest, and allayed his curiosity, "It is called *Mo Cion Daonnan*. It's Gaelic for *My Love Eternal*."

Timmy's eyes widened with surprise when he matched the title to what he saw on the canvas. It was one of the grimmest paintings he had ever seen, and he started to question her notion of love.

"A most arresting piece, this one," he commented.

She conveyed the meaning behind her work.

"The naked man in the foreground, the one attempting to run, was reckless with a girl's heart many years back. He regrets what he did."

She paused.

"The gnarled leafless tree atop the hill and the snow-covered ground, tells you he is going through winter, perhaps the coldest of his time."

"Is that the Vergina Sun behind the clouds?" Timmy enquired. "It's a Macedonian symbol right?"

"Very perceptive."

She was impressed he spotted that.

"Actually, I painted this when I was sixteen, and the sixteen points in the star represent that."

"I see."

"Actually, it appears as if the sun is crouched behind a cloud, but it is not. The sun is actually turning into cloud. When I painted this, Macedonia had just removed the Vergina Star from their flag. Greece, for many years, had maintained that the Vergina Star was their symbol, and that Macedonia had stolen it. After much dispute between the countries, Macedonia conceded. And the sun faded from existence."

"Interesting."

"In this piece, the star represents something that once existed, but doesn't anymore. After the sun fully dissolves, the man in the picture will be stuck forever in the cold."

"Ouch!"

Cambria pointed, and squinted, to draw focus to a small detail on the painting. "If you look closely, within the tears flowing from his petrified eyes, you can see the image of the girl whose heart he broke."

Timmy leaned forward, and narrowed his eyes. "Yeah. I see her."

"The man is hoping that crying will bring her back, and that his tears will melt his winter. But instead, his tears freeze his feet to the ground, along with the image of her. He can't go back, and he can't come back."

"Can't go back, can't come back? What do you mean?"

"You can't smoke a cigarette twice. He can't go back in time to correct his mistakes."

"The mistakes that drove the girl away?"

"Yes. And till today, she has not forgiven him."

"Oh, so she won't let him come back to her, and he can't go back to fix the past,"

"Precisely."

My love eternal. Timmy now saw the significance of the title. It was of a person who squandered his chance at love, and now had to pay for his mistake. Forever.

He turned and looked at Cambria. "Brutal," he muttered, his tone so serious she knew he wasn't serious.

Cambria eased into a controlled grin, and Timmy smiled with her. Quickly, she pulled a stern seriousness back onto her face, and in a lecturing tone cautioned, "Yeah, so you better be more careful with the next heart you hold in your hands."

Timmy caught some semblance of a smile as she spoke those words, and wondered if the heart she was referring to was her own.

They moved to the next painting, and the next. Timmy was baffled by the amount of thought that went into her work, and he could tell that she had shed her naiveté at a very early age. He saw from the bold and fluid striations of her brush, that she painted with purpose, passion and great confidence.

~.~.~.~.~.~

Mid afternoon, Greg took Timmy to the back of the house, into the converted barn that was now his personal hideout cum work area. Inside, it had all that you'd expect to find in a wood-shop; sturdy hardwood benches, lumber storage racks, a floor drill press, a table saw, hand tools, chisels, planes, hand saws and marking instruments. At the far corner from the entrance, there was a couch and a TV, and beside that, a fridge full of beer and dip. This was where Greg took the guys to hang out. And Timmy felt honoured to be shown it.

The smell of the woodshop was familiar, and triggered a wave of nostalgia for his summers on Laeso. The full-bodied musk of hardwoods, the sweet fragrance of cedar, the revit-alising scent of pine, the camphorous fumes of resin gum and lacquer.

Timmy recalled the times he used to assist his grandpa with the repairs. One summer, he spent a couple weeks helping his granddad re-thatch their roof, and another summer building and replacing a windmill blade. When Timmy was fifteen, he helped reconstruct the hull of their uncle's fishing boat which had run aground. That was the last project Timmy completed with his gramps, before a stroke took him in the winter.

With a curious eye, Timmy browsed Greg's workspace as if he were on a museum school trip. He noticed that Greg owned many tools from far off times, and he got excited each time he came across a rare something he was familiar with. Even more excited when he found something he knew nothing about. He asked Greg a lot of questions, and Greg was all too happy to nourish his curiosity. Two hours passed in a blink.

~.~.~.~.~.~.~

A dull knock rattled the door frame. Before either could answer, Cambria poked her head in. She had come to invite Timmy out for a run, just as she had promised him she would. Before Timmy left with her, he made Greg promise one thing, that they would continue their discussion on the wabble saw.

Greg winked.

The sky was starting to take on the hues of evening, so Timmy wasted no time getting changed. When he emerged from the house, he found Cambria jogging lightly on one spot. She was wearing a loose white T-shirt rolled up at the sleeves, and underneath that, a black tank top. Her pair of tight-hugging three quarter Lycras caught every curve of her lower body; and this was accentuated further as she went through her warm up routine of forward lunges, back stretches and knee lifts. There was an instance when her oversized T-shirt slid to one side, exposing her shoulder, elegant and smooth like ivory. Timmy, like a schoolboy discovering his pubescence, got excited at the reveal.

Timmy reckoned that their run that evening was going to be part trail, part road, and he was impressed by Cambria's shoe choice, a Saucony ProGrid Xodus. It had a really durable outsole, which was ideal for rougher terrain, and a light, cushiony midsole, that also made it good for the road.

To stretch out her quads, Cambria folded her leg backwards and held her heels to her buttocks. This allowed Timmy a glimpse of her shoe bottom. He noticed wear on the inner side of the sole, which suggested she was an overpronator.

Maybe that's why her heels clank when she walks down the basement stairs. Overpronators are normally flat footed. Her low heel arch doesn't afford her sufficient bend. Yes, that must be it. Because she can't bend, she can't press her shoe insoles close to the bottom of her feet. Hence the clanking.

Timmy felt smug that he had solved the mystery of her signature walk. But he also felt like such a running nerd for arriving at that conclusion.

As Timmy shook out his legs and proceeded with his warm ups alongside Cambria, he realised his body felt less limber than usual. His infatuation with Cambria had frayed the reins he once had on his life, and caused him to break from his usual running routine. Plagued by sleepless nights, it had been weeks since he had run at sun up. He still made it a point to run over lunch though. He needed the stress relief. Each morning, despite his body crying for more sleep, he took special effort to be at work earlier than usual, to catch that first glimpse of Cambria as she descended down the stairs. The tumultuous weeks had taken a toll on him.

"Cambria," a voice called out from behind them.

The pair looked over their shoulders. Lenka had stepped out of the house for a smoke. She frowned as she lit up, but in the twinkling of an eye, untwisted her face into a smile. Cambria tensed up when she caught the glimpse of mischief across her sister's face.

"You were right about his shorts," Lenka laughed. "It leaves very little to the imagination."

Cambria very nearly had a coronary. "Lenkaaaaa?" she yelled, fists on her hips.

Timmy was quick with his response.

"I picked my smallest pair in hopes that your sister would take my lead, and attire herself in something of equal reveal."

Lenka burst out laughing. "I told her earlier to lose her T-shirt and just wear her tank top."

"Lenkaa," Cambria warned her sister in a low, reprimanding, *you'd-better-not-go-there* tone.

Lenka proceeded anyway with her salacious remark. "But she was afraid that her nipples would show."

"Lenkaaaa!!!" a mortified Cambria shrieked, her face red and warm in embarrassment.

Timmy could not shake his big grin. He had never before seen Cambria lose it quite like this. Before this trip, the most he had witnessed of her frustration was a low growl under her breath.

Impartial to his amusement, she ushered him on with a ghost of a smile, "Come on silly. We ought to be getting along before it gets dark."

The lovebirds pushed off, down the gravel path leading away from the house, and onto the main road. Timmy ran slower than his usual, but Cambria surged forward little by little, until they arrived at a pace he was more accustomed to.

Cambria displayed immaculate running form. Impressed, he asked, "You run competitively?"

"Why do you ask?"

"You've got exquisite technique. Smooth and pendulum-like. Arms nicely tucked in. Well abbreviated breathing. Feather light footfall... like a spider threading across a pond."

She smiled. "I used to run 10Ks. Back when I was in school."

"Oh!" Timmy was surprised. "You still run?"

"Yes, I run occasionally on weekends," Cambria lied, hopeful that Timmy would ask her out for a run one day.

"If you're up to it, we should get together on weekends to run. I've been looking for a worthy running partner for some time now."

An even bigger lie from Timmy. He hated running with a partner. Conversation was an inevitability when running in tandem. And it threw him off his pace.

Cambria was delighted that she was going to see more of Timmy on weekends.

"You always wear that?" Cambria asked.

"What? My heart rate monitor?"

"Uh huh."

"Yes, I wear it all the time."

"Why?"

Timmy told Cambria about the time he died. And how since, to not tempt providence and suffer another heart arrest, he ran with a heart monitor strapped to his wrist. He also told her about the game he played with himself; to guess his own heart rate. She tested him. He guessed 55. His wrist showed 55. She was impressed. And then amazed.

"55? That's ridiculously low. What's your resting heart rate?"

"32."

"Absurd!" she remarked.

"MHR is about 188."

"Alright, now you're boasting."

Timmy flashed a guilty grin.

"So your Heart Rate Reserve is 156. That is off the trolley." She knew her terminology. Timmy was blown away.

Cambria took Timmy through Lechlade's high street and past St Lawrence, her primary school. From there she led him out of the town centre. They went off the main road onto supple terrain, down into a meadow that led to the brook that she used to sit by. She went there when she wanted to be alone, and Zen-ed out by its mossy banks, under a shady overhanging tree. For hours, she listened to the gurgling water and the rustle of long grass swaying in the breeze.

From the brook, they progressed up a hill, to the highest point around Lechlade, a spot that offered a view of the town. Timmy was struck by how the light fell on the valley below. The sun was starting to set, and from the hill, they could see lights starting to be turned on. Atop the hill was a lone tree, under which Cambria received her first kiss, from a boy two years her senior, a boy by the name of Jacob. It was the same tree that Cambria featured in her painting, *Mo Cion Daonnan*.

Cambria did not, at any time, stop at any of the points of interest. She merely explained the significance of the landmarks to Timmy as they passed them. He was impressed that she was able to comfortably hold a conversation while running at that pace.

"From here, it's about a mile to the house. Care to race?"

Timmy was surprised at the challenge Cambria threw at him. It seemed a little out of character.

"You bet. Are we wagering on anything?"

"How about if you win, I take off the shirt shielding my tank top?"

Timmy was stunned, shocked that she would bet on something of that nature. He let out a clap of laughter, realising that his punishment for losing would probably be far worse than what she was putting out.

"And what happens if I lose?"

"You'll have to..."

A mischievous grin formed on her face.

"Ah, this is a good one. Wear your running shorts to dinner."

The dare was not even close to what Timmy had feared.

"You're on."

Cambria quickened her step but Timmy matched her speed and reeled her back in. Accustomed to running much further than they had done that evening, Timmy had ample left in the tank, so he went full throttle and pulled ahead of her. To his dismay, she segued effortlessly into a higher gear and drew even with him, her feet falling with his.

Sensing that Timmy had pledged everything and was at peak velocity, Cambria was almost certain that victory was hers. With half a mile to go, she broke into full stride. All Timmy could do was watch helplessly as she surged past him, her elbows slicing air as she ran. Overwhelmed by her speed, his legs became prematurely heavy, as if tendrils had emerged from the earth and curled around his ankles. He knew that unless she tired at the last minute—or tripped—that she was going to reach the house first, and that he'd be wearing his skimpies to dinner that night.

Cambria was still reclaiming her breath when a discomfited Timmy arrived at the doorstep.

"Alright hombre," she huffed. "Better be prepared to show your sexy legs tonight."

"No worries. I'll keep my end," Timmy assured.

"Oh, by the way," Cambria mentioned between breaths, "I forgot to tell you." She laid a reaffirming hand on Timmy's shoulder. "We're having dinner at my aunt's. You'll get to meet everyone."

Timmy was completely amused and taken by her playful deceitfulness. He wanted so badly to wrestle her to the ground and mash his lips against hers. He shook his head and smiled.

An Evening Gathering

The night was cold, just like the day before. To stay warm, Cora and Greg stood by the fireplace while the rest got ready. Timmy was the first to come out of his room. Sporting a really smart turtleneck and a paltry pair of running shorts, he joined his hosts by the hearthside and waited for the girls.

Timmy was deeply amused that Greg and Cora wanted to make a comment about his attire, but were too polite to do so. From the brevity of their knowing him, they weren't sure if it was a fashion signature of his they were unaware of, especially with him being a running freak and all.

Dressed the way he was, Timmy tried his best to look dignified. Just to make conversation, he made some comment about the weather. Sensing Timmy's unease, Cora started to query him about the work he did, which fell well within his comfort zone of topics to be discussed.

Cambria and Lenka emerged from their room looking vibrant, dressed for an evening out. Standing there in his lean pair of shorts, Timmy felt more naked than before.

Lenka wore the eccentricity of her usual Bohemian self, dressed in a chiffon top the colour of dark plum, and a long black skirt that teased the ground she walked on. She glimmered with every sway, this because of the mirror sequins in her skirt. As Timmy had come to expect of her, she bore a well-orchestrated percussion of costume jewellery that melded seamlessly with her persona. Bangles, anklets, earrings, neck-laces and a shimmy belt. It was musical just to hear her jangle down the hallway.

Timmy turned his focus away from Lenka, and was seized by a moment of breathlessness as his eyes fell upon Cambria. In a black strapless one piece, her hair pulled back into a pony tail, Cambria's shoulders were fully exposed, and begged to be feathered with kisses. A faint shadow of cleavage vied for at-tention. Finding harbour within the slender curve of her neck, diamonds of light danced on a vine of silver earrings, casting a candescence on her already naturally radiant face. Timmy's gaze progressed downwards, starting from her face, down her neck, past her breasts, through her thighs. Her dress concluded three fingers above her knee, and showed ample of her take-no-prisoners legs. He consciously had to retract his slumping jaw.

As Cambria approached Timmy, her sultry gaze turned into a broad smile when she caught on to his bare legs. Stopping a foot short of him, she remarked, "Hey, sexy."

Timmy unravelled a smile, as if nothing were amiss, "Hey."

"You know you really didn't have to, right?"

"No, I insist," he replied smugly.

Over to the side, Lenka informed Cora and Greg of the bet between Cambria and Timmy. Cora tried to contain her smile, but a flicker of amusement escaped her conceal.

"You'd better get changed," Greg called out to Timmy. "If you step out of the house in that, son, you're going to freeze your Easter eggs off," he remarked jokingly.

Laughter lifted into the air.

Lenka chimed in, "And besides, I don't think your date would be seen with you dressed in that," using her eyes to make reference to Cambria.

Cambria chided her twin with an angry gaze.

Cora interjected, to everyone's surprise. "Actually, I think you will find Lenka on your arm most of the night if you insist on wearing that."

"Yes, I think Lenka will have you," Cambria supplemented, offering a feather-like pat of reassurance on Timmy's shoulder.

Lenka grew aware of the alliance that was starting to form against her. "Hey, how did I emerge as the desperate social outcast, left with but the pick of the crumbs," she laughingly shot back at her sister and mum.

"The crumbs?" Timmy rose in defence.

"Actually," Timmy looked at Greg as he spoke. "I figured that with these two lovely dames by my side, I would need all the cooling this pair of shorts afford me."

Greg let out a light chuckle.

"But it appears that I'm not on the side of the majority, so I should probably change into something more constricting."

Following his display of quick wit and flattery, what Cambria regarded as *Classic Timmy*, she smiled and shook her head, the words *My Timmy* forming in her mind. As Timmy made his way back to his room, the Lanes looked at each other amusedly.

"Where'd you find this fella anyway?" Greg asked jokingly.

~.~.~.~.~.~

The house was frothing with conversation when they arrived. It was the same each year.

After taking Timmy for a quick round of introductions, Cambria ducked into the kitchen to help with the food, leaving him in the care of her dad. As Cambria had come to expect, when she came out of the kitchen a mere ten minutes later, Timmy was already holding court, laughter erupting around him. With the ease and candidness he shared with the group, one would have made the easy mistake of assuming he had been born into the pack.

Throughout the night, Cambria was teased with Timmy. At first, she found herself tongue-tied for a response. Growing up, such teasing triggered knee jerk responses like "Never in a million years." But with Timmy by her side, she was careful not to say anything that would deter any advances from him. As the night wore on, she became more adept at parrying jokes of their couplehood, and countered with replies like "Oh, I'm sure Timmy has better taste" and "Don't scare the poor fella off." Much later, after the ale had lent her some daring, she ventured into responses like "if I should be so lucky" and "if he would have me, I don't see why not."

~.~.~.~.~.~.~

Cambria was a different person amongst her family than when around her work colleagues; full of life, a jokester, a charmer, goofy. As Timmy watched her in her element, he caught himself making comparisons between her and Monica, the vivacious goddess from work.

He noticed that like Monica, Cambria had the gift to hold an audience in silent fixation, but more with her eloquence than Monica with her beauty. As with the goddess, Cambria carried herself with great confidence, candour and charm. But absent, was Monica's prowess, which Timmy felt was a good thing. In his Eden, Cambria emerged more and more Eve-like; Monica, more serpentine.

The party crackled healthily throughout the night, and looked like it would go into the wee hours. But at the stroke of midnight, Greg's brother, Joe, excused himself and his family from the get-together; his two boys had to sing in the early mass the next morning. Those who remained did not remain for long.

Timmy found it interesting how parties always met an abrupt end after the first group of people peeled away; a real pity when the party was good, and a blessing for the ones that were a drag. Timmy had a great time that evening, and found it refreshing talking to farm belt folk. They were a simple people with close to nothing in common with him. And that led to some interesting conversation. Throughout the night, many of Cambria's relatives were compelled to share stories about her she did not want told, and Timmy was all too happy to be afforded this glimpse into her past, to be acquainted with the environment she grew up in, and with the people she grew up with.

Perfect as the evening was, Timmy was troubled by one thing—his sunset race with Cambria. Like a general scrutinising a defeat, he dissected the run over and over, to try and derive what he had done wrong. He knew in his mind, that if it were a real race, he would have emerged victorious for sure. He would have set a much quicker pace in the initial stages to wear her down, leaving her with insufficient fuel to burst to the finish the way she did. Distance running was all about proper fuel management, and he was denied that opportunity to plot the race.

He looked forward to their next encounter.

It was a long day, and although his body was tired, his mind bounced all over, like Styrofoam balls in a wind tunnel. As he lay in bed, and blinked at the ceiling, snippets of conversations from the party played back in his head. He thought he connected well with the people he met, and he wondered if he would ever see them again. Shifting away from the party, his mind naturally fell on Cambria, these words stencilled on his mind: *If he will have me, I don't see why not.*

Was she serious? Did she mean it? For a long time he pondered... and tossed... till he was drawn into a deep slumber.

~.~.~.~.~.~.~

Rapture wrapped her warm arms around Cambria. As she lay in bed, she wondered how it was that she was dreaming before sleep had even arrived. Her final reflection of the night was of her run with Timmy, a route that took them through town, past Willow's Brook and over Samsden's Hill, 10.2 kilometres in all. In her opinion, she would have beaten him by a much greater margin if she had kept her fitness up.

When she was fifteen, she owned the 10K race in the district, and was the clear favourite to win the nationals in her age category, until a calf injury ruled her out of competition. Plagued by the same injury for two years, she gave up running altogether, and this became a sore subject in her life. She tried to blot out her past by stowing away her trophies, certificates, wall photos, news articles; anything that reminded her of the promise that never materialised. Her family shared in the pain of her extinguished hopes, and the topic of running, for years, lost mention in all conversation.

Rather than hang up her running shoes, Cambria decided to burn them, using the remaining kerosene her mother dabbed on her hair when she was eleven—to kill off her head lice. In her mind, she was incinerating two painful memories with one light of the match.

The cremation took place in Greg's woodshop, and the fire from her burning shoes caught on some rope that hung from the ceiling. No one was injured and they were able to salvage the building. But Cambria never heard the end of it from Greg. After the incident, her shadow never again darkened the floor of her father's shed, until ten years later, when she walked in to invite a boy out for an evening run.

Post Easter

God, it is cold. What were you thinking Cammy? Sitting out here like this. I should have brought ma's shawl with me. The one she just knitted for me. What good is it sitting on the desk at work? Oh no. Was that rain? Or a drop of dew? It's too deep into the day for dew. Oh misery. It must be rain.

Just a couple minutes more. Please, just a couple minutes.

God. I need to tinkle. It's freezing today. Isn't it supposed to be spring already?

Was that another drop? Heaven help me. Where is he?

Ah, there he is, like clockwork. My Timmy. My running angel. My favourite three seconds. Grace unfurled. Cottony footfalls. Floating on a low cloud. Coasting like a peregrine falcon. Those legs, how I love thee, O sleek intertwine of silky muscle, the day I shall impose myself on thy fulcrum. I'm yours to be trespassed, Timothy Malcolm Smith, to be, ahem.. pollinated. [naughty giggle]

Well, at least he had the cow sense to wear a hat and gloves. Oh no, it's starting to rain for real. And..... aiyaiyai need to peeeee! Just a few more seconds. And he'll be off. On his way.

Oh misery. I think he's seen me. Oh, no. He's coming this way. What do I do? Bugger. What do I do?

Don't look. Just melt into your book. Pretend you didn't see him. Breathe.

Look calm. Just be lost in your book. Oh no it's getting heavy. It's starting to pour.

Breathe. Act surprised. Just be calm.

"Oh hi Timmy!"

He must think I'm such a numbnut. A dorky bookworm dork. Reading out here in the pouring rain.

Hmmmm, I think he's going to ask. I'd better think of an excuse. Why I'm out here, reading in the rain, like a weird weirdo.

I'll just tell him I was at a really gripping part of the book. And didn't even notice the rain. No, that's dumb. Urrrmmmm!

Rats, he really did ask. What should I say?

"Oh, I was at a really gripping part of the book. I didn't even notice the rain."

Oh, that just sounded so daft. Well, what was I going to say? That I walk all the way to this park every lunch break to stalk him? Oh, I so need to tinkle.

He wants to know what book I'm reading. Stall.

"Oh the book I'm reading? You want to know the title?"

Golly, what book am I reading?

"This book is..."

Just look at the cover dummy. No wait, don't. Look at the top of the page. It should be there.

"... the Change of Times. By urmmm, Shelly Wilson. One of my favourite authors."

Phew. That went pretty smooth. Boy, I'm freezing. The wind seems to have picked up.

Oh heck, he wants to know if I come here all the time.

"No, I don't come to this park all the time."

Liar.

"Yes, I know. I really should get out of the rain. I'd love to join you for coffee. Where'd you reckon we go?"

Oh, please suggest some place near. I really, really, really have to tinkle. Oh look at that. The wind has blown a leaf onto his crotch. And it's stuck on his wet shorts. This is too funny. He looks like

Adam. The leaf is flitting. Don't laugh, or you'll spring a leak. Don't laugh.

Oh bugger. He wants to know what I'm laughing at? Oh, should I tell him?

Just look at your shorts dummy. I'll tell him once I catch my breath. Oh this is too funny.

Oh misery, it's coming. Squeeze it in Cammy. Squeeze it in. Oh bugger. Too late. It's out the gates. Forget it, it's too late. No point fighting it now. Might as well just let it all out. Mmmm, it feels warm. Oooh, that feels so much better. Rats, I hope he doesn't smell it. Check for smell. Inhale. Oh, please, let there not be any. Phew, I think the rain has masked it. Oh misery, we'll be going to the café. What now smarty pants? More like smelly pants. Ha, ha. I'll just wash in the ladies. I'm all drenched anyway. He won't see a difference. Good thinking Cambria. You know, you're pretty smart sometimes. Man, I'm freezing.

"Look at your shorts silly!" Cambria pointed.

Timmy looked down, and they both laughed. He peeled the leaf off his shorts and asked her if she wanted to keep it, as a bookmark. She took it from him, and they adjourned out of the rain, into a toasty delicatessen a short distance from the park.

~.~.~.~.~.~

A bond of familiarity formed between Timmy and Cambria following their Easter weekend together, and to Timmy's relief, he regained some normalcy in his life: the butterflies made their way back into their cocoons, his heart regained some of its buoyancy and he rediscovered the friendly spontaneity he enjoyed with her before. The ritual of asking her out for coffee also lost its awkwardness, and their conversations and dalliances grew more intimate. Single knuckle punches to the arm and shoulder-to-shoulder nudges became common between them. And Cambria sometimes walked up to his side and pendulumed her hip against his, as a way of saying, "Hi, I'm here."

Despite the developments in their friendship, Timmy's sleepless nights did not completely leave him, his pent-up feelings for Cambria keeping him awake most nights. He was comfortable with the rate at which their relationship was progressing, and he sensed an eventuality to their union. He was just waiting for the right time to tell her.

They started to go on runs together; during lunch, and sometimes over the weekend. Cambria gave Timmy another shot at beating her at the 10K and let him pick the route. They met early one Saturday morning at Birdcage Walk, and took an anti-Clockwise route along the Thames, sliding past Cleopatra's Needle, up Queen Victoria Street, looping back through Fenchurch, Leadenhall Market, Puddle Dock and back to where they started. The gloves came off this time round. For someone who was not used to run that distance, Timmy put in a dazzling performance. He clocked a time of 30 minutes and 14 seconds, a showing worthy of a top 20 spot at most world competitions. To his chagrin, Cambria beat him again, this time more convincingly than she had done through the uneven terrain around Lechlade. Finishing a whole ten seconds ahead of him, it wasn't much of a contest.

Cambria made her move seven kilometres into their race. As she had done previously, she unleashed a straining burst of speed towards the end, and outstrode Timmy to the finish. Timmy had the wind worked out of him trying to keep up with her, and it took him several minutes to reclaim his breath after he crossed. He asked her for her time, and she told him. It took a while to set in. One of the world's fastest female runners in the 10K had just come out of retirement. And he was madly in love with her.

~.~.~.~.~.~

That morning, right after Cambria's landmark performance, they stepped into Shelley's, a modest dinette by St James' Park. The place served breakfast for most of the day before fading into a charming candlelit dining establishment in the evening. Cambria and Timmy ordered a hearty breakfast to replenish what they had expended on their run.

An omelette, a slice of toast and half a banger into their meal, Cambria revealed her painful past to Timmy, of how she lost her place in running history when she was fifteen, and how she almost burned down her Dad's converted barn two years later. Timmy, who before wondered how Greg worked dark swirls into the wood, got his answer. After learning of Cambria's past, Timmy felt a little better with himself, now knowing that he had conceded to a once professional competitor, and not some complete novice whose weekly workout consisted of time on a stationary bike and an hour in step class.

Timmy spent every Saturday being beaten by Cambria in the 10K, each time progressively worse, always to her devastating final burst. Each time, they proceeded to Shelley's afterwards. They chatted endlessly, like lovers reunited after a war, and their breakfast dates often turned into lunch, lunch into tea. Their weeklies never progressed into dinner, this a result of them feeling a bit underdressed as the formal evening crowd arrived at the dinette. To not cheapen the place, they always called for the cheque. The restaurant owner appreciated the courtesy.

Sunday afternoons, Cambria started to join Timmy and Kim at the movies. Kim was initially not too happy with the intrusion. But it did not take long before he grew to like her, and the three eventually became inseparable, both at work and on the weekends.

The thing that Kim liked the most about Cambria was that there was nothing to dislike about her. No annoying habits, no limiting phobias, not a finicky eater, nor nitpicky over toilet conditions. No annoying laugh, no irritating overuse of words like 'like. No feminist agenda, no OCD, no anger issues, no bossiness.

But Cambria was in no way uncontroversial. She had a mind of her own, but with a healthy dose of agreeableness and compromise. And Kim appreciated that about her.

Cambria also possessed a restrained frankness. Politically correct with her political incorrectness, she always apologised before saying something that could be construed as insensitive, unladylike, or coloured. A result of her country upbringing, she was reserved and held herself well in public, but could be persuaded to abandon social etiquette for a good laugh. Her humour was well-timed, piquant and in good measure. Kim could see how some people would regard her mannerisms a little uppity, slightly high brow, but he wasn't one of those.

~.~.~.~.~.~.~

Over weeks of running almost daily, Cambria exceeded her form from before and started to clock in times that made her a world class contender in 10K competition. She looked forward to the possibility of making a comeback. Her running time eventually plateaued slightly outside the world's top five woman runners.

Technically, Timmy's knowledge of running mechanics was far superior to what Cambria had acquired when she was a teenager. And she spent hours on end with him to discuss ways she could improve. The two were thrilled to discover this shared interest.

As the weeks passed, Cambria started feeling bad about beating Timmy every weekend. This was despite him taking each loss in the highest spirits—he always joked that her drool-inducing derriere brought about crucial fluid loss, which cost him the race.

To help Timmy regain his pride, Cambria one day suggested

that they run a 26.2, which was in Timmy's wheelhouse. Timmy suggested they run the official route of the London Marathon. They both looked forward to the day.

It was on a sleepy Sunday morning in the third week of May that Cambria attempted her first marathon-length run. They set off from Blackheath, heading east through Charlton, looping back at Woolwich. Like on their other runs, they felt each other out in the early stages, and settled on a median pace. Six miles in, as they were heading towards the Cutty Sark dry-docked at Greenwich, Timmy made a break. But he couldn't quite shake her. To his surprise, she passed him as they entered Mudchute at the Isle of Dogs, but he stayed close on her heels and regained his lead at the halfway point, as they crossed Tower Bridge. At the twentieth mile, Cambria hit a bit of a wall and started to wither away. Victory within his clutches, Timmy went on a final burn to ensure his win was safely in the books. To his shock, Cambria caught a second wind and closed in on him with re-newed vigour. As they passed Blackfriars at mile 24, Cambria, holding nothing in reserve, unravelled her length and surged past Timmy. Already running as fast as his legs could carry him, Timmy felt like a compromised speedboat that was taking on water. Easing her way out of view with her long ground eaters, it appeared certain that Cambria was going to take the race, eas-ily. And she did. A whole minute ahead of Timmy.

It wasn't as effortless as she made it look. She was complete-ly spent by the end of it, gagging crudely as she repaid her oxygen debt. Her heart thumped with the ferocity of a climax-ing night club. Her mouth no longer conjured saliva. And her tongue stuck to the roof of her mouth each time she gobbled for air. She, for a moment, a moment that felt like it would not cease, thought she was going to die.

Timmy was brutally outclassed. Looking at his watch as he reached the finish line, he stared at Cambria as if he had just seen a ghost. Pale from the retching, she wasn't too far off looking like one. She was copiously covered in sweat, and crystals of light dangled on every precipice of her face.

Hands on his hips, Timmy walked in circles around her. In between breaths, he squeezed out.

"Cambria..."

"... you finished..."

"... a minute short..."

"... of the world..."

"... the world marathon record."

Cambria was well aware of the record: set by Paula Radcliffe at the London Marathon, on the same exact course they had just run.

At fifteen, after Cambria's running career went up in ashes, she averted her eyes whenever she came across any news of the sport. But when fellow country woman Paula Radcliffe obliterated the world record in 2003, the English press made sure to fog every mind in the country with the news. Almost a decade later, no one, not even Paula herself, had come close to beating that time.

Depleted, having embezzled every iota of energy and will from her stores, she rested her weary eyes on Timmy's and looked at him quizzically. A minute seemed an insurmountable gap to close.

"Cambria, you don't understand. Berlin is a much faster course than what we ran today."

She finally got it. Berlin was tamer, easier. If she were running Berlin today, she may actually have bettered Radcliffe's time.

"So you're saying, if I were running Berlin today, I would have broken Paula Radcliffe's record. And become the fastest woman on the planet?"

"No, Cambria. The record I'm referring to is not Radcliffe's. But Gebrselassie's. If you were running Berlin today, you very possibly would have been the fastest person on the planet, man or woman."

Walk On The Pier

The ripples on the puddles of water were the clearest indication that the heavens were still tearing. From the charming curtained windows at Shelley's, they peered out at the sky every few minutes. The sun was stubbornly elusive that day, except for a brief moment, when it kissed the rain and birthed a rainbow. The gloom was for a while lifted, then drawn again into the powdery grey.

Each completely absorbed by the other, the hours fell through their hands, and before they knew it, the late afternoon was upon them. Not wanting to carry the luggage of a meal, they chose not to eat from morning, hoping the whole time that the rain would lift long enough for them to proceed with their Saturday run. Confronted by the late hour and fading light, they grew resigned to the fact that their run just wasn't going to happen that day. So they decided to get some dinner.

Cambria expressed a craving for Chinese food of the most exotic variety. Timmy was game. He knew of a restaurant by his place that pushed the limits of the palate; fried duck bills, buttermilk jelly fish, pickled tripe, deep fried durian ice cream, salmon macaroons and numerous other peculiar things in the miscellaneous category.

They hopped onto the Jubilee Line which had a direct route from Westminster to where Timmy lived, in Canary Wharf. The Jubilee was unusually crowded, which Cambria reckoned came from the conclusion of the tulip exhibition in St James' Park, an event she wanted very badly to attend but forewent because she cherished her time with Timmy more. Of all living things, she considered tulips to be the most sensual and effeminate on Earth, their elegant curvature and smooth satiny texture oozing sex appeal.

At Waterloo, the train got a lot more crowded, and turned from a can of sardines into a can of shredded tuna. The force of the crowd, leaning itself onto the train car, washed Timmy up against Cambria. Firmly packed with barely any wriggle room, he gave her an apologetic look. Through their giggles they conveyed to each other, *This is London for you*. When the railing above became overcrowded with white knuckles, Cambria released her hold of the bar, and placed both her hands on the outer edges of Timmy's chest, below his shoulders. Tightly pressed against him, she could feel his chest rise and fall, steadily and surely, his breaths deep and long, true to that of a distance man.

When they arrived at their stop, the train emptied rapidly, like an aquarium full of fish that just had its glass broken. It was Cambria's first time to Canary Wharf. As they emerged from the tube station, she was pleasantly surprised to see they were close to the water's edge, and she was instantly drawn to it.

Timmy ran his fingers along the pier railing as they meandered quietly, looking downwards most of the time. Every now and then, he peeled up to steal a glance at her.

"Earth to Timmy!" Cambria reined him in. "You haven't been talking much. Like you usually do."

"Is everything alright?" she softened her tone.

Funnily, that was the first time she had said anything herself the last ten minutes. Her mind, just like Timmy's, was in a distant place, trapped in her private musings. She had never felt so close to him as she did that day—discoursing at length with him about everything and nothing, basking in their similitude, trading laughs and subtle flirtation, and after that, being mashed against him on the crowded train.

Cambria's silence breaker knocked Timmy off his cloud of faraway thought.

"Everything's fine," he threw back as he leaned over the pier railing and faced the declining sun. She parked herself next to him, the fabric of her shirt lightly brushing against his arm. Timmy wanted badly to ask her. Ask if she had any feelings for him. He grew more and more breathless as the words started to gather in his throat.

As they stared off into the horizon, Cambria mentioned to him that *Before Sunset* was her favourite romantic movie of all time. Timmy's was *Reign Over Me*, a tragic love story of a man who lost his wife and kid in the 9/11 attack. It had Adam Sandler and Don Cheadle in it. She had not watched it so Timmy tried to regurgitate the movie to her. He could not quite convey the true depth and emotion of it.

"It's just one of those movies you have to watch to get."

"My favourite Adam Sandler movie is the *Wedding Singer*," Cambria admitted. She knew that it was a bit of a silly movie, unrepresentative of her true tastes, so she felt the need to defend her choice.

"Well, ... I know it's a bit schmaltzy, stereotypical..."

"No, the *Wedding Singer* is one of my favourite flicks of all time," Timmy jumped in before she tore the movie apart any further.

"Really?" Cambria replied, a bit excitedly.

"Yeah really. You know, it's funny. We discuss movies almost every weekend, and I never would have thought this movie would be one you'd be into."

"Well, it's light and fun, as most of his movies are. I reserve Sandler mainly for Friday nights, when I need to unwind."

Timmy started to sing *Wanna Grow Old With You*, the soundtrack to the movie. Cambria joined in.

They sang the parts they knew, and hummed the rest.

I wanna make you smile whenever you're sad
Carry you around when your arthritis is bad
Oh all I wanna do is grow old with you
I'll get your medicine when your tummy aches
Ta dum dum da dum
Oh it could be so nice, growing old with you
I'll miss you
Kiss you
Ta dum dumdum
Dum dum da dum
Dum dum da dum
Even let ya hold the remote control
So let me do the dishes in our kitchen sink
Put you to bed when you've had too much to drink
Ta dum dum da dum ta dum da dum

They remembered and sang the final line together, "Oh I could be the one, who grows old with you. I wanna grow old with you."

They stared at each other for what seemed like an eternity. Something hung between them, something so real they could reach out and touch. Timmy's feelings for her had never been so strong. And never had he been so sure she felt the same way for him. He leaned in to kiss her. Cambria was taken by surprise and instinctively leaned back, away from Timmy. Timmy panicked, and realised he may have misread the whole situation.

Hers was a knee-jerk reaction from all the non-potentials who tried to kiss her in the past. After she realised what she had done, it was too late. Just as she was to reverse her direction to meet his lips, Timmy, trapped in a quagmire of uncertainty, withdrew his advance. And he turned to face the sunset. He was relieved he pulled away in time, but felt as if his chest had imploded, and left a deep dark hollow within.

"What a blessed sunset we have here?" He puffed his cheeks and blew.

It was one of the most anaemic conclusions to the day each had ever beheld, void of any fanfare or splendour of flaming colours.

"Yes, the pale pink tinge is rather calming huh!?" Cambria contributed.

"Yup."

Each stewing in their silence, in their solitary worlds, they stared off into the remains of the day, their minds locked onto a different moment, of the kiss that almost was.

Cambria kicked herself for squandering her chance to endorse her feelings for Timmy. She considered turning to him and saying, "All set, I'm ready now. Kiss me."

"You can't smoke a cigarette twice," she sighed to herself. Her regret recycled in her head.

"I'm famished. You?" Timmy asked.

"Let's have dinner."

They turned around and headed for *The Palace of the Golden Sunset,* the restaurant they had appointed to test their gastronomic limits. When they got there, they were sorely astounded by the line that had formed outside. Just to get in, the estimated wait was an hour and a quarter. For the day, between the two of them, they'd had eight cups of tea, nibbled on some saltine crackers, and shared two muffins—a blueberry and a banana nut. Their scant eatings weren't going to see them through to dinner at the Palace.

"Hey, I live a couple doors from here. We could go back to my place and I could rustle up something."

"That's right. You live in Canary Wharf."

"Shall we?"

Over At Timmy's

The reception area was disconcertingly grand.

"Good evening Mr Smith."

You only saw that in movies; a concierge at the lobby of your abode greeting you by name. Cambria was impressed.

Cambria noticed something odd when she entered the lift. There wasn't a menu of numbers you could light up to get to your floor, merely a card slot. Timmy slid his card in, and the doors closed. She liked the music in the lift. They played Lisa Gerrard. Not the annoying instrumental arrangements looped in hotel elevators, shopping malls, dentists' offices or when customer service put you on hold. She expected a *'ping'* as the elevator decelerated to a stop, but there was none. When the doors parted, Cambria thought she had woken in a dream. She batted her eyelids a few times to see if her eyes would correct themselves.

"We're here," Timmy announced. And he exited the lift. Cambria stepped out with him, into a lush roof top garden of Eden-like abundance—ferns, flowering shrubs, bamboo, yuccas, trailing plants and foliage shrubs—all part of the faunal composition. Turning her eyes upwards, she saw the sky. Water, cascading from one rock pool to another, produced a light murmur that she found calming.

Timmy escorted Cambria toward the house, along a palm-fringed path of loose powdery pebbles. The sound of crunching stones under his feet always triggered a special feeling in him. It reminded him that he was close to home. He experienced that same sensation of homeward-boundness in Lechlade, that evening when he raced with Cambria, as he ran on the loose gravel road leading to their cottage.

"Wow, it's gorgeous up here. So is this where you take all your dates?" Cambria asked jokingly.

Curiously, she brushed aside a curtain of drooping green fronds, and found the edge of the building. She spotted a line of pigeons perched along one of the roof walls, their glossy eyes staring out into the darkening sapphire sky.

"We having them for dinner tonight?" she asked as she pointed.

Timmy chuckled, and watched adoringly as Cambria continued to explore the grounds in amazement.

"Wow, there's even a house up here. Does anyone live in it?"

"Mmm-hmmm," Timmy replied. "Me."

Cambria knew that modern day luxury condos came with an open area that tenants were afforded the use of, to hold garden parties and the like. To see how far he was planning to go with it, she decided to oblige him his gag.

"Nice home you have," she complimented, her voice thick with sarcasm.

"Come on. I'll show you inside."

The steps that led to the front veranda were flanked by sweet smelling blooms. Cambria admired them as she brushed past. On her ascent, she spotted a shoe rack by the front door with six pairs of running shoes perched on it, all of the brand Timmy wore. It hit her like a spade in the face. Timmy wasn't joking. This rooftop nirvana actually belonged to him.

"Seriously. You live here?"

Timmy nodded, a little embarrassed.

Cambria was stunned, or overly impressed, she did not know which. All she knew was that Timmy was always a bit eccentric, so it fell well within his character to live in a place like this. Standing on the veranda, she asked him about the inscription above his front door. A piece of driftwood, carved with the word *Ankhura*, dangled from a low beam.

"It's the name I've given this house. It is Sanskrit for *East Meets West*. I thought it was the perfect name for a Balinese hut sitting in the heart of London's financial district."

"Do you read Sanskrit?"

"Hell no," Timmy admitted through his grin. "Kim has a cousin, Tina, over in Tuscany. She is a Chinese Malaysian married to Chris, a Swedish bloke. Together, they run a B&B by that name."

"Oh, so East meets West because he is from Sweden, and she, from the Orient?"

"Yup. Kim and I spent a week in Italy and rented a room from them for a couple of days."

"Nice."

"I've also assigned my own meaning to the word *Ankhura*." Timmy went on to explain, "It combines the word *Ankh*, which in Egypt is the symbol of life, and the word *Pura*, which in Bali is a temple."

"So, the Temple of Life?" Cambria pieced together.

"Yup. Welcome to my dream home. The architectural manifestation of me. So I hoped anyway, back when I was building it."

Timmy pushed open the intricately carved double doors, and they entered.

The interior was not lavish, but well-coordinated. Cambria liked how the different levels in flooring defined the different spaces of the house. She also noticed that Timmy employed a very natural, earthy palette: deep olive, sisal, sage, terracotta, wine red. She was impressed with how everything just seemed

to come together. The wood and wicker furniture complement-
ed the rice paper lamps. The decorative bowls and mother-of-
pearl vases matched the beaded scatter cushions. The seat fabric, the towelling and the rugs were all well-coordinated. And
the bamboo matting used for the ceiling held it all together.

Timmy pointed out the key areas to Cambria, to give her a
general feel of the place. And then he headed for the kitchen to
get dinner going. He told her she was free to wander, but she
chose instead to stand by the kitchen doorway, and watch.

She was amazed by how smoothly Timmy sashayed around
his kitchen, almost like a ballerina gracing the stage.

Timmy's first order of business was to put water on the stove
to boil. After that, he pulled a bag of frozen mussels from the
freezer, washed them, and placed the colander of clams atop
the boiling pot to thaw.

"You a wine person?" The question came out of nowhere.

Cambria nodded.

Timmy drew a bottle from his wine cooler and held it up.

"*Vino de Casa Leona*. Marks and Spencer's best." He wore a
boyish grin to underline his delight.

Cambria smiled back. Pulling a cork screw from a drawer,
Timmy worked the bottle with the ease of a waiter who had
waitered half his life. He poured Cambria and himself a glass,
they toasted, and he proceeded to chop up some basil, parsley
and yellow pepper. To not taint his knife, he slivered the garlic
last (he took special effort to point that out).

Cambria was amused by how Timmy described everything
he was doing as he was doing it, as if he were filming a cooking
show. The character he was, she wasn't surprised if he made
this play-by-play even if he were by himself.

"Tip in a glass of white wine. Wait for it to reduce. Now, toss
in the herbs and thawed-out clams. Be sure not to cook them
through, the freshly boiled pasta will do that."

"The fettuccini is done. Let's drain it and put it into the pan.

Make sure we work in the sauce. Some parmesan. A few twists of pepper. Voila, *fettuccini al quicko*."

It was the best seafood pasta Cambria had tasted in her life, and she savoured each mouthful. There was a pureness and refinement to his viand. The delicate notes it carried came from his talent to expertly draw—from each ingredient—a different and distinct hue of flavour. His culinary touch was clearly of the sort that could not be taught, but that which was obtained through trial and error. What amazed Cambria more was that the meal was prepared in the time it took the fettuccini to boil.

They ate out on the veranda, in candlelight.

~.~.~.~.~.~

As Timmy was in the kitchen making them both a cup of coffee, Cambria proceeded to the living room and settled herself on the couch. She ran into some scrapbooks of Timmy's in the enclave of his coffee table. Figuring they were in a public area, she started to browse through them. She could tell from the montage of ticket stubs, holiday photos, un-mailed postcards, stamps and foreign currency, that Timmy had the bug. In one of the scrapbooks, he had many pictures of a girl, and poems he had written about her.

"I nosed into some of your poems in here. I hope you don't mind."

"No I don't mind," Timmy called from the kitchen. "But I think I would cringe if I read them again. Probably over-the-top cheesy. You know how it's like when you're in love?"

"I actually thought they were all pretty good. Especially the one titled, *Two Forks And A Spoon*."

"Ha, ha, ha. I forgot about that one." Timmy set her mug on the table. "Here's your coffee."

"Thanks Timmy."

"So. Do you write poems about every woman you fall in love with?"

"Hmmphh. Nah, I think I've only written poems about my true loves."

"And just how many true loves have you had?"

"Four."

"One second. Isn't everyone only supposed to have one true love in their lifetime?"

"Nah, I don't subscribe to the belief that there is one who exists on the planet just for you. I mean, let's get real. You'll never, ever find someone who is the perfect fit, someone who complements all of you. That only happens in movies. In every relationship, some degree of compromise is necessary. And that is not a bad thing. When you compromise for someone, you are saying to the person that you care enough to give up a part of yourself, you know... to make the relationship work."

"But you can't give up too much of yourself right?"

"Well, I believe with your true loves, the compromises actually turn you into a better person. You just may not know it at the time."

"So how do you know you've found true love?"

Timmy squinted at her question.

"Do you get hit by an arrow or something?"

"Actually, I don't really believe in love at first sight. The women I've fallen deeply for, I've normally known for some time."

"So you start out as friends?"

"Yarrr."

"Isn't the transition from friendship to 'more-than-just-friends' a bit awkward?"

Timmy knew he had to get this question right. "Yeah, always. But there's no substitute for what you feel afterwards."

"And at what point do you know she is the one?"

"You just know."

"You just know? How?"

"Well..."

"Are there signs?" She tried to urge him along.

"Actually there are. *True love snapshots*."

"*True love snapshots*?"

"Yeah."

"Urrrrmmm, I think you need to explain this one, Timmy."

Timmy thought about it.

"A *true love snapshot* is the moment that fossilises in my mind at the point of discovering true love. I feel blissful and full of awe when it happens, and it normally occurs when she does something that encapsulates the essence of her. *True love snapshots* are taken when you least expect it, and it can come in any form."

"Like?" Cambria asked. "Maybe you could share some of your *snapshots*," she suggested, a sheepish grin forming on her face.

Timmy smiled and considered whether to share. "Let me see. My first love was an English teacher I had in school, from the time I was fourteen. Her name was Heather Kingsley, a real looker. Back then, in an attempt to impress her with my writing, I acquired a voracious appetite for reading and compiled notebooks of exquisitely worded phrases. And I emulated those styles in my writing."

"Ah, that's where you got your reading interests from."

Timmy acknowledged with a nod.

"Well, my *true love snapshot* of Miss Kingsley happened after class, when she accidentally dropped a bunch of papers on the floor and knelt down to gather them back into a pile. I rushed in to help her. After we recruited the last sheet into the stack, she looked up, her eyes into mine. No voice left her throat, but her lips moved to form the words 'thank you'. That image burned itself into my memory forever."

Timmy felt a tingle across his skin, and was amazed by the power the memory still had over him. Cambria was touched by the story and started to consider all the moments she had shared with Timmy. None stood out as 'the one'.

"How about your second?" Cambria asked.

"Wow, you're on a war path, aren't you?"

She flashed a guilty grin.

"Well the second actually took place in Iowa. At the time, I was working towards a degree in advertising, in the neighbouring state, at the University of Missouri-Columbia."

"Why Missouri? Of all places."

"I picked that school because they parked advertising under their journalism program, and they were arguably the best journalism school in the world. Even though my interest area was in advertising design, I always had a love for writing and wanted to stay close to it."

"Still trying to impress Miss Kingsley I see."

"Ha, ha. Yeah," Timmy admitted. "Back to the story. Nicole and I had known each other since we were kids, and we left to further our studies at the same time, she to Iowa, I to Missouri. One weekend, I paid her a visit. The weekend passed in no time, and she and I fell into the gloomiest of moods on the day I was to leave. We were in her room, on her bed..."

"Yes, I'm sure you were," Cambria interjected, flashing a wide naughty grin.

"Hey, you wanna hear the story or what?"

"Alright.... alright," she stifled her amusement and rolled her hands outwards, to motion Timmy to get on with the story.

"We were on the bed staring at the ceiling. Then Nicole turns her head to look at me. I turn to look back at her, but before our eyes could fully meet, she looks back up. And I do the same. I then hear the sheets rustle, and realise that she had turned to look at me again. So I turn, but she immediately stares back up at the ceiling. The third time, our eyes connect and we hold each other's gaze. A tear forms and rolls down her cheek."

Timmy paused for a second.

"Well that's *snapshot* number two."

"Wow, that was a really sweet moment. Hey, you seem to be on a roll. Tell me about number three."

"Ahhh! That I'd rather not do."

"Awww come on. Your reluctance has gotten me even more curious."

"Well, I was actually going to marry number three. Even got a ring and all. And then something tragic happened on the day I was to propose. But it's in the past now and should be kept in the past."

"What happened Timmy?" Cambria asked with a concerned voice, "Did she pass away or something?"

Cambria was at a new level of ease with Timmy, but her question sounded awful when spoken out loud. She regretted her candour and quickly added, "Well, it's really none of my business. I shouldn't have asked that question."

"No, she did not die. But she is dead to me. Maybe we'll just leave it at that."

There was dead air for a while. Not wanting to leave the conversation on a negative note, Timmy continued, "Well maybe I'll tell you some day. When we're both old."

Cambria liked the notion of them growing old together, and felt a velvety warmth flow through her.

"How about number four? Am I entitled to that story?"

Amused by her tenacity, Timmy burst out laughing.

"Sure... I'll tell you about number four."

Cambria perked up, sat straight and was all ears.

"I actually have a title for the fourth story."

"Oh! What is it?"

"It's called... none of your damn business."

Cambria picked up a pillow and smacked Timmy with it. He retaliated. The pillow fight escalated into a full blown pillow war. At first, Timmy thought it would be like in the movies, the pillows bursting into a plume of feathers. But his pillows were too sturdy for that. The series of exchanges eventually led to rough and tumble. Timmy managed to overpower Cambria, and pinned her down by the wrists. They were both breathing hard, their chests heaving heavily, his breath on hers.

Timmy made a request for her surrender, "Mercy?"

Cambria thought about it. She crooked her finger and gestured for him to come closer, so she could whisper something to him. Timmy drew his ear to her lightly parted lips. Her breath enticed him even closer, till he was upon her moistness.

Drawing on everything in her lungs, she let out a bellicose battle cry "Freedommmmm!" like William Wallace had done in *Braveheart*.

His head tilted to one side, and off balance, it did not take much to topple him and slip out of his grasp.

Timmy sat up, deeply amused by what had just transpired. Cambria was on her feet bubbling with giggles, a pillow in hand to defend herself. It was a childish girlishness Timmy had never seen in her before, and he was smitten. His ears ringing, he wriggled his little finger in his ear passage to try and restore his hearing.

"Why don't you want to tell me?" Cambria asked through her mirth, making sure she kept her distance. "Is it someone I know? I won't tell a soul. I'm good at keeping secrets."

Timmy was amazed by her resolute hunger to ascertain who it was. Bereft of all words, he rolled his eyes upwards and feigned a fainting spell, dizzily slumping to the ground while waving his make-belief white flag. Cambria felt it was safe again and moved in to sit beside him, her pillow clutched to her chest.

She tried to tease it out of him, "Is it someone from work?"

Timmy could only shake his head.

"How about you? I've been telling you love stories all night. When are we going to hear about your love life?"

Those weren't the words Cambria were hoping to hear. But

she realised a rare opportunity had reared itself. She now had a chance to open an intimate side of herself to Timmy. And she was partly thrilled at the prospect.

She hugged her pillow close, and smiled with the honesty of one indulging in a warm and fuzzy memory. "Well, there once was a boy,"

"Oh, only one?"

"Noooo," she countered defensively.

"I've shared my bed with scores of men. I just thought I'd tell you about the one unforgettable," she professed, looking straight at him to search for any signs of surprise or uneasiness. He tried not to show it, but his face betrayed a shade of displeasure. Her lips curled into a smile.

He was relieved she was kidding.

"So this guy? Does he have a name?"

"Gael. Gael.... mmmm.... I don't remember his last name."

"Wait! Is this one of your one night escapades you're relaying to me."

"Trust me. It wasn't only the one night. Gael and I shared many mornings, afternoons and nights of simmering passion. Steamy. Raw. Unrestrained. No, actually, sometimes there were restraints."

Timmy's mind plunged off the edge of the earth. And it showed on his mug. He looked straight at Cambria to see if she was pulling another one on him. But her eyes convinced him of the truth.

When she knew she had him, she uncuffed her grin. Timmy was in total disbelief that he was suckered twice in less than a minute. This was another side of her he had never seen before. A dry, cute wit that he found extremely provocative. He felt he could just sit back and watch her all night, giggling and laughing. Completely unguarded. Conjuring trickery at every turn and doing a great job of concealing it, a new bouquet of endearing expressions revealed each time she found success.

Jeremy Chin

"When I was nineteen," Cambria continued, "the Uni I was attending gave us the option to spend a semester abroad. So that year, I found myself in Paris, in a World Religion class with Gael. We were assigned to do a paper together, and ended up as lovers two days later. Gael was quite the Romeo. He always drew my chair out for me, always afforded me a half rise when I had to take leave from the table. He used to hold my eyes with his as he kissed the top of my hand to say *I love you*."

Cambria's story pricked a little. Timmy realised that over dinner he had not conformed to the proprieties; had not drawn her chair, nor made an attempt to stand when she excused herself to the restroom to — in her own words — 'tinkle'.

Cambria continued with her story. "This is my *true love snapshot* of Gael. He was sitting with his legs stretched out on the grass, his back against a tree. I was lying down on his lap, staring up at him. It was a cool day in the summer. In his hand was a book he just bought from a second-hand bookstore, a collection of romantic poems by a Spanish poet. He read it out to me in French. I didn't understand half of what he was saying but it sounded impossibly beautiful. Midway through one of the poems, Gael paused and placed his hand on my cheek. I looked up and saw him staring into my eyes. And he says this to me in his gorgeous French accent."

She fed her voice through her nose and did a really good imitation. *"No poem about you should ever be attempted. For words of this world just cannot describe you."* Cambria hugged her pillow tight as she reminisced the moment.

Timmy rolled his eyes upwards.

"What was that?" She leaned in to look at him.

"What was what?"

"That?" She fluttered her eyes and struck an exaggerated look of inquisitiveness.

"What?" Timmy maintained his countenance of innocence.

"That thing with your eyes. You were pulling a face."

"It was dust."

"Yes, I'm sure it was." She shot Timmy a sheepish grin.

"Hey, so what happened to this Gael fella?"

"Well the story has a bit of a bitter end."

"Good," Timmy humorously injected.

Cambria crinkled her nose and flashed him a mouthful of gritted teeth.

"Gael gave me my first sexual experience, and I he. Well that's what he told me anyway. A few weeks into our relationship, Gael took me up to the Basilica of Sacré Coeur at Montmartre. I still remember the awe I felt when I walked in. The entire dome was covered in gold mosaic. The image of Jesus in his white robes, his arms outstretched, graced the centre. Never had I witnessed such majesty. We walked down the centre aisle, genuflected, and shifted ourselves into one of the pews. A long moment of silence passed before Gael turned to look at me. He held both my hands in his. Our knees touched. My heart sank when I realised he wore the jitters of one about to propose marriage. Nervously, he broke it to me that he always had plans to join a seminary in Provence. And that he counted himself blessed to have been able to share the pleasures of the flesh with me before entering the priesthood."

Timmy offered a sympathetic droop of the jaw.

"My heart broke into a million pieces. And I really didn't know what to think of the whole situation. All I knew was that I would have furnished him with my hand were he to have asked for it."

"Wow! It must have really rankled."

"Lenka used to joke about how I scared the guy into celibacy."

"Hey Sunshine, with your good looks, you'd be able to talk me out of priesthood any day."

Cambria chuckled. "You're funny. You always make me laugh."

Cambria looked at the clock and saw that it was getting late. She was in two minds whether to leave.

"Hey, I just noticed the time. I've got to catch the last train to Whitechapel."

"Oh," Timmy remarked, a little crestfallen.

"Let me drive you," he was upbeat with his offer.

"No it's fine really."

"Seriously. It'll be no problem at all."

"Really Timmy. It's quite a drive. I'll be fine."

"I insist."

~.~.~.~.~.~

It was musky on the inside, the glass unspeakably yellowed through the years. And a spring poked her in the bum. Judging by its age and state of disrepair, Cambria reckoned that Timmy's ride could not have been a far off relative of Lenka's car. Pumping furiously on the gas pedal as he toiled at the ignition, Timmy was eventually able to get the clunker to rumble to life.

Both a little downcast that their day together was coming to a close, they did not say much on their moonlight drive through the quiet city. She did, however, learn that Timmy's car was a gift from his parents, who bought it for him as a practice car. Which explained why he still tolerated it.

A vacant spot in front of her apartment building allowed him to park his car and walk her up. His mind raced as they took the elevator up to the third floor. He was thinking of what to say in the event she invited him in for coffee. An invitation for coffee in the late hours was synonymous with an invitation for sex, so to say 'yes' to coffee just seemed too forward.

But it'd be moronic to say no. Timmy thought to himself.

Maybe I'll just say it's late, and see how hard she convinces me. But what if she doesn't convince me? Then I'll be kicking myself all night. Oh I know. Maybe I'll decline the coffee, but ask to use the bathroom. And whatever happens, happens.

To wring out every second of their time spent together, they pootled along the narrow corridor, just above a pace that kept the whole thing from looking ridiculous. Cambria issued a regretful smile when they exhausted the length of corridor leading to her door. Her head at a mild tilt, she combed her hair behind her ear.

"Thanks for the ride home, Timmy. I had a really, really good time tonight." Fully conscious of herself, she avoided his eyes when she thanked him, her voice breaking and sensual at once.

Timmy smiled. Mustering the courage, he took her hand in his own, and brought it to his lips.

"Tout le plaisir est pour moi." He lured her deep into his eyes as he planted a kiss on the top of her hand.

"The pleasure is all mine," Cambria took a while to make the translation.

Making a play on the story she told him about Gael, he muttered, "Je t'aime, je t'aime, je t'aime, je t'aime."

I love you, I love you, I love you, I love you, Timmy confessed, his lips travelling upwards from her wrist to her elbow. Cambria giggled uncontrollably.

Timmy took a step back, and with an arm across his waist, took a bow, his eyes fixed on her the whole time. Still bent, he shuffled backwards, using his hand to draw circles close to the ground, in the manner of a jester withdrawing himself from a king's court.

Cambria could not stop giggling, and watched adoringly as he backed his way to the elevator and disappeared into it. Her face glowed from the warmth that was emanating from within her. That image of Timmy secured a place as her life's most precious memory, and became her *true love snapshot* of him.

Let The Good Times Roll

Spring kept her promise, and brought with it the warm sun, the sweet scent of flowers, and a brilliant mélange of colour. They drove with the windows down. Cambria's hair flowed with the breeze, like a silk scarf carried on the wind. Timmy found it sexy how her hair sometimes caught on her lips.

Timmy kept it as a surprise, and only told her on the car ride there, that they were going for the cheese rolling event at Cooper's Hill.

Cambria had only watched the event on TV, people tumbling uncontrollably down a hill in pursuit of an eight pound chunk of cheese. She was really thrilled that she was now actually going to see it LIVE. There was barely a moment of quiet between them the whole way there. Although they had spent the previous day together, they chatted as if they had not talked in years.

It was a short walk in from the parking lot. They spotted the hill through a scramble of trees. From the roar of the crowd, they could tell that the event had already started. As they were approaching the base of the hill, a nasal voice they distinctly recognised called out behind them.

"Cambria. Timmy. Hey!"

They turned to look. It was overly well-meaning Jasper from Video Editing, thin as a rake, the protrusion of his Adam's apple like a septic boil begging to be speared. He was quite a caricature.

"Hey, Jasper. What a surprise?" Timmy responded.

Jasper high-fived Timmy. He then awkwardly bypassed Cambria's outstretched hand and plungered her cheek with a kiss. Timmy was a little irked.

"Your first time here?" Jasper asked.

"Yes, it's our first time," Cambria answered on Timmy's behalf.

"Did you guys just arrive?"

"Yup. Two minutes ago."

"Oh, so you missed the first cheese roll." In spritely form, he brought them up to speed, "They had to stretcher two people off, a man and a woman. They crashed into each other at the base of the hill. I was thirty metres away and heard a loud crack. Someone broke something for sure. The guy was out cold."

"Youch!" Timmy and Cambria twisted their faces.

"Hey, we should head up the hill," Jasper suggested, "we'll get a better view from there."

Timmy did not really want Jasper's company, but he was right. On the way up, Timmy curled his fingers around Cambria's hand and led her up the slope.

"This here is a decent spot," Jasper stamped his foot and turned to them. Their hands reluctantly drifted apart, miserably stayed apart, but were kept close enough to enjoy the thrill of the occasional brush. Camped slightly below the half-way mark, they watched in amusement each time cheese was rolled.

"Either of you planning to roll down?" Jasper jokingly enquired.

"Yes. I am."

"You are?" Jasper and Cambria asked in tandem.

"Yeah. It's something I've always wanted to do."

"Are you sure you want to do this Timmy? It looks rather dangerous." Cambria was deeply concerned.

"Hey, I know this sounds crazy," Jasper excitedly injected, "but why don't we all do it together. It'd be great fun. Some story we'll have tomorrow."

"No Jasper, I don't think it's a good idea. It's not safe."

"Oh, so it's alright for you, but not alright for us?" Jasper countered. "Come on Timmy, we only live once."

Another big round of Double Gloucester cheese, the fourth of the day, was released. The hill tremored with cheers as hordes of death defying participants came hurtling down after it. When it was done, another two people were whisked away by the medics. Preparations were being made for the final roll of the day.

Timmy was very annoyed by Jasper's suggestion that they all take on the hill. With the last roll moments away, Timmy capitulated.

"Well, fine. You can come. But Cambria stays. I don't want her getting hurt."

Cambria did not know whether to feel flattered by Timmy's attempt to protect her, or take umbrage. If she had her way, she would rather they all remained spectators, safe by the wings. The thought of something happening to Timmy was unbearable.

"Actually Timmy, I think Jasper has a point. We only live once. I say let's all do it."

Cambria knew that Timmy would not run down the hill if she insisted on coming. This she thought was the best way to keep him safe.

"No, Cambria," Timmy objected with a low stern voice.

Like bubblegum under one's shoe, Jasper continued to irritate. "Come on Timmy. Cambria's a big girl. She can take it slow with me. Cambria, maybe we'll just slide down on our bums."

An imbecilic proposal. Timmy was taxed to the limit, and his forbearance turned into full-fledged anger. Desperate to make it up there on time, he snapped at the two.

"Jesus, Jasper, will you stop encouraging her... just, just, just quit your deleterious goading. And Cambria, for fucks sake, would you please... this one time, not persist with your stubbornness and stay here. I don't want you getting hurt."

Fazed by the hostility in Timmy's voice, Cambria conceded with a nod.

"Jasper, let's go. Just you and me," Timmy barked.

Timmy was really unhappy with the way his words came out. But he was glad he got Cambria to stay put. He wasted no time clambering his way to the top. Jasper followed after him, first two steps behind, and then three, and then he lost Timmy through the trees. By the time Timmy reached the crest of the hill, his calves burned and he was gasping for air. He tried to look for Cambria in the crowd, but did not see her there.

~.~.~.~.~.~.~

Timmy's words really singed, and tears started to well up in Cambria's eyes. Over the course of knowing him, she had seen him raise his voice to many people. But never once at her.

Cambria, for fucks sake, would you please... just for once, not persist with your stubbornness and stay here. His words echoed in her head.

His voice eventually gave way to her own.

Did I read the signs wrongly. Him holding my hand up the hill. The almost kiss on the pier. His butterfly kisses up my arm.

Have I been blinded by love, wandered unknowingly into a penumbra of unquestionable desire. Perhaps everything he did took on new connotations, became some kind of truth, merely because I was over indulgent in my musings.

You are a fool Cammy. A damn fool. For reading the signs wrongly. With eyes of desire rather than of reason.

Overcome by a swarm of emotions, she decided not to stay for the event any longer. She drew one long, last lingering look at Cooper's Hill, and in her heart, bade her Timmy a final good-bye. And she started to make her way down.

It was less crowded down at the foot than it was on the sides of the hill. As final preparations for the concluding roll were made, players from a professional rugby team formed a human wall at the base, ready to assist those who needed help stopping. Further back, giant bales of hay offered a soft landing to anyone who slipped past the players. Off to each side, St. John ambulance medics stood on alert. Each year, approximately fifty injuries were reported. Scratches and bruises aside, the most common injuries were dislocations, fractures and injury to the spine. Three ambulances were normally assigned for the event. Sometimes, that wasn't enough.

The crowd started to chant. *Roll that cheese. Roll that cheese. Roll that cheese.* The atmosphere was electric.

While weaving her way through the milling crowd, Cambria slipped on a patch of mud. She collided into one of the volunteer nurses and knocked the nurse's first aid kit to the ground, scattering its contents.

"I am so sorry. Really, I am," Cambria apologised.

Roll that cheese.

"Don't even worry about it, dear. It's slippery. The ground is a bit gooey from all the trampling."

Roll that cheese.

Cambria helped the nurse gather her things back into her kit. The nurse had her daughter there with her; a young pretty girl with tight curly hair and a fetching personality, no older than six. She too knelt down on the ground to help, muddying her knees. Once all the items were collected, they all stood up.

"I am so, so sorry.... Marsha." Cambria read the name on the nurse's name tag.

Roll that cheese.

"No worries, dear. It's fine. Really." Marsha squeezed Cambria's shoulder lightly to reassure her.

"Is everything alright?" Marsha asked with a concerned voice. "You look as if you've been crying,"

"Thanks for asking. I'm alrig..."

The bell sounded. The chants suddenly ceased, replaced by a healthy roar. The final cheese roll was under way, and it became impossible for Cambria and Marsha to hear each other. Unlike the previous ones, the final roll ended with the crowd letting out a huge groan, followed by a deadly silence, and then oohs and aahs.

Augustina, Marsha's daughter, tugged her mother at the wrist and called, "Mummy!"

Marsha looked down at her daughter, "Not now Augustina. Mummy's talking to this lovely lady." And she reverted her attention back to Cambria.

"But Mummy, you have to see this. Really, really have to see this."

Marsha turned to see what her daughter was pointing at. Cambria looked up as well, and saw that blanketing the entire slope of Cooper's Hill, was a massive white sign. There were purple tulips imprinted on the fringes. At the centre of the sign, in a sea of words, was a man on one knee, trying his silliest best not to slip down the sixty degree slope. The words on the sign read, "Cambria Sarah Lane. I wanna grow old with you."

In a Century Gothic font.

Planning

The grandiose hillside announcement aside, Timmy was determined to do it the old-fashioned way. So before proposing, he opted to first ask Cambria's parents for their blessing. It had been three weeks since his Easter visit to Lechlade, and he was really looking forward to seeing Cora and Greg again. Thinking back, he was surprised by how quickly they warmed up to him, and he to them. Despite only a scant two days with them, he already felt like part of the family; it was a feeling of acceptance and a sense of home he had not enjoyed since his parents were taken from him.

His day packed with work appointments, Timmy left *Ankhura* long before the sun came up. It was delightful driving through London before it was sludged up with traffic and it did not take him long to get to the outskirts, past the densely populated areas. In the distance, the morning fog formed a dreamy cotton veil close to the ground, obscuring the earth. Timmy relaxed at the wheel, and his mind started to recall the countryside hospitality he was shown over Easter, warm like a bun just out of the oven. The memory of it served as good company on his lonely drive.

Although Timmy did not spend a lot of time with Cora, he felt a connectedness to her that was far more complex than the jock camaraderie he had struck up with Greg. Cora possessed an inner calm and steady confidence that Timmy found comforting. He felt that they shared a common understanding of the world, and that with her, some things didn't need to be spoken. Just as he discovered in Cambria, there was a deep wisdom buried in Cora, a clairvoyance. He saw the potential of a far deeper relationship developing between himself and Cora, a friendship that would traverse the plane of layman chit chat, and find its way down the tunnels of intellectual exchange.

The sun had singed away much of the morning fog when Timmy's car pulled up their driveway. Cora, who was in the middle of weeding, looked up to try and figure out who the sorry white Fiat belonged to. Timmy's car door announced its age as he opened it. The loud awful creak signalled that its days were numbered. He stepped out, and savoured the warmth of the ripening sun on his face.

"Got to get that oiled, son," Greg threw out as he lumbered from the back of the house.

"Hey there pops. How's it going?"

"What a pleasant surprise, Timmy!" Cora expressed as she walked up to him. To make sure the dirt on her gloves did not soil his clothing, she turned her hands outwards as she leaned in to give him a hug.

"Don't you young-uns ever call before popping by?" Greg growled in a pirate voice.

"What? And give forewarning to the pigeons of my approach?"

Timmy extended his hand out to Greg. Greg reeled him in for a hug.

"It's great to see you again. What brings you to these parts?"

"Well..." Timmy turned and stepped towards his car. "I got you guys a gift."

"A gift?" Cora exclaimed her surprise.

Timmy opened his car trunk, and reached in.

"A new weather vane."

Timmy held the beautifully painted weather vane close to his chest. Proud of his gift, he flashed a grin that stretched the corners of his face.

Greg noticed the detailing on the vane and burst out with a bellyful of laughter. There were red concentric circles on the rooster's head, with points assigned to each band. The points got higher as they progressed inwards. A target for Timmy to hit.

"Oh you really shouldn't have," Cora managed to put in through her amusement.

"Nah, I figured you already have a bent cock under your roof. Last thing you need is one atop as well."

Cora laughed uproariously. Greg ha-ha laughed. Timmy chuckled.

Putting his arm around Timmy's neck, Greg invited Timmy in.

"Come. Join us for a cuppa."

The three entered the house, and Cora proceeded to steep some tea.

"Timmy, dear. You needn't have driven all the way for this."

Timmy smiled at Cora as they settled at the round kitchen table overlooking the back garden.

"Well," Timmy confessed, "my trip to Lechlade goes beyond the purpose of helping you find the direction of the wind."

"Alright..." Greg waited for the real reason.

"I came here to tell you that I've found my true north..."

A smile started to form on Cora's face. She knew what Timmy was alluding to.

"... and I wanted to get your consent before I asked for her hand."

Deep inside, Cora had developed a genuine liking for Timmy. Even before they met, when she had first learned of him, she secretly wished that her daughter would find happiness with him.

"Our daughter's hand?" Greg enquired.

Timmy nodded.

"Cambria or Lenka?" A baffled Greg asked.

Cora looked at Timmy and rolled her eyes upwards. *Please disregard his obliviousness*, she beamed to Timmy.

"Cambria silly," Cora verbalised to Greg, patting him affectionately on his thigh. Despite Cora and Greg appearing worlds apart, Timmy always sensed a deep and abiding connection between them, an unspoken appreciation.

"Wow!" Greg's eyes widened. "This is wonderful news. Surprising, but wonderful." Greg leaned back in his chair, and grinned with delight. "You have my blessing. One hundred percent."

Timmy was delighted by the enthusiasm behind Greg's approval.

Greg suddenly grew aware of Cora's silence and wondered if he had been too quick with his mouth. He realised he might have got too caught up in the moment and answered too hastily. He cleared his throat and stated the conditions of his approval, "Well, that's if Cora is alright with it too."

The two boys shifted their eyes to her.

A wave of nervousness passed through Timmy when he realised that Cora was still deliberating on an answer. A wry yet comforting smile formed on Cora's face. She reached for Timmy's hand and gave it a light squeeze.

"Walk with me."

Cora's chair scraped backwards as she straightened herself into a standing position. Something in her voice inferred that he had nothing to worry about. He followed her outside, where they walked companionably along the low drystone wall dividing their property.

"Cambria's special, isn't she?"

Timmy met Cora's smile with his own.

"I've known that from the moment I watched her eyes open, how special she is. And throughout her life she's proven me right. You know Timmy, I could not have asked for a better daughter," Cora professed with great pride.

"As a mother, you try and protect them as much as you can, for as long as they will allow you. Beyond that, you just make yourself available to them, be there when they need you."

Timmy agreed.

"I've nursed her colds as a child, umpired countless sibling disputes, broken more fevers than I can count. Nursed away her troubles, cured her of head lice."

Cora smiled to herself as she reminisced the day.

"Not sure if she told you that story?"

Timmy dipped his head smilingly.

"I recall watching her sleep as a baby. From the early morning rise to the last breath of the day, I watched her. In a world of her own, much like today. I've helped her through heartbreak, watched her laugh again, and cry again, and watched her blossom into the sophisticated young girl she has become today, quiet on the outside, giggly on the inside."

"And when I see her with you, Timmy."

She stopped walking, and turned to look at him.

"When I see the two of you together, I can see how special you are to her. Even though she tries her best to conceal it, it still shines through."

Timmy was delighted hearing those words. But he knew there was a bigger reason behind the request for their private walk. And that realisation discomfited him.

"How long have you known my daughter, Timmy?" Cora asked.

"Coming to five years," Timmy replied.

"And how long have you had feelings for her?"

Timmy shuddered at the question, and hesitated on his reply. Though she had asked in an inquisitive voice, he was unsure if she was making an enquiry or a remark. He knew that in calendar days, his feelings for Cambria were nascent, and that normal guys would court the girl first. Go through a period of discovery till each was certain of the other. And only then consider marriage.

But Timmy had never in his life been more sure about anything. His was a decision of the heart. But he didn't know if that qualified as a valid answer.

"I started having feelings for her six weeks ago," he nervously admitted.

A deep heaviness formed in Cora's chest, and her eyes squinted close, her deepest fears confirmed. Her eyes still shut, she voiced her concerns.

"Timmy. You have come here today, not only to ask us for our daughter's hand in marriage, but for her heart."

She opened her eyes, a thin glaze now coating its surface. Tears crowding her voice, she asked, "With your feelings for her merely in adolescence, how can you be certain..." she paused to gather herself. She continued, her voice breaking, "...how can you be sure, that my little girl, my Cambria, is your 'forever'? That you will love her till the end of your days? She, and no other?"

Timmy was himself on the verge of tears. He squared himself up to Cora and held her hands in his. Dipping his eyes into hers, he allowed her a glimpse into his centre.

"I just know Cora. I just know."

She sensed his earnestness.

Convinced by the ardour in his voice, a tear ran down her face. His was the answer she was looking for. That and no other.

~.~.~.~.~.~.~

It took Timmy a month to mastermind and execute his wedding proposal on Cooper's Hill. After Cora and Greg gave him his blessing, Timmy approached the event organisers for the green light to unveil his sign during the event. It took a fair bit of nerve.

One evening, Timmy walked into a classroom of fourteen organisers, uninvited. They were gathered at Gloucester College.

"May we help you," someone asked.

"Yes. Very much so."

All fourteen shifted in their seats, surprised and curious.

"My name is Timothy Malcolm Smith. And I have found the
woman I will love till the end of my days. She is the rock upon
which I stand, from which I speak to you today. From the moment she won my heart, my life's only fear has been that she
would be absent from it, and the only truth I have since been
convinced of is this, that love hath no emblem as curt as that
which exists between she and I. When I'm with her, time is
swift but at the same time stagnant, for she is, and forever will
be, my eternal now. She is the source of my needing, the person
without whom I would not be whole, and my feelings for her
have reached a juncture where near is not near enough, a hair
apart suddenly now a hair too far. I exist for her. And now I
would like to exist with her. In perpetuity."

"In a month's time," he looked them all straight in the eye,
"I intend to ask for her hand in marriage... by way of a goliath
sign. One large enough to blanket the entire slope of Cooper's
Hill. Will you help me?"

The organisers looked at each other quizzically, amused
by what had just unfolded before them. One in their group
scanned the room with his eyes, up, down and behind him,
looking to unearth a hidden camera. As each confided in the
other, nods slowly started to fill the room. Timmy had crossed
the second hurdle.

~.~.~.~.~.~.~

In the weeks leading up to the event, Timmy worked closely
with the event's organisers to make sure everything was pegged
down right. For the big day, twenty volunteers were recruited

to help roll the sign down the hill. This was to happen after the final wave of tumblers took off after the cheese.

To print a sign the size of two football fields was no easy feat. It had to be printed on 80 different pieces of vinyl, assembled, and neatly rolled up atop the hill the day before. Kim and Chloe, Timmy's present and past personal assistants, spent the night in the damp coldness to watch over the sign, to make sure it wasn't tampered with. Following the event, Kim and Chloe became an item. Timmy never got around to asking them what they did that night to stay warm.

Cambria was in awe when Timmy's sign was revealed to her and to the world, and it took awhile before she was fully aware of what was happening. Funnily though, she never said 'yes' to Timmy. After his grand declaration, she made her way back up the hill. The crowd waited anxiously as she gingerly crossed the slippery tarp to get to the centre where Timmy waited—a hand on one knee, the other hand holding a ring box propped open like a clam. Before he could pop the question, she lunged into his arms to kiss him. Lips locked, and in a tight embrace, they slid down the sea of vinyl to the base of the hill. As she held Timmy tight against her, she wore the resigned look of a woman with nowhere to go, having found herself in the only place she wanted to be, in the arms of the man she loved.

Post Proposal

Mankind, despite contributing daily to its own destruction, likes to remind itself occasionally that it is worthy of preservation. Though reports of war, natural disaster, philandering politicians and failing economies predominate the news, the media seem always able to salvage from the chaos, proof that humankind is capable of comedy. That people can put aside, even if for a little while, their differences, their inhibitions, their pursuit of gold, and just live. And it is for that very reason, that mindless acts of feel good silliness, found in events like the Running of the Bulls in Pamplona, the Tomatina in Bunol and the Cheese Roll down Cooper's Hill, never fail to make the news globally. Year after year after year.

News of Timmy's engagement to Cambria spread like the stain from a freshly steeped tea bag, appearing in the world's furthest-flung regions; in the papers, on TV, in someone's inbox. Videos of the proposal were passed around on the internet like a baton that multiplied itself, and sprinklings of Timmy fan sites surfaced around the world.

Following their much storied union, the pair had to get accustomed to their overnight celebrity, to being stopped on the street by inquisitive strangers. Their spotters all asked or alleged with the same serendipitous expression of voice: "Hey, you're that guy" or "Aren't you that girl from..." or "You two are the ones..."

They entertained the first flurry of public acknowledgements with great excitement, and chatted at length with their admirers. But it did not take long for the novelty of their fame to lose its enthral, chaffed away by the wear of repetition. Cambria and Timmy eventually found themselves making a conscious effort to hold little or no conversation with their spotters, most often limiting contact to a templatised closed-mouthed smile, followed by a frosty nod of acknowledgement. But though their engagement was a little more public than each would have liked, they were too preoccupied with their discovery of each other to really be irked by public intrusion.

Not wanting to spend a minute apart from the other, Cambria eventually moved her things into Timmy's place. They spent day and night trading stories, cuddling, watching each other, playing out their rehearsed intimacies. Timmy conveyed a passionate account of his ordeal, confessed how he fell stupid for her after the party, after he saw her rocking her arms. Cambria was bewildered by how something so mundane, so innocent at the time, totally altered the course of their lives.

Each day, Cambria continued to be amazed by Timmy's rooftop oasis. Up there she relished the different rhythms of the day, welcomed the fleeting treasures prescribed by the different hours. In the morning, she loved how the light over the city was misty and muted, the sky's colour—graduated. At midday, the sun at its zenith, the air carried a sensuous warmth and was heavy with the scent of flowers. If the day got too hot, she moved over to the side of the house with the cooling pool. The water, still and glassy, sometimes caught a ripple—unsettled by the wind, an insect or a falling leaf. Cambria found it soothing to watch the concentric circles bloom on the water's surface and then settle back into the stillness.

In the evening she liked to observe the sky as it changed, how it shed its usual day colour for the hues of a ripening peach. She also loved to watch the water slink down the rugged rock pools, loved the way it danced and caught the golden light of sunset. Night was her favourite time. Lit by outdoor lanterns, Timmy's sky garden glowed with a magical allure under the stars. Most nights she felt as if she were on top of the world, above worry, far from the ills that plagued the world beneath.

Following their engagement, it took Timmy and Cambria two weeks to regain some normalcy in their lives, after which they shifted their focus back to Cambria, to the possibility of her making a comeback in running competition. With her gift to excel at marathon distances now revealed, they considered her options.

Timmy salivated at the possibility of her debuting at Berlin. It was the fastest course on the circuit, and the ideal place to attempt the world record. But they shuddered at the scant amount of time she would have to prepare—three months to the day. Also, the forty thousand participant cap for Berlin had already been reached, so it would have taken quite a lot of string-pulling to slip her into the race.

After much consideration, they both agreed Berlin was a no go. Also, the last thing they wanted was for her to be stripped of her title due to legitimacy issues.

It was Timmy in the end who decided they should run New York. Cambria was reluctant. She knew Timmy had prepared long and hard to win that race. And she did not want to take his dream from him. But New York made the most sense. She too agreed.

~.~.~.~.~.~.~

Wow. It's finally going to happen. My moment is finally upon me. The years of striving towards running purity and aerobic efficiency—the months of tedious study, of sowing the seeds, refinement, all the laborious morning runs through the fog and the rain, the blisters and raw ankles, blackened toe nails, hyponatremia, the weeks of nursing sprains and pulls —it all is going to be put to the test—finally— culminating into a single two-hour moment, pit against the world's best, pit against Cambria.

He still felt he had lots of room to improve, that he had not arrived at his prime. This was the same feeling that visited him each year, when it came time to decide whether or not to participate in New York. For the past two years, on his monthly practice runs, he had consistently clocked times that brought New York within his grasp. Everything hinged on his ability to strike the perfect run, to stay focused throughout, to allow his adrenaline to carry him past the field.

Timmy realised that his dream of taking New York risked derailment with Cambria in the race. But he knew deep inside, that if she were to prevail, he would feel a joy greater than if he were to win it himself. The gap between the fastest male and female in the marathon was massive—twelve minutes. As the day drew closer, Timmy found himself more and more lost in reverie, as he fathomed the possibility of Cambria achieving what no woman had even come close to doing. Just the thought caused his chest to swell with pride.

Although registration for the New York Marathon had already closed, Timmy had for many years lent huge support to a number of charity organisations affiliated to the race. Each year, entry was automatically granted to supporters of those causes. Kim made all the arrangements for their trip to New York, making sure they arrived a couple of days in advance to get settled in. All Cambria and Timmy had to do was arrive in the city prepared, in the best condition of their lives.

Training

With only four and a half months to race day, Timmy and Cambria had to get on the ball with their preparations. Their time was cut even shorter because they had to figure in their tapering period. Three weeks before a race, long distance runners progressively cut down on their training, to give their muscles a chance to regenerate. This grace also allows runners to carboload their bodies, so that their energy stores are at their fullest. With less than four months before they had to taper, Timmy configured a rigorous training regimen for Cambria, to get her adapted to running marathon distances.

The first order of business was to resolve any problems she may have encountered on her first run. She informed Timmy that she experienced side stitches, around the 18K mark. She was mildly amused by how intently he listened as she conveyed her discomfort to him. Wrinkles on his forehead, he nodded as if he were a doctor taking note of a patient's symptoms.

Side stitches are often linked to the way a runner breathes. Upon examination of Cambria's breathing technique, Timmy found she did everything right. She took breaths from her belly not her chest. Inhaled from both her nose and mouth to maximise her oxygen intake. She also exhaled fully to expel as much of the carbon dioxide her body had produced. And this cocked the lungs to its fullest for the next inhale.

Cambria's problem, after she reported it to Timmy, hung in his head all day. That evening, as they took a short run around the park, Timmy observed her closely, and he watched how she timed her stride. All good runners synchronised their breathing to their footfalls. This allowed them to strike a steady rhythm. Cambria exhaled at every four footstrikes, her right foot hitting the ground as she breathed out. Timmy, in comparison, exhaled every five footstrikes–three footstrikes per inhale, two for every exhale. Cambria had more breaths incorporated into her technique because she used to run a shorter format, at a more rapid pace, and this required faster oxygen turnaround.

Timmy wondered if Cambria always landed on her right foot when she exhaled, and if she was conscious of it. To verify his observation, he made an excuse to stop, citing that his shoe was too tight and needed to be re-tied. Cambria stopped and waited for him to make the adjustment. When they resumed their run, Timmy noticed the same thing again; she exhaled on her right foot, inhaled on the left. A minute later, to fully confirm his finding, he asked her if they could stop again, this time to tie his other shoe which had come loose. She did not know whether to laugh or to frown. After Timmy tugged his laces tight, they continued, and it was the same as before. Timmy was quite sure he was on to something.

At the conclusion of their run, it suddenly hit him, and he mumbled to himself, "Your liver is on the right."

"Excuse me?" Cambria looked at him quizzically.

"Your liver is on the right." Louder this time.

"Your liver is on the right!!!" he excitedly announced, like he were crying *eureka*.

"Yes, and so is yours silly," Cambria teased. "And everybody else's."

He proceeded to explain to her that when a person exhales, the ligament between their diaphragm and liver is fully extended, and vulnerable. Each time her right foot impacted the ground on an exhale, it sent a shock up that side of her body, and this put undue strain on the extended ligament, causing side stitches. Timmy never encountered this problem because he exhaled every five footstrikes. The odd number created an alternation that distributed the stress evenly on both sides.

Cambria was very impressed that Timmy found the stone in her shoe. What they did with their discovery was another thing. For running a long format, it was best for her to adopt Timmy's 3:2 breathing technique, but that was a complicated adjustment, and they did not want to risk the wheels coming off before New York. Rather than rewire her circuitry, Timmy came up with a patch that worked for the short term. Each time Cambria started a run, she merely had to lead off with the left foot and exhale as she did so.

~.~.~.~.~.~.~

Summer was a little lackadaisical in its arrival. When it finally came, families went on outings together, parks stirred with laughter, sidewalk cafés brimmed and hemlines rose.

On the weekend, so as not to be hindered by the city, Timmy and Cambria set out really early on their second 26.2 miler. This time it was Timmy who emerged victorious, clocking 2 hours, 6 minutes and 33 seconds, his best time ever. Cambria finished 30 seconds behind him. Timmy was ecstatic, absolutely proud of his performance. All marathon routes being equal, his new best would have secured him the top spot at the New York Marathon the year before. Cambria's time was remarkable too. Though not as good as her first, it reinforced that the marathon format was better suited to her.

To celebrate, Cambria and Timmy had dinner at a romantic quayside restaurant overlooking the Thames. Overwhelmingly proud of his record time, Timmy carried his jubilant smile from the morning.

Midway through dinner, Timmy realised that something sat not quite right with Cambria, that while she displayed the same level of elatedness as he, she was a little withdrawn, as if something weighed on her mind. He wondered if he had overdone his merriment, if he should have been more sensitive to her 'lacklustre' performance, which in his real opinion, was in no way unspectacular. She still was, by a long shot, the world's fastest female, and only short of the men's record by three minutes, something she could easily overcome as she proceeded deeper into her training.

Timmy also questioned if his victory over her in the morning might have sparked off a rivalry between them. He knew the prospect to be silly, but one that he should not totally discount.

"Is everything alright?" he decided to ask. "Something seems to be troubling you."

"No, everything's fine," she threw back without hesitation. "Why do you ask?"

"No reason really. Just got a feeling something is hanging over your head."

Cambria initially thought she had done a good job to conceal that which had troubled her for weeks. She hadn't realised her disingenuous smiles and concocted laughter showed.

Her dilemma was one she initially tried to ignore. She feared that to acknowledge it would open doors to a past she had laboured so hard to forget. For days after her first 26.2 with Timmy, Cambria felt a strain in her right calf, and feared she had awakened a dormant injury. Her fears were confirmed during their second run, during which her compromised muscle progressed through different grades of pain. It initially felt tight when she pushed off, and she hoped it would pass, which it did. At the halfway mark, the discomfort returned, and reiterated itself for a few miles. And then it grew sharp. First a pinch, then a poke and finally a stab. By mile 23, she could no longer renounce the pain. She had no choice but to let Timmy pass her.

She found it hard to break it to him—seeing how his face would light up each time they discussed the enormity of what she was about to do. What made it worse was that his hopes for her seemed to intensify with each passing moment, making the subject harder and harder to broach. But she finally decided she could not keep her injury from him any longer, and told him that night.

Cambria was surprised by Timmy's response after she revealed what she thought would be crushing news to him. He first received her disclosure with great concern, as one naturally would when a loved one gravely initiates a conversation with: *There's something I've been meaning to tell you for some time but could not pick up the courage.*

Timmy was a master of running mechanics, and his mind's first instinct was to sieve through all the possible solutions to Cambria's problem. He knew from past experience, that when solving a running problem, you shouldn't always look at the obvious. Timmy always had a deep fascination for the interconnectedness of the human body, by how you could prevent a toe injury merely by angling your head differently, how a tightly clenched fist could sometimes cause a neck strain. It was as the song went: *the foot bone's connected to the shin bone, the shin bone to the knee bone, and so on.*

The very next morning, Timmy used a video camera to record the way Cambria ran. And he analysed her movement frame by frame. He discovered she was a toe striker. Because her foot struck the ground close to the front, it put more strain on the calves than if she were to land mid-foot.

Timmy had the opposite problem years ago. He was a heel striker. Because he lacked length, he overcompensated by over striding. This resulted in him striking the ground with his heel. Landing the way he did caused his body to brake unnecessarily, costing him precious energy.

Timmy ran up excitedly to Cambria and shared his findings with her. Drawn into his excitement, she started to celebrate herself. And then a veil of discouragement fell upon them. To get her to land mid-foot was not going to be easy. It was a practice that was simple in concept, but virtually impossible to imbibe, not in the time they had.

The body is like a stress ball, and is inclined to return to its original shape. It took Timmy half a year to land mid-foot, to re-condition his body to accept his new stride as part of its natural. Steep as it seemed, they had no choice but to attempt that hill.

Over the next month, Cambria concentrated wholly on altering her run. The adjustment felt awkward, her body at first refusing to abide. She also started to experience blisters in new parts of her feet. So as not to put too much pressure on her strained calf, they never ran more than 5K over their workday lunches. While in light training, Timmy imparted everything he knew on the psychological and emotional aspects of running the long format. He also stressed to her the importance of fuel management in a marathon, that the human spirit only takes a runner past the limits of pain, but not beyond the limit of one's energy.

To prepare their bodies for New York, Cambria and Timmy got stricter with their diet. They introduced more complex carbohydrates into their meals, foods like pasta and whole grain breads. Timmy also gave Cambria tips on how to get around *the wall*, the point at which one's glycogen stores run out, usually around the twenty-mile mark. Upon hitting *the wall*, he advised her to engage in self-talk, to say to herself something along the lines of, "I'll have water in ten minutes, and that will give me renewed energy."

Although he had never himself participated in an official race, Timmy also believed in the importance of pre-race rituals. The act of engaging in something familiar, he shared with Cambria, drew you into your own private bubble. This he felt took your mind away from the race and stopped it from gnawing on the nerves. Like the Yogis of India, Timmy always believed you could rise above the sensory realm—beyond the noise, the fatigue, the pain—and still be in tune with the real world. Through years (and many miles) of practice, he learned how to bring the world around him inward so that he did not have to reach out to experience it. With the external internalised, he had full reign over it. So rather than fight the physical punishment running a marathon subjected on him, he was able to merely regard it, experience it and embrace it.

~.~.~.~.~.~

A month into her training, Cambria grew more comfortable landing mid-foot and was able to sustain her new running movement for the entire length of their 5K runs. But she found it mentally draining because she had to be conscious of every step. She attempted several times to free her mind of her technique, and just let her limbs do what came naturally, but her body always reverted back into its pre-programmed ways. For seventeen weeks, she tried, but her body did not yield. Week after week, as failure continued to visit her, she grew more and more frustrated. She reached a point where at the end of each run, she would unleash a scream and tambourine her thighs in anger. Each time she did that, Timmy walked up to her and reassured her, "It takes time. We'll try again tomorrow." Though discouraged, she did not waver in her effort, and showed up the next day steely-eyed, ready to pour her heart into it.

Late one night, under the silvery light of the moon, Timmy found Cambria crouched in a hidden corner outside their house. Her body convulsed as she fought to smother her sobs. To mute her cry, she had one hand clamped over her nose and mouth. Timmy's heart fell to pieces when he found her like that. He did not ask her why she was crying. He knew. He sank next to her, kissed her crown, absorbed her into his arms. He held her till her body surrendered, till her grief became his.

Despite Timmy trying to dissuade her, Cambria was still determined to debut in New York. She decided she had come too far not to. Through the weeks of training, she found herself in the fittest condition of her life. She knew in her mind that she had come close to breaking the world record once, and there was no reason she could not do it again, mid-foot or not.

The Final Weeks

At Timmy's apartment, Cambria spent hours on end soaking up her surroundings. More than once, she found herself gently falling asleep on the veranda lounger, to the roundish tinkle of the wooden wind chimes, to bird song, the buzzing of insects, the rustle of palm fronds stirring in languid breezes. Sometimes she woke to the dull patter of raindrops on leaves, sometimes to the taste of Timmy's lips on hers.

Indoors, she liked how the gauzy voile curtains became dreamy once the wind caught them, how the potted plants on the window sills scented the breeze that blew through the rooms. The ample windows and doors brought the garden into the house, and provided a living panorama, a theatre of continuous change.

Cambria got on well with Iqbal, the gardener cum botanist in charge of the garden's upkeep. It was he who helped Timmy grow the garden from scratch. And he was very proud of the achievement, seeing that he had far from ideal conditions to work with. He took time each day to proudly explain to Cambria the horticultural challenges that he and Timmy had to overcome, the miracles they had to perform to get their tropical garden to flourish the way it did, where it did. He also pointed out how everything was designed according to the principles of *asta kosala kosali*, the Balinese version of Feng Shui. Timmy, he conveyed to her, was not particularly concerned about appeasing the gods. But he always believed in the wisdom behind the building laws of the ages. The people from long ago, Timmy felt, always found a practical way to make spaces functional, to make sure harmony existed between the home's occupants and their surroundings.

On Mondays and Thursdays, Gloria, the cleaning lady, dropped by to straighten the place. A burly, motherly figure, she always brought food for Timmy–baked goods, stews, desserts, soups as thick as her stews. It seemed her life's purpose to fatten Timmy up.

"You need to put some meat on them bones. Thin as you are, I don't think you can provide shade for more than a couple of ants."

Cambria was highly amused by how Timmy got lectured each time Gloria was around. This was until she too became a target, after a bond of familiarity formed between Gloria and her.

"Just look at the two of you. A twig and its shadow."

"She seems to have a thing about shadows," Cambria once amusedly shared with Timmy, only after Gloria had turned her good ear away from them.

Cambria took a liking to a sumptuous red armchair of Timmy's; it wrapped itself around anyone who sank into it. The chair looked a bit out of place amidst the Balinese interior, but it was a family heirloom that Timmy could not bring himself to dispose of. So he shoved it into a discreet corner, by a window that barely caught any sun. Cambria instantly fell in love with the chair and laid claim to it, to be used for her reading. The way the chair cushily enveloped her reminded her of cold winter days as a child. While she used to sit on her mum's lap, her mom would wrap her shawl around her to bundle in their collective warmth, the same way the chair folded around her.

Cambria did not get any reading done in that chair, however. She discovered that books had lost their place in her life, now with Timmy in the picture.

~.~.~.~.~.~

Even with Cambria living with him, Timmy still loathed *Ankhura*. No matter how hard he tried, he could not quite fall into harmony with the place. He likened his home to one of the make-belief hotels in Las Vegas, built not from the earth but with money, dripping with a type of fakery and forced abidance that lasts but for a fleeting moment. Similar to how he approached running, his 'natural' surroundings at *Ankhura* felt manufactured, rigid, lacked *genius loci*. Timmy hoped to one day move to the countryside, to a home like the one Cambria grew up in, or to a cottage like his grandparents'. Anxiously, he waited for that time to come.

Finding Cambria in such a pitiful state that night really broke Timmy's heart. He used to enjoy watching her run, free like the wind, full of joy and abandon. And he felt guilty for subjecting her to his rigid methods, for trying to alter what came naturally to her. That night, as Cambria wept in his arms, he knew they could not continue on the path they were on, that it was best they took a break from their normal routine. For a few days at least.

The next morning, Timmy found Cambria on her favourite veranda lounger, in pensive silence, a little sullen, hugging her legs close to her body. The sun was rising in her eyes.

"In competition, one of the greatest challenges a marathon runner faces is the crowd," Timmy's voice cut through the stillness. "Good morning."

She thought those were odd words for Timmy to start the day with.

"How so?"

"When it is crowded, it cramps your style, taints your stride. Forces you to brake when you don't plan to. Causes you to swerve, making your route longer than it already is. It's always best to start strong, and break away from the crowd. That way, you can maintain a straight line. And you can concentrate on keeping your motion fluid. And this saves you fuel for the rest of the race, and makes up for the energy you expended early on."

"Makes sense."

Timmy thought of a fun exercise. His idea required them to go down to Oxford Circus. When they arrived, as Timmy expected, it was shopping mayhem. The sidewalk was teeming with people, all trying to elbow their way from one store to the next. Sun dresses were torn off their racks faster than they could be replaced.

Cambria was very puzzled as to why Timmy brought her there. And then he told her the goal of their activity.

"OK, what we've got to do is run through the crowd as quickly as possible. We'll stop once we get to the first of the three bookstores. Our purpose here is to hone our ability to anticipate crowd movement, and make quick flight path adjustments without breaking our run."

The competitor she was, Cambria darted off before Timmy could say *go*.

They both found themselves lost in giggles as they ploughed through the crowded pavement. When they reached the bookstore, Cambria considered all the people she accidentally bumped out of the way, and erupted in laughter. Realising how much fun it was, she readied herself in the next instant to re-run the gauntlet in the opposite direction. Timmy was really glad that he had thought of the activity, and it brought him great joy to see Cambria smile again. After running a dozen or so laps, they got so proficient at negotiating the crowd that they consistently emerged at each end unscathed. The exercise had achieved its goal.

The second activity that Timmy had planned for the day was also a light one, but more fun for him than it was for her. After a quick lunch stop at a sandwich place, they popped into a sports store to shop for a sports bra. It was important that Cambria found one suitable for long distance running; one fashioned of moisture wicking fabric—and to prevent chaffing—one with rolled edges, preferably without seams. Each time she tried on a new bra, she teased him in for a viewing by curling her finger through the side of the changing room curtain.

To play a prank on her, Timmy asked one of the male store assistants to take his place on one of her invites. When the assistant slipped into the cubicle with her, she yelped so loud that all the people in the store turned to look. Timmy burst out laughing and in the process fell backwards into an occupied cubicle. The customer, her face blanched in terror, gripped her clothes close to her body and shrieked till her voice became hoarse. In her late forties, bearing more makeup than a Kabuki performer, she stared Timmy down as she fumbled to reinstate her clothes. And then the real shouting started. Timmy apologised profusely and endured a long tirade of expletives. It turned out to be quite a scene. Cambria was deeply amused by the whole incident. So was everyone in the store.

Cambria eventually decided on a sports bra with wide shoulder and racerback straps, not because she needed the support, but because she found them more comfortable. Timmy insisted that he pay for it, that it was a gift from him. Cambria looked at him funny, and waited for a punch line, but he didn't offer one. The two did a good job of holding in their laughter the rest of the time they were at the store. This was despite Timmy being uncomfortably trapped in the same payment line as the seething woman he had offended, right in front of her, her breath of fury steaming his nape. From a distance, Cambria mischievously made funny faces at a nervous queuing Timmy, to hook him into a laugh. He funny-faced her back to tell her to quit it. As they walked out the door after paying, they erupted in laughter, right in front of the store they were too embarrassed to ever return to. Cambria's side stitches came back.

~.~.~.~.~.~.~

The next day, Timmy followed up their fun filled day with an exercise that many amateur runners failed to consider the importance of—the water stop. For this they went out to the garden, onto the flagstone pathway that ran parallel to the house. Off to the side, Timmy had set paper cups of water on a high stool.

He explained the purpose of the exercise to Cambria. "During a marathon, runners bunch around the water stations like caribou to a body of water. Because people are mostly right handed, the congestion is always on the right hand side, especially at the first table where all the rookies feel compelled to stop at. Because every second counts, it is crucial that you get used to receiving water from the stations on the left, with your left hand."

It all made sense.

"To drink without spilling, you need to press the paper cup gently into a V, like you would purse the lips of a fish to remove a hook."

"Jeez, you didn't have to paint it quite like that," Cambria voiced to Timmy, trying to keep in her amusement.

Timmy smiled. "Well, you get the idea."

Cambria took her spot at the end of the pathway, and started to run. As she flitted by, she snatched the cup from Timmy with her left hand. As she drew the cup to her mouth, she stopped abruptly, and doubled over, her hands clutching her stomach.

Colour drained from Timmy's face. Thinking something had gone terribly wrong, he ran up to her.

"Are you alright?" he asked with great concern. Tears ran down her cheeks and her body jerked back and forth, like a car that wouldn't start on a cold morning. She was quaking with laughter.

"As I was... oh misery..."

She used the back of her hand to wipe away the tears on her cheeks.

"As I was drinking the water, I felt as if I were kissing a fish."

A shade of relief leaned into Timmy's worried face. He was glad that she was alright, but was also a little flustered that her foolish imagination had gotten him worried sick.

"Come on, we really need to get this right," he flatly muttered as he marched back to the water station.

"Hey Nemo!" she called out to him.

Timmy stopped and turned. He saw her bounding towards him. She leapt, trusting he would catch her in midflight, which in the nick of time he did. Arms and legs pegged around him like a koala, she looked down into his eyes. Casting a pleasing shadow over him, she proclaimed in a voice most gentle, "There are plenty of fish in the sea."

She touched his lips lightly with her forefinger and looked upon him with exceeding tenderness.

"But only one has taught me how to swim. Thank you Timmy Malcolm Smith. For letting me in on everything you know about running."

He always liked it when she called him by his full name.

Her voice turned from sweet to stern.

"Now pucker up fish lips."

And she redeemed from his depths a kiss that lasted the morning.

~.~.~.~.~.~.~

On the final week of their training, before their tapering off period, Cambria caught herself landing mid-foot as she ran, and it felt natural. She could not believe it, and wondered if she did it consciously or unconsciously. So she forced her mind to think of other things. Of the movie she, Timmy and Kim watched over the weekend. Of the time she rescued Lenka when they were four, after Lenka fell into the toilet bowl buttocks first. She thought of her *true love snapshot* of Timmy and of Timmy apologising to the half-dressed customer at the sports shop.

Each time she emerged from her reverie, she was greeted by a pleasant surprise—her feet touched the tarmac square in the middle. Flowing into her stride, she felt light as a feather, free as willow in the breeze, and she thought she could run on forever. It was the same feeling she experienced at nine, when she first learned to ride a bike. She smiled to herself as she recalled the day. She cycled up and down, and down and up the gravel road; the one leading up to her parent's house. When that lost its exhilaration, she ventured onto the main road, turning off before the old mill, across the meadow and down the dirt path to the creek. She recalled the sinking feeling when the light failed before she could find her way home. As she sat in tears under a tree, in pitch darkness, she remembered the relief she felt when she heard voices calling her name. The whole village skipped dinner that night, and swept the area with their torches. It was Jacob who found her in the end, the boy in her painting. The one she sentenced to an eternal winter, his feet frozen to the ground. Years after he became her hero, he broke her heart. Badly.

Cambria wanted to tell Timmy right away that her feet were landing right, but she chose to first savour the moment by herself. She contained her joy till they concluded their run. And then she let it all out.

She jogged backwards in circles around Timmy.

"Guess what?" she asked excitably.

"I don't know. What?"

"Just take a guess."

When she got dizzy, she skipped sideways, still in circles around him, like a boxer taunting an opponent. Timmy was highly amused.

"You got me tickets to go see Celine Dion? I don't know. What?"

"I'm running right Timmy."

"Running right?"

"I landed mid-foot our entire workout," she shared, giddy with delight. "And it did not feel forced."

"No way?"

"Yes way."

Timmy could barely contain his excitement and jounced with her, in circles.

"Who da man?" Timmy initiated with a throaty voice.

She caught on. "You da man."

"No you da man."

"I da man?" she asked in a high pitch, like she didn't believe it.

"Yeah, you da man." Timmy reinforced, still skipping.

Cambria slipped her thumb into the top of her shorts, and peeked in.

"You sure I da man?" She giggled.

Timmy broke out laughing.

"Yeah, I sure you da man."

"Ok, if you say I da man, then I da man."

"Well, just to be sure I should probably check for myself." Timmy reached for her shorts. Cambria yelped. She twirled away and took off running. He went after her.

With new fluency, she led him along the river bank through Limehouse towards central London. Feeling unhindered, free like a bird enjoying first flight, she did not want to stop, and kept running, preserving the integrity of her stride the whole way. She ran till daylight dissipated, the sky slipping from pale blue to fiery crimson to deep sapphire to twinkly. Cambria had never felt her limbs fall into harmony as smoothly as they did that night, and she experienced everything that Timmy had described as the perfect run—a coming together of your mind, body and soul, where you feel no tiredness even though you are running heavy. The face of one who is having the perfect run is composed and tranquil, with a wisp of a smile. Cambria wore that face that night.

Timmy and Cambria had so much fun they completely lost track of time and distance. That night, they ran a total of 33.6 miles. Unbeknownst to the two of them, they had along the way, claimed the world record. Both of them, by fifteen seconds.

Flight To New York

Timmy and Cambria spent the entire day at the airport. A snow storm had blown in from the north, freakish for the time of the year. All of New York was snowed in.

Unlike Timmy who was biting his nails and pacing up and down, Cambria sat demurely in the lounge, looking reflective and composed, a book half an arm's length from her. Timmy was a little irked by her stoic composure, unaware that a turbulent undercurrent swept under her complexion of calm, that while she appeared relaxed in her chair, emotionally, she was on the edge of her seat.

As she hid behind her book, Cambria was every bit as unsettled as her fiancé, and her mind was impermeable to the words on the page. Timmy was too caught up with the flight delay to notice that she had made four trips to the book stand, and made away with a new title each time. No matter how hard she tried, she could not lose herself in the story, and never got past two chapters. She refused to accept that her highly disturbed state could have had a bearing on the book's merit.

Timmy felt helpless knowing that his and Cambria's shot at making history was eroding with each twitch of the clock. He returned to the black and green screen every five minutes, his fingers crossed each time, wishing for their flight status to change. It finally did. From 'Delayed' to 'Cancelled'.

Cambria lifted her eyes when she saw Timmy walking over. He carried the gloom of a soldier sent to claim the dead. She braced herself for the worst. He flung himself heavily into the chair next to her, and buried his face in his hands. Speaking through his fingers, he relayed the news to her. The waiting lounge started to empty as word of the cancelled flight spread. The two marathon hopefuls sat in silence, despondent.

A half hour passed. And then Timmy's phone rang. It was Kim.

"Luke chapter 7, verse 14," Kim uttered through the phone in a low sombre voice.

"Huh!?" a baffled Timmy exclaimed.

Summoning the fire of a Southern Baptist priest, Kim commanded, "YOUNG MAN! Get upPPP, I tell YOU!" He continued, "Was just in touch with New York. The sodding storm has ceased."

"That's great news!" Timmy's face lit up.

"I've got you on the next flight to the Apple. Eight-thirty tomorrow. Looks like history will be made after all."

"Any chance you were able to get us into business or better? We're really weary from the day. We could use some proper rest en route."

"Hey buddy, thank your lucky stars I even bloody got you on. It was a full flight."

"Thanks for pulling this off. How'd you swing it?"

"Don't thank me. Thank my inamorata."

"Chloe?"

"Jesus, Timmy. Have you seen how she works the Rolodex?" Timmy chuckled.

"She called all over. The Minister of Transportation. The person in charge of the person in charge of ticketing. Ministry of Sports. Got through to bloody Branson himself. You know

Timmy... your little stunt on Cooper's Hill has won you some fans."

"I really appreciate all you've done. Thank Chloe for me will ya."

"Just go get 'em Timmy. Bring back the bloody title. You or Cambria. *Yichalal.*"

"*Yichalal?*"

"Never mind, I'll explain it to you when you get back. Go get some rest. Goodnight."

"Goodnight."

Because of their flight's early hour, Timmy and Cambria declined the complimentary accommodations offered by the airlines, figuring they would get more rest roughing it in the airport lounge than transiting to and from the hotel. After getting off the phone with Kim, Timmy left Cambria for a bit, to go to the washroom. He needed badly to splash the tenseness off his brow. The water felt good against his skin, and he felt rejuvenated, full of promise again. When he returned to the lounge, Cambria was gone. Looking around, he spotted her at the far end of the hall, on all fours, ironing out their jackets on the ground for cushioning. She had found them a quiet corner to spend the night. When he reached her, she was fluffing her backpack as a pillow. Aware of how fussy he was about their running shoes, she removed them from the bag to make sure they weren't squashed.

Timmy insisted that they each brought two pairs of running shoes, one in their check-in luggage, and another in their hand-carry. This was in case either got lost. Cambria initially wondered why he didn't want to just wear the shoes he was going to run in. Surely, no one was going to steal them off his feet. He had his reasons. Each of their shoes were worn with just enough mileage left in them to survive one more race, the soles thinned to a point they would be aware of each twig and pebble on their path. The reason for such lean footwear was to ensure that as much of their energy was transferred into propelling them forward, rather than be absorbed and dissipated by the shoe's cushioning. This was contrary to what modern day marketing preached—that the more air, springs and foam the better. If you were running to arrive, maybe. If you were running to win, NO.

"That is how elite runners maintain the appearance that they are always running on air. Their feet are expelled from the ground the second there is contact, allowing them to be in the air more than they are on the road," he explained to her.

Proud of the makeshift bed she had put together, Cambria tapped the ground with her palm, to invite Timmy to take the spot beside her. She offered him the side where she laid the backpack.

"Why don't you take the pack?" he suggested to her.

"No, it's fine. Really. We should get our rest. Come on."

"No I insist. Take the pack." Timmy's face twisted into a cheeky grin, "I'll just lay on your bosom."

"Ahhh," Cambria retorted, "for a moment I thought chivalry was dead."

"And because it is pretty bright in here, I'll probably have to sleep face down."

Cambria sideway-stared him in amusement as she pulled the makeshift pillow over to her side. "Fine you goof. Just no drooling."

Timmy lay down beside her. He was about to settle his head on her chest when she bolted upright.

"Wait. I almost forgot."

She started to rummage through their bag.

"I know you told me this was unnecessary, seeing that we were checked into First Class and all, but..."

Cambria smugly pulled out an air shoulder cushion. She waved it like a matador's cape. Timmy could not help but grin at her self-delight.

She started blowing. She blew and blew, but was unable to move the pillow out of its flaccid state. Her face turned red from the effort.

"Love, you're supposed to squeeze the valve as you blow." Timmy smiled with adoration.

"What? Squeeze it into fish lips?"

Timmy nodded. "Yeah, like you're giving CPR to it."

The stressful events of the day took a lot out of the pair. Sleep came easily to them both. They woke up at five feeling well rested, and were amongst the first to crowd onto the plane. They could not get seats next to each other, but it didn't matter. They were happy just to be onboard. Head slumped against the window, Cambria re-attempted one of the four books she purchased. And she found it to be one of the best reads of her life.

~.~.~.~.~.~

Timmy and Cambria rushed out of the airport and wasted no time hailing a cab. Their driver was a native 'Noo Yawwker' who dominated the front seat with his size. He had the complexion of a crumpet and a big face that was enlarged further by a hairline that reached to his nape. He distributed disgruntle fairly and widely on the road, to all who dared cross his path, tossing his hands each time he dished out a string of choice words. Occasionally he paid them compliments. "Hey wise guy, you're a real class act y'know." And he would shake a sarcastic thumb. Negotiating the traffic with surgical accuracy, many of his manoeuvres caused Timmy to say to himself, "I can't believe he just did that." Funnily, he and Cambria both felt this, that they could not have fallen into better hands.

Before heading to their hotel, the two hopefuls first had to collect their race materials from the Marathon Expo at the Jacob Javits Convention Center. En route, they peered out of the cab window with a childish awe, and excitedly pointed out to each other landmarks that they recognised. It was a beautiful New York day. The sky was clear, the sun, intense. Except for the two-foot banks of snow flanking the streets, there was no evidence of the freak storm from the previous day.

When their cab driver caught on that they were going to be participating in the marathon, he jokingly asked in his baritone, "So, which Kenyan do you think is going to win it?"

"I think a woman is going to win it this year," Timmy replied, his voice full of conviction.

The Noo Yawwker received the absurdity with a low croupy cough. Through the rear view mirror, he planted a scowl on them, and never said another word... to them anyway.

When they emerged from their taxi, they realised that the city looked, sounded and even smelled like what Hollywood had portrayed it. The streets were gridlocked with yellow cabs, car horns crescendoed the busy cacophony of the street, smoke breathed out of vents in the road and newspaper vendors reiterated the headlines out loud. People walked like they were making away with stolen goods, past street sellers who were busy autographing hotdogs with a common signature; two lines of ketchup atop a squiggle of mustard. Timmy promised himself one after the race. With everything on it.

The expo featured hundreds of exhibitors promoting anything and everything to do with the sport. Sports bras and nipple chaffing cream included. The running nerd he was, Timmy wanted badly to browse through the entire hall. But with the staleness of the previous day still clinging on them, they wanted badly to get out of their clothes, and catch a breather. After acquiring their official race packet and goody bag, they checked into a snazzy boutique hotel in Brooklyn, one that Kim had booked for them. After their long, tiring journey, they were thankful Kim had spared no expense in arranging their accommodation. As Cambria bounced on the bed to test it, Timmy stepped out onto the balcony to take in the view. The Manhattan skyline, twinkling under the sun, was visible from their room. When deciding on a hotel, Kim also made sure they were not too far from the Verrazano-Narrows bridge, the starting point of the race.

The weary travellers managed to shed their tiredness by squeezing in a short nap before dinner. Dinner was pre-arranged by Kim, at Tony's, an Italian restaurant serious runners ate at before a race. Before leaving the hotel room, Timmy insisted on bringing their backpack with their shoes in it, just in case a fire ashed the hotel. Cambria initially had wanted to wear her shoes to lighten the pack, but Timmy insisted that she not do that, stressing to her again the importance of her shoes' life.

"So what if the soles fall out? Abebe Bekele won the 1960 Olympic Marathon barefoot."

"It's not 1960, Brie. And the bottom of Bekele's callused feet were thick like elephant hide. Compare that to your pale, prissy, little miss daisies," Timmy huffed back at her.

She gave in, begrudgingly. *Prissy little miss daisies*, huh. Those words brought a rise in her. To wiggle under his skin, she proceeded to pin her race bib to the shirt she was wearing to dinner. *Let's see what he has to say about this* was encoded on her face.

Highly entertained by her antics, Timmy did not know whether to feel amused or exasperated. His gamine in all her glory. He smiled to himself and shook his head.

"Don't blame me if you look like a dork, wearing your number the night before the race."

"Being a dork is better than being seen with one," she countered as she fastened the final corner to the front of her shirt.

Tony's was only four blocks from their hotel, so they set out on foot, using the directions they received from the concierge. The air was more chilly than it appeared from inside the hotel. Cambria clung to Timmy's arm as they made their way there. The sun was setting, casting a golden glow that made the neighbour-hood feel more warm and less grey. Although the streets were still full of people and cars, the place was emptying, not filling up. Timmy always enjoyed this feeling of a city in unwind.

The walk was short and pleasant. The only unpleasantness was when they almost got run over by a car while crossing the street. Cambria felt they needed to have signs like they did in London, the words 'look left' or 'look right' tattooed on each curbside crossing. They could hear the restaurant from a few doors away, and knew right away it was a very popular place. As they entered, several people turned to look at them. One by one they withdrew their stares, once they realised Timmy and Cambria were not from their running fraternity. Timmy scanned the interior. Offering a mix of table and cubicle seat-ing, and trimmed with creamy white wood panelling that reached the waist, the restaurant carried the appearance of a neighbourhood joint with a family feel. Though it was crowd-ed, the enlivening pale scheme made the place look bigger than it was. Behind the cash register, jars of pesto, spaghetti sauce and homemade jams sat on shelves, each with a price scribbled diagonally across its label. Decades of photos, many bronzed through the years, hung on the walls and offered a window into the establishment's long history.

The wide plank floors creaked as they walked deeper into the restaurant. Casting their eyes about, they looked for some-one to seat them. They were greeted jovially by Tony himself, a portly larger-than-life figure with really thick arms and an equally thick Italian accent.

"Hi, I am a Toenee," he greeted them buoyantly.

"Hi Tony," Timmy threw back with equal enthusiasm.

Opening both his palms, an excusatory droop on his face, Tony broke it to them.

"I'm afraid a... that we have a foool house tonight. This crowd will probably leave around, a maybe eight, a maybe nine," he apologetically shrugged his shoulders. "Would you like to swing back later? I could reserve a table for you."

Timmy took a quick glance and saw that there wasn't a vacant table.

"But I believe we made reservations for seven o'clock. A friend of ours, Kim..."

"You must a be Timmy and Cambria," Tony expressed with serendipitous delight.

"Yeah," Timmy accepted, greatly relieved that their reservation might not have been lost after all.

"This way please."

They were shepherded by Tony to a private room with a tastefully prepared ambience. The table was set for three. Certain that Kim had planned something special for them, they wondered who their mystery guest was. Tony poured them each a glass of water.

"If you need anything, anything at all, I'll be outta side. Just poke yer head out and yell fur me." Tony closed the door as he left the room.

Although they were cordoned off from the rest of the restaurant, they could still hear the murmur of conversation through the walls. After about five minutes of waiting, the chatter outside abated, and immediately after, broke into cheers and claps. Timmy and Cambria perked up, their curiosity heightened. The commotion gradually died down, became susurrus. Their eyes fixed on the door, they waited in great anticipation.

The knob turned, and in came an African man of small stature, his smile brighter than bone. Timmy and Cambria recognised him immediately, and looked at each other dumbfounded, as if undeserving of the honour. *How in the world was Kim able to swing a dinner date with Haile Gebrselassie, on the eve of a race?*

"You must be Timmy? Cambria?"

He shook each of their hands with animated energy, without breaking the smile he entered the room with.

As they resumed their seats at the table, Cambria had to satisfy her curiosity, and beat Timmy to the same question.

"Haile, I'm really curious to know. To what do we owe your presence this evening?"

"Ha, ha, ha! I guess your friend Kim has kept this a secret from the two of you."

They nodded.

His eyes twinkling, Haile cheekily held his reply for a bit, for the suspense to build a little longer.

"How far that little candle throws his beams! So shines a good deed in a naughty world,'" Haile grinned, his smile like a magnesium flash. "From the *Merchant of Venice*, I believe."

The pair tipped their heads.

"Every year, for the last five years, on the 18th of December, a huge lorry would pull up to *Right To Play*, the charity organisation I support in Ethiopia. In it would be over a thousand presents for the children, each one gift wrapped. The sender always chose to be anonymous. For years I'd always been curious. Wondered who was sending these gifts. Now I'm happy to finally meet the person who puts smiles on so many faces, year after year."

Cambria shot Timmy a look, and saw that he was smiling to himself.

"Haile..." Timmy started to scratch his head, "what puzzles me is that no one knows I send these gifts each year. Not even Kim. So how is it that..."

"No, it wasn't Kim who contacted me. I contacted him. One of my assistants, after some poking around, learned of your identity about a year back. When I was in London this year for the marathon, I called the place you worked at. I hoped to meet you. I was thinking maybe for dinner or lunch. I wanted to thank you personally for all you had done. Kim answered the phone on your behalf. After he learned who I was, he asked if I could do him a favour."

Before Timmy and Cambria could ask Haile any more questions, Tony, now shimmering with sweat, entered the room. Though a little breathless from the busier than usual night, he still bubbled with joy.

"Hey there old friend. It's great to see you again." Haile stood up to receive the hug Tony had prepared for him.

"It's wonderful that you've decided to return," Tony expressed.

"What can I say? It's a wonderful city."

After pouring Haile a glass of water, Tony burst out of the room with the same hurriedness with which he entered. "I'll be back with your food in a minute," he announced as he left.

He returned as he promised, in a minute, with three large plates, one in each hand, and another balanced on his forearm. It was the blandest looking spaghetti Timmy and Cambria had ever set their eyes on, even with the light sprinkling of herbs on the top. They wondered if Tony would return with the sauce, but he never did. They started to wonder if the restaurant had risen to acclaim not for its cuisine, but as a spot for old friends to gather. It was only after their first mouthful that they realised the pallid complexion of their food bore false testament to the rich flavour that burst from it, and they understood why Tony's restaurant commanded the kind of popularity it did.

Dinner conversation focused mainly on Haile, of his past accomplishments in running, of his future aspirations in politics, of his present participation in the New York Marathon. In his early days, Haile preferred to not run New York because the route had too many turns, too many inclines, unpredictable wind conditions, which made it a really slow course. To optimise his chances at breaking his own world record, he focused his effort on faster courses like Berlin and London.

Timmy always viewed Haile in the highest regard, not just for his racing accomplishments, but for what he lived and fought for. Timmy knew of Haile's genuine effort to eradicate poverty in his home country, of his love for children, of the support he lent to other runners—just so doors could open for them as they did for him. In Timmy's mind, Haile was undoubtedly the greatest ambassador the sport had ever seen.

For over a decade, Timmy culled the best running techniques from the world's top runners. But as much admiration as he had for Haile, he never looked to him for technique. Haile had his own style, born out of the circumstances with which he grew up. As a child brought up on a farm, Haile used to run ten kilometres to and from school each day, this while carrying his schoolbooks in one hand. Over the years, all the book carrying led to a very distinctive posture which Haile had not been able to shake off till this day. Haile also, just like Cambria before, was a toe striker. That made him more prone to injuries than other runners.

Timmy instead fashioned his running technique to that of Kenenisa Bekele, a protégé of Haile's who many in the running world have hailed to be the best 5K and 10K athlete of all time. Kenenisa's fluid grace was a paragon of efficiency—his ability to retract his leg the moment it hit the ground lent him the appearance he was floating on air. He was a natural front runner with little need to rely on a kick finish, his relentless pace crushing enough to see others fall back. Kenenisa had already re-written most of the records set by his mentor, with plans to take on marathon length distances later in his career. It was a matter of time before Haile would be superseded. With a pinch of irony, no moment would make him prouder.

Timmy and Cambria were completely absorbed by Haile's candour, his humility, his childish vibrancy. They both felt a little guilty that this was the man whose record they intended to break.

Before they called it a night, Timmy asked, "So what would you say is the one thing that has made you so successful?"

Haile obliged smilingly in a manner that suggested he had answered this question many times before. *"Yichalal."*

The English pair shot the Ethiopian a puzzled look.

"In Amharic, it means *everything is possible*. To be successful in running a marathon we really need to believe in ourselves. That is the most important thing. In all sports, training is important. But in our sport, you need more than training. You need to last. And to last long you need heart. Plenty of it."

Timmy and Cambria nodded in agreement.

Haile added to his advice, "The fire that burns in every person is different. Some people run in anger. Some people run for love. Some run to escape poverty, and some run just to be with friends. But in a marathon, all the fire in the world, without the proper training, will only earn you a bed in the hospital. But at the same time, if you have all training but no fire, you will give up at the first hurdle. And as you two probably already know, when you run twenty-six miles, you will have to cross many hurdles, and the hurdles get higher each time. You agree?"

"Yes," the two said with one voice.

"I believe it is when the two come together, belief in yourself and training, that greatness comes," Haile wrapped up his advice with a smile. "Oh, and one more thing. Lots of rest." He laughed. "So I should be heading back to my hotel now."

They rose from their chairs simultaneously and exited the room. Outside the restaurant, Timmy and Cambria exchanged best wishes with Haile, and they went their separate ways.

Yichalal

"Wow, can you believe that you're finally here? On the cusp of living out your dream."

"Ha, ha," Timmy laughed cynically. "Well, I've got to get past Haile first," he rolled his eyes upwards to communicate the magnitude of the task. "Well, that's actually the easy part. Getting past my wife? Now, that's the real bitch."

Cambria elbowed him in the ribs.

"Tell you what. I'll wait for you on the 10-yard line. And we can cross the finish together."

"Flush that thought. Don't you dare do that," Timmy clamped Cambria's neck in the crook of his arm and playfully knuckled her head. "Promise me."

She ducked out of his hold, and walked backwards, in front of him.

"Fathom this, a photo of the two of us, on the front page of the Times, crossing the line together, hand-in-hand. Emblazoned above that, the headlines will read.."

Cambria wiped the air in front of her, excitement leaping from her eyes, "*Couple go the distance and win the New York Marathon.*"

Timmy rolled his eyes.

"No, I'd rather that the headlines blare, *Man marries trophy wife.*"

Timmy was a little irked that his witty comeback did not catch, skimmed right off Cambria like water off a duck's back. Her mind was someplace else, scrabbling for her next headline.

"Or maybe, the front page could read, *The perfect day.*"

Timmy squinted his eyes to see the humour in what she was saying.

"And DAY,'" Cambria made quote marks with her fingers, " will be spelled, T-H-E-Y." She flexed her eyebrows and looked smug.

While Cambria was conjuring that line in her head, she had not noticed that she had backed herself all the way to the edge of the curb. "Whoopsie doodle," she comically yelped as she stumbled backward over the edge. To restore her balance, she back paddled her arms like boat oars. Upon steadying herself, she giggled uncontrollably, realising how silly she must have looked as she fought to keep her footing. Timmy's heart sank when he realised she could have twisted her ankle in her moment of silliness. But he was glad that she was alright.

Like a soldier, Cambria playfully stamped one foot on the ground, saluted Timmy, and spun on her heel to face where they were going. Timmy could not believe her goofiness.

Making off like an army scout leading her company, she gingerly crouched her way to the edge of a line of parked cars. She peeked right, and seeing that the coast was clear, waved him on.

As she proceeded to cross, she called out to him, "Coast clea..."

Timmy heard a loud thump, and she was gone, swept out of view. A vehicle screeched to a stop. Everything happened so quickly. It did not fully register in Timmy's mind what had just taken place. All he knew was that it was something terrible, and that he had to go to his Cambria. He spotted her ten feet to his right. A pool of blood was starting to spread. He dashed to her.

When he reached her, she was already gone. Timmy crumpled to the floor by her side, and pulled her close to him. He cupped her face with his hands. He squeezed her arms, her hands, searching for life. Engulfed in a miasma of despair, he felt like an asthmatic at the onset of an attack, and his body heaved as he struggled for breath. He reached deep into the hollows of his soul, hoping to find the God he had abandoned.

"God, please help her. Just this one time," Timmy wheezed, "...just this one time."

His voice got more desperate, destitute.

"I beg you."

Eyes turning upwards, "Jezza, are you there? Can you hear me?" Timmy shuddered as he sobbed.

God replied. But Timmy did not hear Him.

"She is with us, Timmy. She is with us."

Timmy squeezed Cambria close to his chest, afraid that if he let go, she would be lost forever. He looked around.

The windshield of the car that took her had caved inwards and was webbed with cracks. A black SUV.

The driver, a woman in her early forties, stumbled out of her vehicle. "Oh my god. Oh my god," her face pulled into a grotesque mask of white horror. Hand over her mouth, she remorsefully begged forgiveness, "I'm so, so sorry. I did not see her coming. I swear. I'm sorry mister. She came out of nowhere. I'm so, so..." She started to weep.

The child in the backseat wailed for his mother. The driver's side door which was ajar, forced a seat belt warning, and beeped a death toll. The woman took out her phone to call 911, but her hands trembled so badly she could not hit the right numbers. Passersby gathered, and watched from afar.

Cambria's face was severely scratched, her nose, badly broken. The accident had left her unbeautiful. But it didn't matter to Timmy. All he wanted was his baby back—to luxuriate in her ebullience, to see the sun trapped in her eyes at dawn, to hear her voice carried on the wind, like church bells across the valley.

Cheeks twitching from the shock, he remained on the ground, rocking back and forth, cradling his *only* close to him. The paramedics finally arrived on the scene. One of them knelt on the ground, and checked for vital signs.

"I'm sorry sir. She's no longer with us."

Although he already knew that, hearing those words on the wind drove a volley of grief into his body, and he started to quake. The ground beneath him crumbled away, like soil shaken from the roots of a plant. He refused to believe he was a part of the ugliness that took her away from him, and he swayed his head left and right, the way the blind play the piano.

"No," he rasped to himself, "no."

The circle of observers shrank inwards to feed their curiosity. Suffocated by the murmurs, the stares, and the flashing lights, Timmy picked himself off the ground, righted his shirt, and fled through the crowd.

~.~.~.~.~.~.~

Timmy wandered the streets in forsakenness, lost in his pain, angry that he had been dealt another of life's cruel injustices. It was unfair that she had been taken from him so quickly, without warning, without any parting words. No *I love you*. No words of reassurance that she would wait out eternity for him. God had taken her. Just like that. In mid-sentence.

He looked around him. And it got him mad. He had just been robbed of his universe, and the world swaggered on like nothing had happened. The sounds of the city were crisp in his ear, but his vision was a hazy blur, a kaleidoscope of neon lights. His tears brought no relief, offered no refuge. As he wandered blindly, he was well cognizant of one thing, of the pointlessness of his life moving forward. The pain—deep and ravenous and relentless—gnawed at his insides, a hollow left in its wake. Even the knot of nausea in the pit of his belly, was ingested.

For hours, he walked through the streets of Brooklyn. He grew angry with himself for bringing her to New York. Angry that he had allowed her to wander out of his reach. Angry for not letting her wear her running shoes. The difference those few seconds could have made.

The trauma Timmy went through that night eventually wore him down, and a deep tiredness started to set in. His clothes suddenly felt heavy, as if he had just emerged from the ocean fully clothed. He slumped to the ground at the foot of a building. Leaning his back against the wall, he realised he was still wearing his backpack. He shrugged it off and started rummaging through it for something soft to cushion his head. He ran into things of hers. A pack of facial tissues for dabbing oil off her face, a hair brush tangled with her silky strands, a stick of lip gloss. Recollections of her, renewed by her personal possessions, tore like a blunt knife into his body.

To Timmy, Cambria was like the rain in May, bringing life to everything she touched, leaving in her wake, the freshness and promise of spring. He wanted so badly to again touch her skin, hear her voice, absorb her into his arms, be lost in the silk of her hair. With hands that trembled from the cold, Timmy unscrewed the cap of Cambria's lip gloss and applied it, to taste her lips once more on his. He waded deeper into the backpack, and found the neck cushion that Cambria had blown up for him, that night in the airport. He felt a sharp pain in his chest, as if the talons of an eagle had just locked onto his heart. Realising that her breath lived within the synthetic walls of the cushion, his eyes clamped shut, and drew tears from the dark unreachable depths of his soul. He started to hyperventilate, and felt as if he were choking on his own breath.

When he was finally able to steady his breathing, he started to think of chestnuts. He thought about the pink-cheeked street seller who set up shop a block from *Cream*. How he lilted, "Two quid for a small. A hundred for them all," his sweet strains rising above the voice of the street.

In the wintertime, Timmy loved to walk up to the cart, and mull over his purchase longer than he needed to. This was so he could hold his hand out over the roasting chestnuts and stir some warmth back into his fingers. As he sat on the rigid, frigid pavement in the darkest winter of his life, Timmy pined for the comfort chestnuts always brought him. He recalled their distinct fragrance, how he could taste their sweetness from the smell.

Like air being let out of a balloon, Timmy's remaining energy left him quickly. His limbs went languid from the fatigue. His eyes fluttered shut, and wrung a final tear from his eyes. As it rolled off his cheek, he forced his eyes open to watch it fall. And he thought of her, of that drop of rain that would never fall again. He drew the valve of the neck cushion to his lips. And he let some of her into him. He held her in his chest for as long as he could. Then he had to let her go.

He slid out of the patch of light he was sitting in, and became anonymous in the shadows. Lying on his side, he clutched the air cushion close to his breast, and curled up like a prawn to embrace his own warmth. His eyelids lowered slowly till they closed, trapping within, the image of his beloved.

The Day Of...

The sounds of the waking city wisped into his ear, and gradually turned from a whisper into a voice. The sound of people getting into and starting their cars. The jangle of keys as someone locked their front door behind them. The thump of newspapers landing on doorsteps. The footfall of feet on the pavement. Timmy's eyelids batted open and he saw daylight. He saw legs walking by, like he used to from the basement of *Cream*.

Paralysed by the cold, he could not move. He was exhausted, more tired than after any of his 26.2s. He closed his eyes and resumed sleeping.

~.~.~.~.~.~.~

He felt something warm, wet and spongy. Like a tongue. It brushed up and down his cheek. He heard a female voice.

"No girl. No."

He bolted upright and saw a woman leaning her body weight backwards, clutching a fully strained dog leash. As she regained control of her butterscotch Labrador, she apologised to him. She was really sorry. He saw the sincerity in her eyes.

"I'm sorry, mister. I really am. She just suddenly just..."

"No, its fine, miss. Really, it's okay," he assured her, shaking off the remaining crumbs of his slumber.

"Alright mister. You have a good day now." The woman continued down the path, her Lab pulling her from side to side.

Despite waking on the ungiving pavement, chilled to the marrow, stiff from head to toe, Timmy felt rejuvenated, and alive. In the moment of his waking, his mind yielded no recollection of what had taken place the night before. And he felt normal. Then he looked at his hands caked with blood. Slowly, the events of the night started to register. Shadows crept in from all corners, and blotted out the normalcy he enjoyed for that brief moment. He grabbed his head with both his hands, and pulled with all his might, trying to uproot his hair. He let out a primal ululating wail that echoed hauntingly within his empty. And his world eclipsed into darkness.

Bob Crawford

Bob Crawford started his career with great promise, but now carried tired eyes. And he had had enough.

He was really good at his job, maybe a little too good. Starting his career as a TV broadcaster thirty-three years ago, Bob covered fringe sports events like canoe races, angling contests, dog shows and marathons—assignments that stations normally threw to rookies looking to break into the field. The thing that set Bob apart from his peers was that he worked the unworkable, and found interesting angles to things that had long lost public interest. To his detriment, the stations eventually found him irreplaceable for the unconventional, less popular sports events he covered. And he was shoeboxed for life.

There was a mix of relief and sadness as he snapped on his microphone headset for the last time. As he had been born in New York, the New York Marathon had always been his favourite event. And he was happy that it was here that he was to conclude his long, unremarkable career.

Bob Crawford was a very lonely man. He was one of those who could die one day, and no one would come to check on him till the stench got too bad. Breathing or un... it did not matter to most; save the two or three people at the station whose livelihoods would temporarily be affected by his pass-ing. Bob's situation was brought about not because he was hard to get along with, or mean, or bad tempered. He merely was non-participative in our world, quiet in his own, a recluse.

Bob was married. Twice. And fathered a child with each wife; a son by the name of Marcus, and a daughter, Tabitha. Because his job required that he be constantly on the road, he found it hard to stitch together a relationship that lasted more than a couple of years. His children only saw him on their birth-days. He never lingered. Just dropped off their presents and left. The last time he saw Marcus was on Marcus's fourteenth. Marcus's mother, Bob's ex-wife, told him not to come around anymore after that.

His relationship with his second wife was much better. They had coffee about once a year, to catch up. Bob still wore their wedding ring on his finger. He liked to be reminded that some-one had once wanted him.

It was Bob's seventeenth straight year covering the New York Marathon. Not just New York, but marathon events worldwide. He struggled in the early days, and fumbled with the obscure names of the runners. He found it tough differen-tiating one rangy African from another, so he used to address them merely by their numbers. But seventeen years on, doing the mile-on-mile coverage of a marathon, whichever one they threw at him, was something he could do in his sleep. He knew all the circuits around the world. All the turns. All the parts of the race runners would start to taper off. The breakaway points. The defining stretches. Eventually, even the tongue-twister names lost their challenge and rolled off his tongue with ease.

Having seen it all in the world of marathon running, Bob decided a year back that he had seen enough. He knew that there was a lot more to life than work. And he wanted to do all the things he always dreamed of doing. Live with the Bedouin in the red sands of Wadi Rum. Check off the seven wonders. Live the life of a Berber in the Ourika Valley. Experience the notorious Fuerte Apache suburb of Buenos Aires. Read all the books he always wanted to read, and complete all the ones he never did.

Bob earned a comfortable salary, led a comfortable life, and had reached a point in his career where the job was tediously undemanding. Although, since making his decision to retire, he was haunted, almost daily, by his choice. He wasn't sure if his nest egg was large enough to see him through the rest of his days. He was aware of how high medical bills could get when one got to an age. And the last thing he wanted was to have to knock on the doors of blood relations for spare change. Or worse still, to have to rely on his estranged children.

Bob scavenged through his notes again, for the umpteenth time that day, searching for that gold nugget that may have escaped his notice. There was nothing in this year's New York marathon that was going to make it more different than all the others. So he reckoned he was just going to do what he had been doing successfully for the past thirty-three years; capture the thrill of victory and the agony of defeat, basically faces contorted with triumph or pain.

The most interesting thing this year was that Haile Gebrselassie had come out of retirement and was going to be in it. He was the clear favourite to win it.

For the American public, there was Karem Amofa, the up-and-coming seventeen-year old who was rising fast in the running world. He currently held a world ranking of 23. Born and bred in Harlem, everyone was counting on him to draw on the energy of home for a good showing.

There was also Kalili Swengi, the forty-four-year old from Kenya who was returning to competition. Many years ago, in a satellite race in the US, he ran with a hairline fracture in his shin, and won. Many doubted that he would be able to regain his step from before. But it was the closest thing they had to a Cinderella story.

Bob was once a serious marathon runner, back in his college days. As such, he was always able to convey what the runners were feeling at each stage, what their strategies were, what went through the interior provinces of their minds. This made him one of the best broadcasters of the sport. Watching the runners prepare at the start of the race always gave Bob the itch to lace up his shoes, to be down there, shoulder-to-shoulder with the herd, instead of watching from a screen in the broadcast booth.

Bob pulled the microphone arm of his headset close to his mouth, and nodded to his crew. A backward count was initiated, and the camera went hot.

"The image we bring you is of the Verrazano-Narrows bridge, where fifty-eight thousand are gathered to take part in the world's largest marathon. A slight chill still hangs in the air, but the sun is out. A beautiful New York day it is."

Bob always felt each pre-race setting around the world inspired its own awe. In Berlin, runners gathered before the six Doric columns of the Brandenburg Gate, in Paris, it was at the Arc de Triomphe looking down the well-manicured greens of the Champs-Elysees. In China, as runners stood on the Great Wall in Tianjin, the sweeping magnificence of its surroundings left you breathless. And at Gorak Shep in Nepal, it was the majesty of Mount Everest. Sometimes the spaces were wide open, boundless even: the blinding white of the Polar Circle Marathon, the rippled Sahara dunes of the Marathon des Sables, the ochre sands of the one in Petra or the parched gold savannah of the marathon in South Africa.

Despite covering New York for seventeen years, that image of everyone lined up at the Verrazano-Narrows still wielded tremendous power over Bob, and stole his breath each year. The generous police presence, the hovering news helicopters and blimp, the brass band, the security crews, the non-stop firing of flash bulbs—they all played a part in casting a veil of importance on the event.

Having covered virtually every major marathon in the world, Bob marvelled at the one similarity. Although everyone appeared calm before the race—easing into their stretches, chatting with the people around them, or silent in introspection—everyone wore a look of resolve, and the undercurrent mood was always intense. It didn't matter if there were lakes, mountains, geysers, sand or snow as a backdrop. Or whether there was rock music blaring through loudspeakers, or live big band music, or the Maori Haka or the pageantry of fireworks over a pre-dawn sky. Before a marathon, runners were aware of the Everest before them, and it showed on their faces.

"That is the signal we've been waiting for," Bob excitedly announced to the world, "the sound of the howitzer being fired. Ladies and gentlemen, this year's New York marathon is underway."

The massive crowd of runners surged forward like a wave creeping onto a beach. Leading the pack were the twenty or so world class runners granted positions at the front of the line. Naturally, they were also the ones afforded the most airtime.

Common in public races like the New York Marathon, are the two-minute fame-seekers. These are the runners who surge to the very front of the race, past the running professionals, just so they can brag that they, at some point, led at the New York Marathon. Mostly they dressed in loud outfits, often bearing some configuration of gimmickry or a written message they wanted to advertise. The pros tended to dislike these runners, for it took energy to swerve around them to get past. What annoyed the running elite more was when the fame seekers did not want to gracefully concede their lead and zigzagged, lengthening the ordeal.

Bob used to refer to these runners as FIPs, which stood for *Flash in the Pans,* as they burned up all their energy in a flash, leaving nothing to continue with.

Five FIPS surfaced this year, and they ran in a group. They all seemed to tire at the same time, around the four-minute mark. They broke formation like fighter jets engaging in battle. All fell to the wayside, bar one. It was a matter of time before he too sputtered. So Bob thought.

Bob was, however, rather surprised at the fluency of the remaining FIP's form. Bob had an eye for good technique, even if it were an ant size image on the TV screen. He saw that this runner kept a fast but steady pace, held a good posture, his stride close to the ground. His arms moved back and forth at waist height, with good cyclical motion, and he fell with ether-like footfalls, his head at a mild tilt, looking perhaps ten to fifteen feet to the ground ahead. It was uncommon to see good form in a FIP. FIPs usually flailed their arms in an effort to maximise their pace. They slowed when they tired, and surged forward whenever they caught their breath. It was different with this FIP though. Watching him flow into his stride forced one solitary word into Bob's mind: runner.

Beautiful as the frontrunner's form was, Bob knew there was no way he could maintain that pace, and that he would eventually relent once his fuel ran out. Most broadcast stations denied FIPs any airtime as to do so was an endorsement of a stunt that wasn't encouraged. But as the race wore on, the stations grew more interested in the maverick who was devouring the road, the resilient runner who had now put an impressive distance between himself and the race leaders—the race leaders who, ironically, were following him.

At the forty-five-minute mark of the race, the FIP was a whole mile ahead of the pack of running elite. Every station covering the New York Marathon could not resist switching their coverage to him, to the ridiculous unwavering galoot with the beautiful stride, who wore an air pillow cushion around his neck, and no shoes on his feet. Like dominoes the broadcast booths fell into a frenzy, as news crews scrambled to gather information on the rogue runner.

From his registration number, 39002, they discovered through the database that he was Timothy Malcolm Smith, a thirty-three-year old Creative Director from a London ad agency called *Cream*. His name did not point to any past participation in marathons, but British broadcasters knew right away that he was the guy who proposed on Cooper's Hill. Bob Crawford was elated when he learned of Timmy's identity. He now had the angle he was looking for. His last day at the office was no longer headed for the unceremonious end he had anticipated.

Back In England

Seven-year old Augustina Powell had the TV tuned to the race in New York. She lived alone with her mother, Marsha, on the outskirts of London, in an apartment lean on amenities. The carpet had shrunk away from the walls, and was curled on the edges. The crimson that it once was, had weathered to a sickly pink. All their furniture were hand-me-downs from relatives, or had come from neighbours who moved away. None of their tableware matched. Most of the plates, mugs and bowls were promotional gifts, and bore a brand name of some kind–canned soup, toothpaste, milk, cereal.

Augustina had never met her father. When she was five, she had asked her mother about him. Though only a seedling, it took Augustina but an instant to realise her question unearthed some very painful emotions. And she never asked about him again.

One day, as Augustina was looking for her favourite ragdoll in her mum's bedroom, she came upon a thin stack of post-cards hidden within the covers of her mother's pillow. She sensed they were private, but her childish curiosity prevailed. Through the postcards, she learned a little about her father. She discovered that he travelled a lot, as each card was posted from a different city. She often wondered if he was someone famous, a news correspondent maybe. As a result, she spent her days camped in front of the TV, and tuned in to the news channel every chance she had.

From the way he wrote, she discovered her father was really good with words and very witty. She could tell that he missed her mum a lot when he travelled. And that she was everything to him. Augustina noticed that the last card her mother received came eight months before she was born. From then on, it had just been the two of them.

She sometimes cried when she considered the possibility of her arrival as the reason for his disappearance. And for this, she always strove to be the model child, to make him proud of her, to prove to him that she was a good kid. That he needn't keep away. That he should return.

Marsha Powell was a nurse at the Royal London Hospital. She worked the morgue yard shift from 7pm to 2 am. She was only thirty-one, but the wear of raising a kid on her own made her look forty.

It was difficult at first, raising Augustina on her own. But as Augustina grew older, it became easier. Augustina was a precocious child, and she picked up life skills that most children only acquired when they were no longer children; after they were packed off to college, or after they got married and became housebound. Augustina did her own laundry, as well as her mum's. She ironed, cooked and did the dishes, all while standing on a low stool.

Marsha and Augustina were very close, as single mothers and their offspring often are. And they meant the world to each other. Independent as they both were, they were totally interdependent on each other for support, for encouragement, for companionship.

"Look Mummy, it's the man from the hill," Augustina excitedly called out to her mother. "He's leading at the New York Marathon."

Marsha looked up and gasped.

"Yes it is."

The phone rang. It was Audrey, a nurse mate Marsha went to medical school with.

"Turn on the tube. The Timmy guy is on TV.... remember the bloke who proposed on Cooper's Hill. He's way ahead at the..."

"Yes I know. We're watching it right now."

"Alrighty then. Let me call Pam. She used to daydream about this Timmy fella, wishing she was the one he knelt down to."

Before Marsha could respond, she heard a click on the phone.

"Thanks for calling," she continued anyway.

Marsha put the handset down and was walking back to the TV when the phone rang again.

"Hey Marsha, do you have the TV on? It's..."

When footage of Timmy hit the airwaves, phones rang all over Great Britain, with news that their most romantic countryman was leading at the New York marathon. Within fifteen minutes of its airing, half the TV sets in the country were turned on, eyes glued to one channel.

The Race Of His Life

The BBC readily had in their possession, footage of Timmy proposing to Cambria on that sunny Monday morning on Cooper's Hill. Of her lunging into his arms and sliding down the hill in a lover's embrace. They were the first station in the world to air that clip. It took no longer than a couple of minutes for their move to be parroted by other networks.

Bob was impressed by how quickly his team turned things around, how in ten minutes they jigsawed together a twenty-six-page brief with details of Timmy's educational and professional background, inclusive of a list of his favourite food, music, past times, movies and books. They also had articles from magazines, newspapers and online publications where he had been featured.

From the old guard, Bob was a proponent of traditional journalism. He believed that everything needed a paper trail, that information needed to be verified, and that it was important to have redundancy. Phrases like "I Wikipedia-ed it", or "I Facebooked him" or "someone Twittered this two minutes ago" made his skin crawl. It was different this time. For the first time in his career, he was willing to abandon the old for the new.

Digesting the brief with great voracity, Bob thought of the numerous ways he could milk the situation. It was inconceivable that Timmy would be able to sustain his blistering pace all the way to the tape. But Bob was aware of the entertainment value of a hypothetical 'what if' scenario. So even though he knew Timmy was going to falter, he had to get the public to entertain the possibility that he was not.

Bob had been around the sport long enough to know that runners could run their hearts out, but not run away from the one law every distance runner answered to. And that was that one needed fuel to run. He remembered the metaphor his running coach used to repeat to the young squirts who had just joined the team. The analogy told of how a car without fuel, would not move a hair. It didn't matter if it had a perfectly working engine and was dressed with brand new treads.

Everything they taught you about the sport was about fuel economy. From the way you strode, to the way you breathed, to the diet you sustained. It was about fuel. How to harness it, how to utilise it, how to conserve it. Serious long distance runners spent all their lives transforming their body to operate on less and less—less energy, less water, fewer pints of air. And the goal of each race was to cross the finish line with just enough in the tank.

In Bob's mind, he wrote off Timmy's display as complete mismanagement by a rookie runner who had not mastered fuel economy. But despite the sad end he foresaw, he was amazed that it was an hour and fifteen minutes into the race, and Timmy was still carrying the inertia of a steed fresh out of the gates. With the impressive lead Timmy had built, he could have halved his pace and still win the race. But Timmy showed no signs of relenting. A cramp was an inevitability. Bob had seen it too many times before, where instead of grabbing a podium finish, a runner ended up grabbing his or her leg in agony, the shadows of other runners eventually sweeping over.

FUEL

~.~.~.~.~.~.~

The TV in Augustina and Marsha's living room zoomed in to a close-up of Timmy, a bleak visage of a man who had lost everything. He was staring at some invisible point in space, and tears glistened on his cheeks. He looked tarnished. The promise that once lived in his eyes was now gone; the fire, the passion, the poetry, dulled into a vague empty glare.

Marsha had seen the exact same look seven years ago. It was the last image she had of Augustina's father, as he turned to look back at her for the last time. Right before he walked out the door. She had confessed to him that she had made the biggest mistake in her life, of sharing her bed with an old flame who had swung by one weekend. She explained to him that it was an error in judgment. That it was the wine. But it was all blather to him.

He was a volunteer at a soup kitchen she used to work at in Bethnal Green. And it was there that she fell in love with him. He was kind to everyone he met, and brought laughter and a sympathetic ear wherever he went. And although it went against the rules of the Kitchen, she always caught him slipping money to the people he thought needed it most.

Marsha often wondered how the future would have unfolded had she kept the truth to herself. She would have loved him. Loved him with all her heart. Augustina would have had a father. A strong pair of shoulders to perch on when they were at the amusement park. He could have read bedtime stories to her. And tickled her silly when she was naughty. They would have travelled the world together, as a family. Laughed together. Cried together.

She had hoped that by coming clean, her honesty—however ugly—would form the bedrock of their relationship. But she was wrong.

Standing in front of the TV set, her young worldly eyes

riveted on the flashing images, Augustina asked, "Mummy, why is the man from the hill crying?"

Marsha knelt down between Augustina and the TV. Her eyes clamped shut, and tears started to stream out of its seam.

"Tina, honey," Marsha's voice quivered. She put Augustina's little hands into her own and drew her close.

"There is something I have to tell you about the man from the hill."

~.~.~.~.~.~

Throughout England, crowds started to gather around TV sets in living rooms, pubs and restaurants. The large TV screen in Trafalgar square, installed for the Olympics, went live with footage of the race. Central London came to a standstill as the city stopped to watch England's son fly like the wind, past the three quarter mark of the New York Marathon.

The reaction to Timmy's attempt at the impossible drew different reactions from different crowds. Some groups were raucous with cheers, some were stunned, some doubtful, some prayerful. Many sat in silence, their eyes fixated on the TV, eyes unblinking for minutes on end, spellbound by the possibility of the impossible coming through. They knew that if any man on the planet could, Timmy could.

Many found the race too nerve-racking to watch and had to tear themselves away. They paced in the background, returning every now and then to check on his progress. Rather oddly, many people stood glued to one spot, subconsciously rocking their arms back and forth, as if it were they who were running.

At the twenty-one-mile mark, as Timmy confronted the Madison Ave Bridge, his left leg cramped. He grabbed his thigh and continued running, his left ear mashed against his shoulder. The prodigious exertion deepened the prominence of his musculature.

Timmy's cramping drew sighs across the country. Those

who were already nervous, grew more nervous. Those who first thought it all too good to be true, claimed that they were right all along. From the way Timmy breathed, which appeared to be heavy and laboured, they could see that he had been pushed to the extremes of fatigue. The nation gasped again, a mile later, when Timmy winced and grabbed at his other thigh. The agony straining the cords in his neck, he raged on like a wounded bull. The nation's dream of a Briton obliterating the world record looked like it was not going to converge with reality.

Timmy's legs no longer bent at the knee, and became straight and stiff like a leg of mounted Parma Ham. Hands clutching the back of his thighs, he powered his body forward by rotating his hips left and right, as if he were nudging a loaded wheel barrow that had lost its wheel. Wrought in pain, his back arched backwards like a bow, and he flinched each time his feet pounded the tarmac.

Viewers nationwide were fragmented in sentiment. A segment cheered harder for Timmy to prevail, to have the strength to bear his cross to the finish. Some wished for the madness to stop. Others started to weep as they watched their crippled warrior soldier on. And as much as they prayed for an end to his mindless gallantry, they also wanted to see him succeed. Mostly they looked on with faded enthusiasm, unaware of the courage he knew.

The camp that was rooting for Timmy to conclude the race started to grow worried because his pace had slowed considerably. The pack of elite runners, led by Haile Gebrselassie, trotted on steadily and surely, like a well-oiled war machinery closing in on a defeated foe. They were a good nine minutes away, even if Timmy stopped running and sat in his shadow. But with Timmy crippled, the gap was closing fast.

As Timmy crossed into Central Park, the final leg of the race, something flashed on the television set that shocked the entire nation. Those who had not wept, started to. And there was not a dry eye in the country.

~.~.~.~.~.~

When Timmy's first leg cramped, Bob Crawford saw it as the beginning of the end he had predicted. With firsthand experience of how crippling and formidable a cramp was, it came as a surprise to him that Timmy persevered through the pain. After his second leg cramped, Bob knew it was game over for sure, beyond ambition, but he was proved wrong again.

"Lunacy," he let slip over the air. With Timmy continuing to nibble his way across the screen, it had become evident that he was committed to enlist everything he had, and more. Timmy's display had progressed beyond a test of stamina, and was now solely a test of endurance.

Bob worked at a frenetic pace to call the race. He was still amazed by how quickly his team extrapolated from the numbers 39002, a detailed report of Timothy's background; scrounging information from search engines, blogs and social networking sites.

As the race was just about to enter its final leg, Bob's producer marched up to Bob, plonked the New York Herald on his desk, and pressed his finger onto the page.

"If it bleeds it leads... this one is dripping,"

The dullness in his producer's voice contradicted the message he was carrying.

The newspaper was peeled open to page 3. It featured a photo showing the back of a man. He was slumped on the ground, cradling in his arms a woman with these numbers pinned to her chest: 39003.

Bob's face fell.

~.~.~.~.~.~

"Ladies and gentlemen," Bob announced to the world in a deep, sombre voice.

FUEL

"A very sad piece of news just came in. We just learned that the man we've identified as Timothy Malcolm Smith, the courageous runner currently leading the New York marathon, lost his fiancé in a road accident last night. The incident occurred on the corner of 4th and Carroll in Brooklyn, around 9 pm."

The BBC switched from the footage of Timmy to the image that was used in the Herald—two broken figures on the ground, slumped into each other, like string puppets that had lost their strings.

Across the globe, jaws started to slump, eyes moistened. What started out as an inspiring display of courage to the world, was now a macabre requiem of a man living his grimmest hour in public. The footage, harsh and undiluted, left viewers stunned, bereft of what to think.

Bob's voice quivered over the airwaves. "Our hearts and prayers go out to..."

He stopped.

Overwhelmed by a heartrending sadness, he choked on his tears and was unable to continue. Forcing himself to take deep, steady breaths, he was successful on his re-attempt, and persevered through the sentence he had started. Just barely.

"Our hearts and prayers go out to Cambria... to Timmy... and... to their families. "

Bob felt another rise of dolour, one he did not have the strength to ward off. He tore off his headset and left his desk to compose himself. Bob had never broken down on air in all his thirty-three years. Standing alone in a corner, his lips trembled as he tried to regain his calm.

From afar he watched the screen, and observed the raw determination in Timmy's face. Instantly he withdrew his reservations of Timmy seeing the race to the finish. And he brushed aside every theory he ever had on fuel. With Timmy's real circumstances now revealed to him, he realised that Timmy ran not with his legs, nor with his heart, but with the most powerful organ in his body, his mind. With what little of it was left anyway. The laws of fuel no longer applied to Timmy. He was a car that had lost control on a downhill slope, the breath of death in its sails. Bob recalled something from *The Imitation of Christ*: 'Love feels no burden, thinks nothing of trouble, attempts what is above its strength, pleads no excuse of impossibility'.

His producer walked over to him, put one hand on his shoulder, and asked if he was alright. Bob looked around, at the excitement that had infected the room of broadcasters. All of them were still on air, unflinching, mopping it all up. On their monitors was the image of a crippled Timmy, nudging his way across the screen. A solitary blip of raw courage. A living, breathing reminder that shadows also fall on the good ones, that life showed no favour, not to hopeless romantics, or icons of the advertising world. Bob glanced back at his thirty-three years. He knew he was one of the best left in the business. And he knew he needed to act it. He pulled himself together, and concluded his career with one of the best closing segments in long distance running coverage.

On the verge of tears, Bob looked straight into the camera.

"Love knows not its own depth until the hour of separation," he paused, "Kahlil Gibran."

"To my ex-wives Moira, and Audrey, to my son, Marcus, my daughter Tabitha, if you're watching, I love you. From the bottom of my heart, I do."

He took a deep breath...

"Yesterday, as death tore Timmy and Cambria apart without warning, he was probably denied such words to his beloved. Let this not be the case for you and me..."

~.~.~.~.~.~

Haile Gebrselassie went through a range of emotions he normally did not experience during competition. He felt a little insulted early in the race when Timmy shot past him in a cold, machine-like manner, no sideway glance or courtesy of a nod. It was as if their heart-warming meal from the night before never happened.

Haile also never felt more insignificant at a race as this one. For more than a decade, he had excelled in almost every competition he entered, and was used to the limelight falling on him by default. By mile-11 of this race, as they passed the Williamsburg Bridge, there wasn't a single camera on him. It felt a little odd, eerie almost.

Haile was able to keep track of Timmy's progress through the giant TV screens that were mounted along the route. As Timmy crossed the Queensboro into Manhattan, Haile grew resigned to the fact that the lead was insurmountable, and that Timmy was well on his way to victory. In his heart, he felt he could not have lost to a nicer and more deserving fellow. But it still irked him that Timmy did not acknowledge him on the pass.

Haile was overcome by great sorrow when he learned of Cambria's death. Susceptible to asthma attacks in the past, Haile detected one coming on. He felt as if he had ingested a plum whole, and that it was stuck in his chest. To ward off a full blown attack, he swiftly shifted his mind elsewhere; to home, to the dirt road he used to run on as a child, past the eucalyptus trees on the way to school, dust kicking up at his feet.

Haile knew the kind of fire that burned inside Timmy. Someone close to him had met a similar fate, his student Kenenisa Bekele, the great runner Timmy studied closely. Kenenisa was engaged to Alem Techale, a runner herself, a pretty young lady who incidentally shared the same first name as Haile's wife, Alem Tilahun. One morning, while Kenenisa and Techale were training together in the hills around Addis Ababa, she collapsed and died of a heart attack. She was only eighteen. Kenenisa was a different runner from that day.

~.~.~.~.~.~

Haile managed to build a thirty-second lead ahead of the pack. This allowed him to slow his pace as he approached the TV screen ahead of him. Timmy was seconds from crossing the finish line, and he wanted to catch Timmy's crowning moment. But a thing most tragic occurred. Timmy grabbed at his chest and collapsed. Paramedics swarmed in.

Haile closed his eyes as he stumbled past the screen, and said a prayer for his friend.

As he came down the final stretch of the New York Marathon, Haile hoped to find that everything was alright with Timmy. From a hundred metres away, he saw that the paramedics were starting to keep away their equipment. They were downcast. He looked into the crowd, and saw tears, and he knew that the worst had happened. He slowed into a walk and went over to where Timmy lay. The runners behind Haile, noticing that Haile had stopped, stopped as well. Haile removed the number on his chest, and placed it on the ground before Timmy's feet. At the broken feet of the man, of his friend, the runner, who had them all beaten. The other elites, doing the same as Haile, conceded.

On that sunny New York afternoon, with birds humming a reckless tune, leaves swooping and diving in the twirling breeze, not a single participant crossed the finish line at the New York Marathon. Timmy was eventually declared the winner.

Last 28 Minutes

"Jezza, are you there?"

I listened, hoping to hear a voice. But none came.

"Jez?"

He still did not answer. I figured I should tell him anyway.

"Jezza, I forgive you. For Mum and Dad. For Cambria. Read into my heart, Jez. Read into it, if you don't believe me."

"It's been awhile Jez. Been awhile since we've spoken. You must understand, it wasn't easy. It just did not make sense then. Some of it still doesn't make sense."

"I miss her so much Jez. I miss her so, so, so, so much."

"Thanks for leading me to her. For allowing me that glimpse of the love you've always spoken so reverently of. It was everything you described it would be. I would not trade this pain. Not trade it for a single second of the time I got to spend with her."

"The greatest pain in the world is to want that which you cannot have..."

"What I'm about to do. It is not a good thing. Not a good thing at all. But what would ya do if you wuz me, Jez? What would ya do?"

"Final words from me. Maybe. I have a favour to ask. The biggest you'll get from me in this life. If they let you, please catch me when I fall. But only if they let you, Jez. Only if they let you."

178.179.181.

I knew I was going to die 28 minutes before I did.

It's funny you know. It really is. Knowing something as final as this.

As I pushed my body to its limit, memories of my near death experience from a decade ago came rushing back, of the time I ran my heart to a stop in Whitechapel, outside the Royal London Hospital. I then thought that would be the lowest point in my life. That rock bottom was as far as you could go. How wrong I was.

Following that incident, after I thought better of things, I had always been cautious about staying within my cardiac threshold. I remember the day I discovered a way to gauge my pulse without a gadget. So thrilled I was. I found that by blocking out my environment and focusing within, I was able to hear my own heart beat. Keeping count. Now, that was the real challenge.

181.180.182.

I ran the first half of the New York Marathon in a trance-like state. I could not recall much of the morning, or of the night before. Sometimes I was unsure if I were dreaming or awake. There were lapses where I felt as if I were wandering blindly in a snow storm, and that I would be lost forever. But in the next instant, my world regained its crispness and certainty, and I brimmed with awareness. My vision sharpened to a point where I saw everything with exaggerated clarity. I grew aware of every bead of sweat on my body. Every sound resonated in my head as if it were spoken directly into my ear. But each time I woke up to the world around me, just as I started to comprehend the circumstances that brought me to the present, the world slipped away.

Past the three quarter mark of the race, my left leg cramped and I was summoned out of the murky netherworld I was moving in and out of. I pressed on with a dour determination. It felt as if there were rusty pins tumbling inside my leg, unleashing punishment severe enough to keep my senses latched to the present. It was at this point that the events of the previous night pricked to life in my mind. It came in a series of wistful vignettes. The images were lucid and lurid, and I felt as if a wrecking ball had hit me square in the chest.

I saw Cambria look back at me one last time. And then she crossed the street, glancing the wrong way. And she was gone.

There was daylight, and the world was sideways. The coldness of the pavement was seeping into my bones. My body felt stiff, hard as the concrete bed I was sleeping on. I was so tired I thought I would cease to breathe, and my eyelids weighed themselves shut.

I was rudely awakened. The woman looked apologetic. She strained her body backwards to pry her dog away from me. I watched her leave. A great sadness filled my chest, and my world slipped into darkness.

I arrived at the marathon check-in point. It was really crowded near the starting line. I 'pardoned' my way through a blur of people to get as far in front as possible. When I could not push further, I stopped. Being close to the open sea, it was frigid at the bridge, and the sensation of the cold wind pricking my skin was vivid. As I stood there, body-to-body, exchanging shivers with the people around me, I felt an assimilation to penguins huddling in the bitter pit of winter to stay warm. But as much as I welcomed the warmth of my neighbours, I felt claustrophobic. I felt as if I were a single grain engulfed in a silo of rice. Trapped in my tracks, my mind started to wander, and I was lulled into a daydream of nothing.

I was stunned into consciousness by the sound of the cannon. And the crowd pushed off. Instinctively, running as fast as I could, I weaved my way through the runners before me. A light breeze, carrying with it the minty breath of dawn, feathered my cheeks as I ran, and that made me feel alive. The sun was bright, and its warmth was starting to seep through the morning haze. I looked over to my left, then to my right, to see if Cambria was beside me.

I felt an abyssal loneliness. My world undulated away from me and became muted again.

I ran into a cacophonous wall of euphoria as I turned at full tilt onto 1st Ave. *Spectators roosted on dividers, ringing cowbells, whooping, clapping large yellow thundersticks. Learning of my participation on TV, a group of Timmy fans had come together — rah-rah girls with red and white pleated skirts. They had a sign with them: 'We love you Timmy. We wanna grow old with you.'*

That was everything I remembered, up to when my first thigh cramped. I lost my other leg a few minutes later, when it went rigid and broke into spasms. Tightening and letting go, and tightening and letting go. The twinge was so severe I cracked two molars gritting my teeth too hard. I buckled at the knees but managed to stay on my feet by stiffening my legs to lend them strength. I regretted each step before I even took it. The pain ate at me without let or pause and I considered stopping. But thoughts of Cambria re-entered my mind, and that drove me to embrace the pain rather than cave in to it. The compounding physical torture, I found, helped quell a far greater pain. Every muscle in my body scorched from the effort. The veins in my neck bulged to a point I thought my eardrums would pop. "*Yichalal,*" I bit down and gasped in my head, "*Yichalal.*"

And so I soared on broken wings, through the five boroughs of New York, into the final leg of the race, through Central Park.

~.~.~.~.~.~

182.184.185.

The sun strained through the leaves of the park and threw a lattice of shadows on the ground. It was nice to get reprieve from the sun. As my pulse rate continued to climb, I was certain that unless I stopped, I was stepping into the final minutes of my life.

Pushed to the extremes of fatigue, I struggled for air. In the last thousand metres of the race, my limbs rose in rebellion against me, and I found it impossible to stay my course. I wobbled left and right. At one point, I left the footpath, and wandered onto a patch of gravel. Shards of stones stuck to my mangled feet. The sound of crunching stones perked me up, alerted me that I was close to home.

186.187.189.

The tributaries of my life's defining moments fed into one extended flashback. It started with my first childhood memory. My cousins were clapping their mouths as they chased me around a wigwam. The inside of the tent was the safe zone—the place you ran into when you needed a break from all the running. I remembered the light in the tent being different. The sun filtered through the pores of the fort's canvas, casting a diffused sense of calm within its slanted walls.

"Come out," my cousins would yell, "it is safe."

When they had backed away enough, I crawled out, and the running continued.

One day, as I was catching my breath inside the tent, my cousins broke the code and rushed in. I slipped out in time, under one of the sides. They ran after me but could not catch me, no matter how long they tried. From that day, being on the run became my safe zone. My bastion. An inviolable refuge others could not reach.

~.~.~.~.~.~

I recalled a memory I had hemmed up and wished never to unstitch. I was at the foot of my parents' coffins at their funeral. It was the first time I realised my world could be taken from me in the blink of an eye. Two phrases entered my mind as I stood staring at Mum and Dad. 'Love is composed of a single soul inhabiting two bodies', Aristotle. And when I considered what they did for a living, I drew from Richard Bach, 'Real love stories never have endings'.

My parents were both best-selling romance novelists. Up to the point of their death, I had never read a single one of their books, something I deeply regretted. After going through volumes of their work, I realised how many details of their lives, of their love, of their friendship with each other, had seeped into their writing. Every paragraph triggered an emotion, unfurled a memory. Albeit painful, I managed to bear each book through. I channelled a lot of my grief into my writing, and this unlocked many areas of my mind I never knew existed. I think this laid the path for me into the world of creative advertising.

It was not easy delivering the eulogy of my parents. Many of my relatives stepped up to say they would do it. But I insisted on it. I felt I owed it to them. And besides, I then thought, who better than me, who like my parents, had the gift of the pen. I did well in holding back my tears, up until the very end, when I read a few lines from Neruda, my favourite poet.

By night, Love, tie your heart to mine, and the two, together in their sleep will defeat the darkness.

~.~.~.~.~.~.~

189.190.191.

At the very end of the race, the finish line in my sight, I felt no pain. The teeth that tore at my body ceased. And I felt light as a kite on a warm breeze. It was at this precise moment that the four *true love snapshots* of my life played through my mind.

My first was of Miss Heather's lips. Lips that moved but breathed no sound; lips that pantomimed the words 'thank you'.

I also recalled walking into an empty classroom on the final day of school. She was alone, packing up her stuff. We talked for a bit. When it was time to say goodbye, I leaned in to give her a hug, to thank her for everything. Facing me, and holding both my hands at their finger tips, she told me that while the romance between me and her could never have played out, she looked forward to coming to work every day. That each day was special because she knew someone in her classroom thought she was special. I asked if it would be alright if I wrote to her.

There was a tinge of gladness in her smile.

"You need not ask that which is not needed."

That was the last time I heard her voice.

~.~.~.~.~.~

I blinked into Nicole's eyes, Nicole, the girl from two streets away, whom I had known since I was a child. On the bed, flank to flank with her, she blinked at me, a tear rolling down her cheek. When I forged this *snapshot* of her in my mind, I was certain she was the one I was going to spend the rest of my life with. I had not realised this. That the death of my parents had made a much more jagged incision in me than I was aware of. While their death opened many doors to my mind, they closed several others to my heart. I lived with the fear that if I gave someone all the keys, they could leave as easily as they came. I think Nicole always felt like an outsider in my world, and she finally realised she could not sleep at my doorstep forever, and she moved on.

~.~.~.~.~.~

I was now in the dimly lit basement of the soup kitchen in Bethnal Green, back at a time when I had different names for the days of the week. There was *Wonderful Wednesday*, the day I volunteered at the kitchen. The day I would see Marsha Powell, the young student nurse who worked there. I had *Thankful Tuesday* because Wednesday was just round the bend. And *Tormented Thursday*, because Wednesday was six days away.

My third *true love snapshot* was of Marsha, her smiling lips glued tight, eyes crinkled in a losing effort to keep in her amusement. While she was doling out the day's cuisine, I had playfully rejoined the line and did as Oliver Twist did. Shyly holding my shallow steel bowl with two hands, I pleaded, "Please mam, I want some more."

I was going to take Marsha to be my wife. On the day I was to propose, she sensed it. And she told me of her weekend love affair.

~.~.~.~.~.~.~

Cambria's nurturing eyes were cast downwards as she gently rocked her arms from side-to-side, with the care and tenderness of a mother genuinely in love with her child. Our child.

This image of her repeated itself in my mind, and I held this memory of her close to me till the end.

192.127.0.0.1.0.0

As Timmy closed his eyes for the last time, the slightest of smiles leaned across his face. Cambria had kept her promise and met him at the 10-yard line. The man with the house of his dreams, was finally home.

Author's Note

One morning, as I lay in bed, I asked myself this question. How would the world define me when I'm gone? A few days later, I quit my job.

It wasn't easy. Leaving it all behind. Ten years of building a successful career in web development. But I knew I was put on Earth for a higher purpose. That God had furnished me with skills greater than what I was using at the time. I felt there had to be more to life than to conjure up one pretty web site after another, that my calling was above devising new methods for corporations to deepen their pockets.

I looked deep into my passions, measured my skills, took stock of my financial situation, and decided I would take a year off to write a book. I stepped off the ledge and let the warm air currents carry me.

I have many books left in me. But until this writing endeavour can put food on the table, I will, for now, be going back to my old life. If you like my work, and would like to see more, please, please, please drop in a kind review of the book and spread the word around.

www.fueldabook.com
itsaparty@justjezza.com
www.facebook.com/fueldabook

Acknowledgements

You, yes you, the person holding this book (you've brought me a step closer to my dream of being a full time writer), my wife **Sophie** (thanks for seasoning my life with the many colourful moments that have made me who I am today... this book would not have been possible without you), my son **Oliver** (for giving me a reason to fight this fight), my **Mom Jacqui Chin** (I know editing my book made you cough blood), **Isabelle Nezeys** (my French connection), **Chris Soyza** (my gunman), **Beng Lin** (hope you feel smarter after reading my book), **Leroy Tan** (my first running counsel... because he ran, I did not need to), **Chris and Tina** (Ankhura), **Nicole Yeong** (2nd true love snapshot), **Paulo Coelho** (your words started me on this journey), **Mitch Albom** (the concept of true love snapshots), **Daniel Tang** (for the quick Paula Radcliffe poll), **Michael Amador** (verification of accomodador), **Henry Hager** (for believing in me... hope I prove you right), **Manas Datta** (thanks for your editing help and pre-ordering my book a year in advance), **Miller Bainbridge** (for showing me what a real work place should be like), **Sharon Tan** (for our terrapins, Bailey and McKenzie), **Hui Mei** (sorry you had to lug my research material half way across the world), **Kirsten and Jorgen** (the many great memories on Laeso), **Bruce Macleod** (how are we doing today?), **Steven Leong** (for the Oliver Twist scene), **Gregory Pezolano** (for taking my NY marathon questions), **Chris & Anner, Noel & Yvonne** (for suffering through my early drafts and giving me that much needed boost), **Joshua Lee** (for being my number 1 fan), **Martha Lee**(for not being my number 1 fan), **Chris Bohrer** (Maker's Mark), **Richard Wong** (for dissecting my work and providing me with insights into the writing world), **Sayre Ribera** (somehow you kept popping into my head when I was crafting Cambria), my **Dad Anthony Chin** (for always believing in me), **Derrick Ng** (thanks for lending me your ear in my lowest times), **Thom Hiatt** (for the years of consultation), **Ingegerd Jorgenson** (part of you became Lenka), **Simon Rutherford** (your pile of shoes), **Lucy** (clanking), **Monica Torres** (for the Mardi Gras car ride), **Hoo Ee Kee** (thanks for inviting me to your rooftop Balinese hut), **David Dass** (for helping me promote this book), **Tan Chip Kim** (my pillar of strength from day 1), **Monica & Victor Guttierez** (for opening up a side of me I never knew existed), **StART Society** (my second home), **Marsha Powell** (the best client I ever had), **Amir Muhammad** (you must regret accepting my Facebook friend request... hey thanks for taking all my book-related questions), **Rosalind Chin** (for fine-tooth-and-combing my book), the **organisers of the Glouscester Cheese Roll** (for helping me fill in the missing bits) and **all the girls I've loved before** (many of whom have never loved me back). This is our book.

CPSIA information can be obtained at www.ICGtesting.com
Printed in the USA
BVOW032324040312

284409BV00001B/41/P

9 781453 886151